BLOOD SPORT

DAVID J. GATWARD

WEIRDSTONE PUBLISHING

Blood Sport
By
David J. Gatward

Copyright © 2021 by David J. Gatward
All rights reserved.

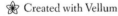

Grimm: nickname for a dour and forbidding individual, from Old High German grim [meaning] 'stern', 'severe'. From a Germanic personal name, Grima, [meaning] 'mask'.
(*www.ancestory.co.uk*)

To Aubrey Parsons,
for bringing Harry's story to life
better than I could ever have imagined.

CHAPTER ONE

SUNK DEEP INTO THE FELLSIDE, THE BARN WAS SO MUCH a part of the landscape that it was as though the surrounding hills had never known a time without it. There was a weight to the place, Harry noticed, the walls thick, the windows boarded in heavy, worn planks. Tufts of grass hung close around its flanks like they were seeking shelter and protection, and the bright gibbous moon gave the grey, slate roof an eerie shine.

Harry, the now full-time Detective Chief Inspector for Wensleydale, approached the building with the care of a soldier approaching an enemy position, something he'd done a few good times in his pre-police days in the Paras. For some reason, he couldn't shake the sensation that he was somehow being pulled towards the barn, as though the place was at the bottom of a pit and he was slipping ever closer. Not a good feeling, he thought. Ominous. And it wasn't gravity that had hold of him, but more a creeping dread which reached out with invisible claws from the stone walls and dragged him forwards.

Trudging on, Harry became acutely aware of the cool air, which still held onto spring's promise, ignoring any sense of summer being just a few weeks away. On it, he could still taste the metallic, icy bite of winter, as though the season's ghosts were breathing on him as he made his way onwards.

'Anyway, I'm sorry I called you,' said the man walking beside Harry, his huge frame moving with surprising grace. 'Didn't really know what else to do, like, so here we are.'

'Not a problem, Dave,' Harry said, doing his best to sound alert and awake at just gone two in the morning. He'd not even had time to throw a coffee down his neck, so it wasn't exactly easy, and he finished speaking with a stifled yawn.

'You've got me started now.' Dave yawned. 'Why is it that they're contagious? Proper strange, really, isn't it?'

Harry had met Dave Calvert back on his first day in Hawes. He was a big man, bull-sized and powerful, but warm and friendly with it, and when he wasn't working offshore, he seemed intent on acting like someone Harry had known for years. They'd shared numerous stories over a few ales in various pubs and the friendship had now moved on to Dave trying to persuade Harry to go with him either shooting or fly fishing.

So far, Harry hadn't taken him up on either offer. For a start, he'd handled plenty of guns in his time. As for fly fishing? Well, he just wasn't convinced that he'd have the required degree of patience to stand thigh-deep in a river and slap the water for hours on end with a stick and a bit of string.

Dave yawned again, the sound like that of a lion with a sore head. And more than loud enough to give warning to anyone in the barn Dave had brought him out here to investigate.

'Sorry about that,' Dave said, covering his mouth a moment too late. 'Used to be good at early mornings, but the older I get the less my body seems impressed with the whole idea.'

'Need your beauty sleep, do you?' Harry asked.

'That's rich, coming from you,' Dave said.

Harry laughed.

'I don't think any amount of sleep is ever going to make much difference to this face, do you?'

Dave stopped and stared intently at Harry, whose face had been scarred terribly by an IED when he was back in the Paras and out in theatre in Afghanistan.

'No, you're right, probably not.'

'Now then,' Harry continued, 'back to you telling me what you were doing out here in the first place at this ungodly hour.'

'There's a badger's sett just ahead,' Dave explained, 'like I said. Just up there a bit and behind the barn. I've got a couple of those fancy wildlife cameras set up, you see. Bit of a hobby of mine, wildlife, that is. I know the farmer and he's happy for me to come out and set them up.'

'Wildlife cameras?'

'You know, the ones with night vision and motion sensors and whatnot? They're fantastic! There's red squirrels up here, obviously, and I keep an eye on those, but I do love me some badgers.'

'How do you mean, obviously?' Harry asked.

'Snaizeholme, it's a red squirrel sanctuary,' Dave said. 'Cute little buggers they are. Difficult to find sometimes, seeing as they're all camouflaged, but that's the point really, isn't it?'

'Red squirrels are camouflaged?'

'No, the cameras,' Dave said. 'Can't have a wildlife camera that's all obvious, can you?'

'No, I suppose not,' Harry said, fighting another yawn.

'I've got some amazing footage of all kinds of stuff,' Dave continued. 'Did you know there's otters now on the Ure?'

'That's the main river that runs through Wensleydale, right?'

'It is,' Dave said. 'You're really getting to know the area, aren't you? I'm impressed. Anyway, they're amazing creatures. Beautiful. I've caught foxes and deer as well, even in my own garden.'

'Seriously?'

'I'll show you some of it, if you fancy,' Dave said. 'You'll be properly impressed, like, I'm sure of it.'

'No doubt,' Harry said, making a mental note to come up with an excuse if Dave ever invited him over for an evening of looking at animal videos.

'Like I said,' continued Dave, his voice rippling with almost boyish enthusiasm for the subject, 'there's badgers away and behind the barn a bit, just in among some trees. I've been keeping an eye on them. The cameras are good, but sometimes it's nice to get out and to see them with my own two eyes, as it were. And I've got some fancy night vision binoculars as well. Cost me a few bob, like, but well worth it.'

'Not used anything like that since I was in the Paras,' Harry said, a flood of memories suddenly crashing towards him. But he stepped to one side and let them rush past; now was not the time.

They were close to the barn now and Harry saw that a

large double door was stood open, swinging a little in the breeze. It was very clearly empty, but the squeal of the hinges only added to Harry's growing sense of unease, and he noticed that the darkness beyond the door seemed to be of a thicker blackness than the night outside.

'So, anyway,' Dave said, 'I was driving along the lane, like, and I saw headlights, which I assumed were just the farmer out and about.'

'And it wasn't?' Harry asked.

'Not a chance of it!' Dave said, shaking his head. 'Not unless his idea of a good time is to rag the bollocks off his truck through his own fields!'

'How do you mean?'

Dave stopped.

'The speed the driver was going? He was shifting. I mean, I'm assuming it was a he, but it could've been a woman, obviously.'

'And where was this?' Harry asked.

Dave pointed back up the track.

'I came round past the trees back up there, on our left, and I think my headlights must've spooked whoever it was. Because the next thing I know, bright lights are coming at me from this barn here. I pulled off the track quick, because there was no way they were stopping, and they just flew past like the devil himself was after them!'

'Bit strange,' Harry said. 'And you're sure it wasn't the farmer?'

'Positive,' said Dave. 'I gave him a call, just to check, in case it was an emergency or something, but it wasn't him.'

'So, you carried on to the barn.'

'I did, but I walked, you see, so as not to disturb the wildlife. I know that was a bit pointless, after that idiot came haring out of there, all engine noise and bright lights, but it's a habit I've got into.'

'And that's when you saw...'

'Blood,' Dave said, cutting in. 'I know my way pretty well out here, but I still need a torch, like. I've got one of those red filters for it so that I don't disturb any of the wildlife as I'm walking through.'

'Very considerate,' Harry said. 'And the blood is inside the barn?'

'I didn't go all the way in,' Dave said. 'I saw it on the ground, just over there by the doors. It didn't register at first, what I was looking at, but then there was that smell, you know?'

'I do,' Harry said. 'All too well.'

And then, with the barn now only a few steps away, and the gaping maw of the open doorway drawing them in, Harry caught the scent himself. He'd experienced it on the battle-field and at too many crime scenes to mention, but it was still an odour he'd never get used to and neither did he want to. If he ever became that desensitised to what he was doing, then it would be time to leave and find something else to do with his life. Though what, exactly, he hadn't the faintest idea, so he generally avoided thinking about it.

Harry swung his torch over to the barn, the sheer-edged beam of light cutting into the darkness beyond the door.

'There it is,' Dave said, the beam from his torch joining in.

Harry said nothing, instead, focusing on what was now before them.

Patches of red were visible on the ground in front of the barn, with some blood spatter on the door as well. To Harry, it looked as though something had been carried bleeding either into or out of the barn, but right now he wasn't sure which. Perhaps it was both. He'd also noticed on their walk to the barn, along a rough track through fields, various fresh tyre marks, and these all came to a halt at the barn. Here the ground was scratched and scuffed up. From what Harry could tell, not from just the one vehicle Dave had seen, either, but a number of them. It looked as though they'd driven to the barn and then turned around to face the other way. Always sensible if you fancied you might need to make a quick getaway, Harry thought.

'I think it's best if you stay out here,' Harry said, turning to Dave. 'I need to see what's what, and that's my job rather than yours, if that's okay.'

'It is,' Dave said. 'But if you need me, just you give a shout and I'll come running.'

Harry turned from Dave and closed the distance between himself and the barn. The building was old, that much was obvious, from the weathered stone and slate roof to the tatty wooden shutters on the windows. There was a battered-looking aluminium ladder along one side of the barn, lying in the grass. Probably left by the farmer, Harry guessed.

The blood was fresh, the wetness of it shining in the light of his torch, slick like oil. Dreading what lay at the end of it, but with no choice but to investigate further and find out, Harry pushed on into the barn.

Inside, Harry caught numerous scents milling around him. The barn was an old place and had clearly seen its way through numerous generations of farmers, and Harry could smell that age now, seeping from the stone walls and the dirt floor. The light from his torch picked out a few crumbling bales of hay up against a wall, some knots of orange baler twine, tufts of sheep wool, an old wrench orange with rust, resting in a gap in the wall.

Above him, Harry could see that the barn had once contained an upper floor, but it must have crumbled away decades ago, though remnants of the rafters still remained, jutting out like rotting teeth from the wall above, and at one end some of that ancient floor was still secured into the walls. The boards on the windows were cracked and worn but still strong enough to protect whatever was either stored here or taking shelter from the elements.

Harry brought his torch back down to the ground and as he did so he caught the glint of something which sent his heart into his mouth, as two bright, wide eyes stared back at him from out of the dark.

'Bloody hell!'

'What is it?' Dave called. 'You okay, Harry?'

The eyes kept staring, then another pair opened next to them and Harry was astonished to find himself under the watchful glare of two owls. They seemed unconcerned by his presence and one of them let out the softest of calls. He swept his torch beam around and picked out another set of eyes, another owl sat high up in the roof of the barn that he'd missed when he'd first looked up.

'Just some owls,' Harry said. 'Keeping a beady eye on me by the looks of things. Must've just come in. No way they'd have been here earlier, all things considered.'

'There's a few around and about,' Dave said. 'Beautiful creatures, aren't they?'

Harry said nothing, dragging the beam of his torch down to the barn's floor, sweeping it slowly, left to right, waiting for it to rest on the source of all the blood. And when it did, he wasn't exactly sure what he was looking at.

'I think I've found what the blood's from,' Harry said.

'It's not a body is it?' Dave said. 'God, I hope it isn't.'

Harry shuffled closer. His first thought was one of relief, because what he was seeing could in no way be human. Yes, there was a lot of blood, and as to its size, it was easily more child than adult, but the main thing which struck Harry was that there was also an awful lot of fur. Which got Harry to wondering, what with Dave's mention of foxes, if what he was looking at wasn't actually a fresh kill. But of what?

'Harry?' Dave called. 'You alright in there? What've you found?'

Harry crouched down for a closer look. As he did so he noticed how scuffed the floor was, and how there was blood spatter everywhere. He saw footprints as well. Thinking back to the tyre tracks he'd spotted on their way in, and Dave's encounter with a speeding vehicle, it was clear that the barn had very recently been more than a little busy.

All at once, the bloody mess in front of him registered in Harry's mind and he knew that he was staring at the remains of a dog. As to what breed it was he had no idea, but judging by the wounds, the amount of blood, the poor thing had died badly. And as Harry stared at the ruined corpse, rage churned a storm in his gut, because this wasn't the work of a fox, of that he was absolutely sure.

Standing back up, taking in what he had already observed—the tyre tracks, the scuffed-up floor, the footprints, the remoteness of the location—Harry's only conclusion was a bad one. Then, as he was about to leave, something caught his eye in amongst the blood and the fur. Harry fished around in a pocket for an evidence bag, then using an old biro lifted the thing out of the gore and slipped it into the bag.

Back outside, Harry strode away from the barn to suck in some of the much needed fresh night air and ponder for a moment on just what the hell was wrong with humanity. Because what had happened in that barn was no accident. Harry knew that the dog had died as people had watched. Torn apart by another dog, he guessed, though he had been on cases where other animals, such as Dave's favourite, the badger, had been involved.

'You're awful quiet,' Dave said, coming over to stand with Harry. 'I'm guessing that's not a good sign. Though you're a hard man to read at the best of times, if you don't mind me saying so. A stare on you that could kill, and that's on a good day.'

'You were right to call me,' Harry said, clenching and unclenching the hand not carrying the evidence bag, trying to squeeze out the anger he felt for those who had been party to what had gone on in that barn.

'Well, that's something, then.'

'It is,' Harry said. 'I think you arriving caught someone in the act of trying to clean up what went on in there. And right now, having had a look around for myself, I'm more than a little relieved that you weren't here any earlier to actually see what was going on in there.'

'Really?' Dave asked. 'Why?'

'Because,' Harry said, 'I'm fairly sure that whoever was out here, doing what they were doing, well, let's just say that they wouldn't have been all that happy to be discovered, if you know what I mean.'

'Bad then,' Dave said, and Harry gave a shallow nod.

'Very. Their sharp exit on seeing you turn up is the only contact you ever want to have with these kinds of people, I promise you.'

'So, now what?'

Harry turned round to face his friend and lifted the evidence bag for him to see. Inside was a dog collar and on it hung a brass tag engraved with a telephone number.

'A phone call, then,' Dave said.

'The first of many, I fear,' Harry replied.

CHAPTER TWO

Rebecca Sowerby, pathologist, perfectionist, and secret collector of absolutely anything to do with her favourite classic television show, *Murder She Wrote*, threw her phone across her bedroom and slumped back down into her bed. The phone thunked against her laundry basket, the vintage one she'd been very happy to find while rummaging through an antiques shop over in Richmond, then dropped to the floor with a dull thud.

She was tired, no, she was exhausted, and the last thing she needed right now was an early morning call to head out into the darkness and on into the dales. A beautiful place it was, but the attraction wasn't really there at this hour. This was the job she had chosen, though, one that she loved, and one that she did better than anyone else, of that she was pretty damned sure, so she pushed herself out of her bed and headed through to the bathroom, stubbing her toe on the way. And that didn't help her frame of mind at all.

Dressed, her toe still throbbing, and quickly fed on a smoothie containing banana, turmeric, spinach, pineapple, and an almost dangerous amount of fresh ginger, Rebecca was soon behind the wheel of her car. The vehicle was some metallic-grey hybrid thing that she'd been persuaded to buy, thanks to a very good salesperson and a momentary lapse of self-control.

Dawn was still some time off, and the vehicle's piercingly bright headlamps didn't so much cut through the darkness ahead, as eradicate it, burning through it like a thermal lance.

To get her brain into gear, Rebecca enlisted the help of a personal Spotify selection she'd entitled *Get The Hell Out Of Bed*, and soon she was feeling a little more energised, the ginger and turmeric doing their thing, and the music driving her on.

When she eventually flew out of the other side of Leyburn, heading on up through Wensleydale to her destination, Rebecca pulled herself out of the music and thought for a moment about what she was driving towards. That didn't really make her any happier, because in the grand scheme of things, the death of a dog, though upsetting, wasn't the kind of crime that got the pulse racing. Not that she would ever admit to finding her job thrilling, that would be crass, but there was no denying the adrenaline, the buzz of a crime scene, of trying to piece together the puzzle of what had happened, to whom and by whom. But a dog?

It was hard to pull in resources at the best of times, which was why, right now, she was heading over on her own. The rest of her team didn't need to be called out for this one, and she would handle it easily on her own, including taking the photographs. And if any additional help were required, there was always DCI Harry Grimm—a detective who was not only Grimm by name, but grim by nature in almost every conceivable way.

As the DCI's name rattled around in her mind, Rebecca rested her head in her right hand, rubbing her temples in the hope of easing, not just her tiredness, but general disquiet about the detective. It wasn't that she didn't like Harry, just that he, like a lot of detectives she'd worked with, didn't seem to quite understand what it was that she or her team did. And if they did, they didn't exactly show it.

What she did wasn't simply a case of pitching up a nice big tent, scratching around in PPE, and as if by magic finding all the evidence needed to make an arrest within hours of the crime being committed. It was considerably more subtle than that, more detailed, and more time-consuming. It was fair enough that those charged with solving the crime were impatient, but sometimes she found herself wishing that they'd just acknowledge the complexity of what she did and give her enough time to do it.

Outside, the night was still dark, the sky a swallowing vastness of black pricked through with the glint of stars, like diamonds cast upon the thickest velvet. And below the sky, the dales were darker still, the ominous silhouettes of the fells rising up around her to touch the sky.

When she eventually came into Hawes, Rebecca found herself wishing it was a few hours later, the shops open. The smoothie had been enough to get her going, but her stomach was crying out for something more substantial. And one of the things she'd learned about Grimm and his team was that they knew where to get a good bacon roll or two, or a tasty pie. Cake as well, though it was perhaps a bit early for that. As for having cheese with it? That was a most emphatic no. Cheese and cake was wrong.

Hawes kicked her out the other side and she headed off

up a hill, a caravan park on her right, before leaving the small market town to disappear in her rearview mirror.

About three miles out of Hawes, Rebecca slowed for a turning on her left, heading up Snaizeholme Road. Though she thought calling it a road was stretching it a bit, the lane little more than a well-used gravel farm track.

Driving on, shadows approached from the left as woodland loomed out of the dark. The trees leaned out as though to snatch her from the road, their branches shivering in the breeze as if some other force commanded them.

The trees soon gave way, their dark silhouettes replaced with open fields and rough moorland ahead. Then the track split, and as directed, Rebecca took the right fork, the lane changing to a narrower, rougher track. It squeezed in from both sides to the point where she found that she was holding her breath as she followed the line of a craggy and grey drystone wall on her left. Ahead she saw more trees, though this was a considerably smaller plantation than the one she had passed just a few minutes ago, and beneath the canopy of the leaves, she saw vehicle headlamps shining out into the gloom.

Rebecca pulled her vehicle to a stop, switched off the engine, and climbed out to meet the least welcoming face she had ever known in her life.

'Grimm,' she said, a yawn chasing the word away as soon as she'd said it. It came on so quickly that she didn't even have a chance to cover it, instead, blessing the DCI with her wide open mouth as a greeting.

'Sorry about this,' Grimm replied, his voice as gruff as usual, though Rebecca could hear in it the same tiredness she was feeling. 'And I know you're probably thinking it's just a dog, but—'

'Actually, no, I'm not,' Rebecca said, walking round to the

boot of her car to collect her equipment, as another yawn came in for an attack.

'Really? Oh, right, well that's good, then,' Grimm said. 'It is early though, but it's not like crime has to happen during waking hours, is it?'

'Sadly, no,' Rebecca said. 'It would be a whole lot more convenient if it did.'

'I don't think criminals are into convenience,' Grimm said. 'Unless it's inconvenience and just how much of it they can cause other people.'

Rebecca, now dressed in her PPE, her various bags unloaded from the rear of her car, slammed the boot shut.

'So, where are we going, then?' she asked.

'Just down that way a while,' another voice said. 'There's a barn, you see. Well, I mean, you can't see it right now, because it's dark, but you will when we get there, if you know what I mean.'

Rebecca was rather surprised that she hadn't noticed the other man before, seeing as he seemed to be about the size of a house. His voice was gentle and friendly though and his smile was certainly genuine.

'This is Dave Calvert,' Grimm said, introducing the large man to Rebecca.

'It's the badgers, you see,' Dave said. 'And the red squirrels. That's why I was up here and ended up seeing what I saw, if you know what I mean. Then I called Harry and he called you. So, blame me if you want. Or the badgers. Though they do get grumpy, so that's probably not the best of ideas.'

Rebecca had no idea what Dave was talking about and her expression must have said it all because Grimm spoke next.

'Dave has a few wildlife cameras set up near here, you see,' he said. 'They look over a badger sett. He was up here checking on them. Isn't that right, Dave?'

'It is, that,' Dave said. 'There's otters on the Ure, now, you know? It's a wonderful place, is Wensleydale. Always something to see. I'm going to be showing Harry here some of the videos I've got of the wildlife we get up here one evening. Aren't I, Harry?'

'You are?'

'Yes,' Dave said, then he looked at Rebecca and added, with an enormous smile, 'And you're welcome, too. Any friend of Harry's is a friend of mine!'

'Right,' Rebecca said with a nod, trying not to think about her cosy bed back home and how it had been replaced by a dour detective and an enormous nature lover. She also found herself somewhat surprised to be in the presence of someone who was clearly Grimm's friend. Up to that point, she'd just assumed that the DCI wasn't someone who, well, had any.

'Ready, then?' Grimm asked, but he didn't wait for an answer, and headed off, his torch picking out the way for them all.

As they were walking, Grimm pointed out tyre tracks in the field. 'Looks like there were a few vehicles up this way earlier,' he said. 'There's scuff marks at the front of the barn as well.'

Rebecca agreed and made a note to collect photos and hopefully some casts where she could.

When the barn came into sight, Rebecca's first thought was that it would be a lovely place to convert into a little bolt hole, somewhere to just escape to, away from the daily grind. Though she couldn't quite make out the surrounding area yet, beyond the looming outlines of the fells, she had no doubt from the quiet of the place and the rich scent of peat and grass and tree in the air, that it was beautiful, the kind of place that would recharge her soul.

'Remind me where are we again?' she asked.

'Snaizeholme,' Dave said. 'But don't ask me where that name comes from. Keep an eye out though, if you can, not just for badgers, but red squirrels.'

'Aren't red squirrels pretty much extinct in this country?' Rebecca asked.

'There's a growing number of them in Snaizeholme,' Dave said. 'Those woodlands you just drove past, that's where they are. They're beautiful little buggers when you catch sight of them.'

'Never seen one,' Rebecca said.

'Same here,' said Grimm.

'Well, this is the place to do so,' Dave said. 'Like I was telling Harry earlier, this whole valley is now a designated reserve for them. The Woodland Trust owns a fair bit of Snaizeholme now and is raising money to plant trees.'

'Sounds like you know quite a bit about it all,' said Grimm.

'Like I said,' Dave said, 'it's a hobby.'

Now only a few metres away from the barn, Rebecca came to a stop and looked at Grimm.

'Best you tell me again what you found, then,' she said. 'Just so I have an idea of what I'm walking into.'

Grimm then described everything he'd seen in and around the barn. When he got to the dog, Rebecca was sure the tone of his voice changed, dropping to a deeper growl, if that was even possible. It was a voice that sent words out into the world only after they'd been ground up with gravel, but right then she heard somewhere in it the sound of cliffs giving way, boulders tumbling down mountainsides. And there was something just hiding behind his eyes, wasn't there? A look, not just of disgust at what they both had a strong suspicion had happened in the barn, but of deep-seated anger, the kind that bubbled and boiled constantly, the lid containing it barely able to do so.

When Grimm had finished, Rebecca pulled the white hood of her protective overalls up and over her head then fixed the regulation face mask over her mouth.

'That's an interesting look,' Dave said. 'Like you've just walked off the set of a dodgy Sixties sci-fi movie.'

'I'll see you in an hour or two,' Rebecca said.

'Watch out for the owls,' Harry said.

'Owls?'

'Gave me quite the scare,' Harry said.

With a confused nod, Rebecca turned from the two men, and walked the final few metres towards the barn, camera at the ready, all of her senses now on full alert.

CHAPTER THREE

Dawn was breaking by the time the pathologist had finished at the barn. In between times, and having sent Dave back home for some shut-eye, Harry had taken the opportunity to try and catch up on the sleep he'd lost that night himself. He could've headed back to the flat, but there was something about where he was right then which just made him want to stay. He wasn't sure if it was the country-side, the air, or the sense of solitude and space, but it held him fast. And he didn't want to go waking his brother Ben up, either.

With the seat back in his old Rav4, Harry quickly dropped off. Only to wake up what felt like minutes later, and yet three hours had somehow passed. Outside, a clear sky of the lightest blue hung above him, wisps of clouds stuck to it here and there like tufts of wool blown into the air.

At first, the snooze seemed to have only made him feel worse, so to wake himself up properly, he pulled his aching body out of his vehicle and into the morning, his muscles complaining as he stretched to try and get them working again. He'd not been running for a couple of weeks at least and the looseness that came with keeping on top of his average fitness had already left him. He made a note to head out again that week, even if it was only a 5K run around Hawes. He'd do it early morning, as well, before his body and brain realised what he was doing and could stop him.

It was in the bright, crisp light of the morning, that Harry was finally able to see for himself the lonely, windswept beauty of Snaizeholme, and once again he found himself at a loss. Indeed, it was as though no matter where he went in the dales, which corner he turned, hill he climbed, path or road he travelled, the place always had something special to show him, a secret to be revealed. And Snaizeholme was no exception.

The first thing that struck Harry was the sense of openness to the valley, which rose gently to each side of him, the earth blanketed in numerous shades of green and patched with faded hues of a peaty, earthy brown. On the wind he heard the cries of birds of prey high up, and straining his eyes he saw them circling, searching for food. Other bird calls joined in, and beneath that came the far off bleat of sheep, though he could see none in the valley before him.

Turning, he gazed back along the way he had driven in, seeing the woodland a way ahead and on his right. As sanctuaries for rare wildlife like the red squirrel went, Harry figured there were worse places on Earth to end up.

Footsteps caught Harry's attention and he turned round just in time for a yawn he hadn't realised was approaching to force itself out of him with an almost desperate sense of urgency.

'Sorry about that,' he said, too late to cover the yawn with a hand.

'Don't be,' Sowerby replied, then she started to yawn herself. 'I did the same to you when I arrived.'

'That you did,' Harry said, though from the look Sowerby then gave him, he wished he hadn't.

'Thanks for the heads up about the owls,' Sowerby said.

'They were there, then?' Harry asked.

'Well, there was one, yes,' Sowerby replied. 'High up. Stared at me the whole time. Bit unnerving.'

'There were three in there when I went in,' Harry said, remembering his encounter. 'These massive eyes came at me out of nowhere. Nearly gave me a heart attack!'

Sowerby laughed, though the laugh quickly morphed into a yawn.

Harry asked, 'What have you got, then?'

'More than enough to be getting on with, that's for sure,' Sowerby said and Harry noticed how the words carried enough weight with them to cause her shoulders to sag just a little. 'Plenty of photos, blood samples, soil samples. I've got some casts of the tyre treads, shoe prints, samples of the soil from each of those areas as well, just in case we can trace something back at some point to their origin.'

'Contamination, you mean?'

Sowerby nodded. 'Even after hundreds of miles, a tyre can carry the residue of where it was parked, that kind of thing. Sometimes, it can help give you a geographical area for where a vehicle's been or spends most of its time.'

'A lot of work for just one person,' Harry said.

Sowerby shrugged.

'It wasn't too bad.'

'Did your team not want to bother with this, then?' he asked.

'And what's that supposed to mean?'

'Nothing at all,' Harry said. 'It's just that you're on your own and usually, you're not.'

'If you think it means we don't take this seriously—' Sowerby began, but Harry held up a hand to stop her.

'If there's one thing I've learned about you,' he said, 'it's that you take everything very seriously.'

'I'll take that as a compliment, whether it was meant as one or not,' Sowerby said.

'Well, that's how it was meant,' Harry said. 'As a compliment, I mean.'

Sowerby raised an eyebrow.

'Compliments aren't your strong point, are they?'

'Not really, no,' Harry said. 'A work in progress, you might say.'

For a moment, neither Harry nor Sowerby spoke, an awkwardness hanging in the air between them.

'What do you think, then?' Harry asked eventually, breaking the silence if only to hurry the morning along because he was getting hungry now, and something told him that getting back to Hawes would very much involve grabbing something for breakfast. The kind of something that Police Constable Jenny Blades would frown at.

'I think that the kind of people who were involved in what happened in that barn should be...'

The pathologist's voice faded and she closed her mouth, sucking in a deep breath through her nose.

Harry noticed her face twitch a little as she clenched her jaw, a storm of anger raging in her eyes.

'Oh, I'm with you on that,' Harry said, stuffing his hands down into his jacket pockets and guessing at the thoughts now playing on the pathologist's mind. 'Dog fight, then?'

Sowerby gave a short, sharp nod.

'I've had a quick check of the body. All that blood, I thought maybe it had been shot and crawled in there, then been attacked by something else.'

'And?'

Sowerby breathed slow and deep through her nose, as though trying to keep herself calm.

'I'm no vet, but I'm fairly confident the poor thing died of its wounds,' she said. 'There are teeth marks, claw marks, it was ripped apart. It's a proper mess.'

'It is that,' Harry agreed.

'I'm assuming the dog that won was taken back by its owner,' Sowerby said. 'Though what state the poor animal was in, I can hardly imagine. The blood outside the barn shows movement, so could be from that animal, its own wounds. Honestly, what the hell is wrong with people?'

'And what kind of dog is it that was in the barn, then?' Harry asked.

'We'll need a vet to tell us that,' Sowerby said. 'The damage was too bad for me to really tell, but I'm guessing some kind of spaniel.'

'What?'

'A spaniel,' Sowerby said.

'Can't be!' Harry said. 'For a start, it looks too big to be a spaniel.'

'Well, regardless of the size, it certainly looks like one,' Sowerby said, and Harry noticed an edge to her voice. 'The colouring of it, anyway. Though it is hard to tell, what with all the damage.'

'Look, I'm not questioning what you think you've seen, but—'

'But what?' Sowerby replied, and Harry heard a knife's edge in her voice. 'I'm just telling you what I think! Obviously, we'll need a vet to have a look as well. But maybe you're an expert at this, too?'

Harry was keen to keep Sowerby on-side and had a feeling that the early morning wasn't doing either of them much good. They were both tired, Sowerby more so, Harry thought, considering the journey she'd done.

'That's not what I meant,' he said.

'Isn't it? Then what did you mean, exactly?'

Harry paused, breathing deep through his nose.

'It's just that a spaniel, well, it's not a fighting breed by any stretch of the imagination, is it? And they're sort of a smallish medium-sized dog, aren't they? Which isn't what we found in there.'

'No, it isn't,' Sowerby said. 'Which makes me wonder how it ever ended up here to die like this in the first place.'

'There's a vet in Hawes,' Harry said, deciding to say no more about whether or not it was a spaniel they'd found in the barn. Because really, there was just no way that it could be. Dog fighting gangs were organised, secretive. They bred dogs specifically for fighting. And they absolutely didn't use spaniels. So, just what the hell was this? It didn't make sense.

'A vet? Good,' Sowerby nodded. 'You know them, then?'

Harry shook his head.

'Not really, no. Don't own a pet myself, or livestock for that matter. Or any kind of living creature, actually, though sometimes I find something at the back of the fridge that comes close. Most of the team are pretty set on me getting a dog, though.'

Sowerby laughed. It was a sound Harry had never heard before and he found himself staring at her.

'And that's funny, is it?' he asked.

'I'm just trying to imagine what kind of dog you'd suit,' Sowerby said.

'Well, don't,' said Harry. 'Because it won't be happening.

'You've resisted, then?'

'I have,' Harry said.

'Why?'

Harry went to answer, but then his voice caught somewhere in the back of his throat, because now, when he came to think of it, he wasn't really sure. The old arguments of no time, nowhere to exercise it, no one to look after it if he was away, well, they didn't really ring true anymore.

'Work,' he said eventually. 'I'm busy, too busy for a dog. That's why.' Harry saw the smallest of smiles break through onto Sowerby's face. 'What?'

'Doesn't one of your PCSOs have a dog?'

'Yes,' Harry said. 'Fly. I mean, Fly's the dog, not the PCSO. That's Jim. Who owns Fly.'

'And Fly's with him most of the time, isn't he?'

'He is.'

'Then you're just making excuses,' Sowerby said.

'It's not an excuse, it's a sensible reason. Well considered and thought through.'

'If you say so.'

'I do say so,' said Harry, then quickly if not exactly subtly, got the conversation back onto what they were actually there for in the first place. 'So, you'll see the vet, then?'

'I'll stop by there on my way through,' Sowerby said. 'Have a word with them about it all. They'll need to do a full necropsy on it.'

'I'll pop by to have a chat with them as well when they're done.'

'Good,' Sowerby said. 'A report's only so good, isn't it?

Sometimes it's best to have it straight from the horse's mouth, as it were.'

Harry hadn't heard the term *necropsy* for a long time but knew that it was simply the same investigation as an autopsy, only one performed on animals.

'That reminds me,' he said and pulled from a pocket the evidence bag containing the dog collar he'd found in the barn by the remains.

Sowerby took it from him and held it up for a closer look.

'I'm assuming you've taken the number?'

'I've not rung it yet, though,' Harry said. 'That's my job for this morning. Not one I'm looking forward to, either.'

'I'm surprised this was here at all,' Sowerby said, holding the bag up between them.

'So am I,' Harry agreed. 'A clear mistake on the part of those involved, I'm hoping.'

Sowerby stowed the evidence bag away.

'Well, thanks for coming over,' Harry said.

'No thanks needed,' Sowerby said. 'It's my job as much as it is yours.'

'Funny way to make a living though. For both of us, I mean,' Harry said. 'Sometimes I wonder what it would be like to do a normal job.'

'Normal?' Sowerby asked. 'What's that, then?'

'You know, nine to five, simple office work, a few meetings here and there about things you can forget about as soon as you go home.'

'Not sure something like that is for people like us,' Sowerby said.

'People like us?'

'We're not as dissimilar as you may think,' Sowerby said. Before he could reply, she turned from Harry and walked over to her car. 'I'll be in touch as soon as I can. And I'll get someone to forward the photographs over as soon as I get into the office.'

'Great, thanks,' Harry said.

Sowerby loaded up the boot of her car then climbed in behind the steering wheel. She started the engine and sent the window down into the door, glancing up at Harry as she did so.

'On the one hand, I know it's just a dog,' she said, 'but that kind of cruelty? It's more than just a random act of violence, isn't it?'

'Very much so,' said Harry and noticed how the pathologist's knuckles were turning white as she gripped her steering wheel.

'To do that, though, to force animals into a death match, for entertainment? I mean, why?'

'Lots of reasons,' Harry said. 'Though usually, it boils down to money.'

'There are kinder ways to make it,' Sowerby said.

'Kinder, yes, but not necessarily easier,' Harry replied.

'That's a very bleak viewpoint.'

'I'm a very bleak person,' Harry said.

At that, Sowerby rested her eyes on Harry's.

'Which is why I'm thinking whoever did this should be more than a little worried. And also why you really should get a dog.'

Harry said nothing, and that was enough.

As Sowerby drove off, Harry turned back to look at the barn. Something terrible had happened there, but to him, it wasn't simply about the one dog they'd found dead. Because he knew deep down that there was no way that what had taken place here was a random event.

Something like this, it took a fair bit of organising to put together. You had to find a suitable location, have access to dogs, know how to keep such activity out of sight of the law. That meant there were a good number of people involved, men and women who found pleasure and profit in the suffering of animals. But there was something else here, too.

If the dog was a spaniel, then that had Harry thinking that perhaps this wasn't as well-organised as similar cases he'd faced. Right now it didn't make any sense. Not just the cruelty, but the way all the details sat together uncomfortably. Harry wasn't sure if that was a good thing or a very bad one indeed.

Whatever had happened, Harry knew that those involved were the kind of people who were the lowest of the low. Weak people who got a kick out of killing something that had no chance of fighting back and who, he had no doubt at all, not only got off on it, but were convinced it made them tough.

Harry was already looking forward to proving them very, very wrong.

CHAPTER FOUR

PCSO JAMES METCALF WAS THE FIRST TO ARRIVE AT the office that he and the rest of the team used in the Community Centre in Hawes. He was early, having been up since six to help his dad around the family farm. Fly was with him, and as Jim unlocked the door, the dog slipped into the room and under a table onto a large cushion. He was a sleek animal with a black and white coat that rippled with the taut, young muscles underneath, and which shone in the sunlight when he was out on the fells helping to bring in the sheep. It was the night which best suited the dog though, Jim thought, when under a clear sky of stars the milky light of the moon would spill across the fells, catching Fly's movements like the scales of a silvery fish in a dark pool.

The room smelled a little stale from the day before, so he opened a window and allowed some cool air to rush in. He caught the scent of the moors and breathed it in, forever convinced that not only was it good for you, but that there was probably no air like it anywhere else in the world. Then it was over to get the kettle on, check the fridge for milk, and to have a nosy around the various information boards which hung from the walls, jostling for space with various other notices and procedures and posters.

For Jim, life in the dales was all he'd ever known. He'd grown up on a local farm, gone to school here, had friends up and down the dale. He'd had friends move away to university, to find work, but other than the training he'd had to complete for his role as a PCSO, Jim had stayed put. The grass, as far as he was concerned, was plenty green enough on his side of the fence, thank you very much, so that was exactly where he was staying. He had no plans to move and couldn't see that he ever would, either.

Now, as a Police Constable Support Officer, he saw himself as not only fulfilling the role of providing a visible police presence in the area, but as someone who was there to help the community, to serve the people around him, many of whom were as close as family. Which was why, months after it had happened, he was unable to shift the guilt he felt about the still-open case of the murder of an old school friend, Neil Hogg. Neil was one of the ones who'd moved away. Except, he'd somehow stumbled into a darkness out there which had then followed him home, and that Jim hadn't known about until it was too late.

The board on this particular crime was up on the wall, the investigation still classed as ongoing, regardless of the fact that the whole thing seemed to be a complete dead end. Add to this the fact, the case was wrapped up in sheep theft, a crime that up and down the country the police as a whole seemed to have little if any success with scoring convictions on, and it only seemed to be more and more hopeless as time ticked by. But Jim knew that he wouldn't let it go and that the rest of the team wouldn't either.

The kettle clicked off and Jim made himself a brew then went to stand again at what they all called Hoggy's board. Front and centre was the face of his friend, staring out into the room from a small collection of photos on loan from Neil's parents. Jim had bumped into Alan, Neil's dad, just a couple of weeks ago. The man looked older since the loss of his son, Jim thought, and there was an emptiness behind the smile he'd offered. It was as though Neil's early and violent death had torn a ragged hole in his soul that was impossible to heal.

Alan had invited Jim over, the unspoken reason behind the request not only to ask about the investigation but to give him and his wife a chance to talk about their son again, to relive the life they all remembered. As yet, though, Jim had avoided going over, coming up with excuses, putting work in the way.

Staring at the board, Jim shook his head at how little there was on it, because in the months after what had happened there had been no leads, everything a dead end. Everyone knew that what had happened to Neil was linked to what had taken place at Jim's parents' farm, that Neil had been involved in the theft of a flock of sheep Jim's dad had spent years breeding into prize-winners. The assumption was, that Neil had not only fed information back to a gang he'd somehow got involved with in Darlington, but also kept Jim himself away from the farm that fateful night. And now he was dead, a loose end tied up in the worst possible way.

As well as some photos of the crime scenes, both of Jim's farm, and also Neil's car, where his body had been found, various other bits of information were dotted around, detailing lines of investigation, relevant information, but nothing really led anywhere.

Neil had been killed by a single shot to the head with a .32 calibre bullet. The skin around the wound had been scorched by the round being fired, so it had been at very close range. So far, though, knowing that hadn't given them any way of finding out who had fired the gun. Unless they found the gun, and if at all possible the person who fired it, that wasn't helpful. And as for DNA at the scene, all they'd found was Neil's.

Forensics had also identified that after being shot, Neil's clothes and car had been searched. Though, whether the killer had found anything or not was impossible to ascertain. As was what they'd been looking for in the first place. The whole thing was one big dead-end, at the end of which was the corpse of a friend.

Jim sensed the pain of his grief bubbling up just a little too much, a sting at the corner of his eyes from the threat of tears. He took a deep breath and turned away and heard the thump of Fly's tail as the dog stared up at him.

'I'm alright, lad,' Jim said, looking down at the dog. 'Don't you worry.'

But the dog did worry, of that Jim was sure, because the animal seemed to have a sixth sense, as though it could read him better than any human. It was uncanny, but it was also helpful when they were out together working the sheep, because Fly was now starting to understand what Jim wanted before he whistled or called a command, and the more they worked together, the closer their bond became.

Jim took a seat over by Fly and reached down to stroke his head, his eyes drawn again to Hoggy's board, his friend's eyes staring back at him.

'You're right,' Jim said, looking down at Fly. 'I'll do it today, okay? I'll visit Neil's parents, I promise.'

'Talking to yourself again, I see.'

Jim turned to see Detective Sergeant Matt Dinsdale standing in the doorway. He was, as he had been known to say himself, comfortably built. However, thanks to his love of the outdoors, which included being a volunteer member of the local mountain rescue team, he managed to burn off most of the calories he took in during the often daily visits to either Cockett's for some cake, or one of the local cafés for a bacon butty.

'Not to myself, to Fly,' Jim said.

'Not sure that's any better.'

'He's a good listener,' said Jim. 'Plus, he doesn't talk as much bollocks as you.'

Matt laughed, the jubilant sound warm and cheerful.

'No, that's a fair point, right enough,' Matt said. 'But then who does and to such a high standard? No one, Jim, that's who.'

'How's Joan?' Jim asked, ignoring Matt's rambling.

'Massive!' Matt replied, then mimed a huge invisible belly on top of his own. 'I mean, she's properly enormous. Never seen anything like it in my life. She's coming up on seven months now and I'm pretty sure she's going to be giving birth to the world's most enormous baby.'

Jim laughed, not just at what Matt had said, but at the thought of the man being a dad. There was no doubt in anyone's mind that he'd be brilliant at it, but at the same time, everyone had a suspicion that not only would Matt's approach to fatherhood be as big and bold and open-hearted as the man himself, it would also be a little unconventional.

'You do know that babies can't be fed cheese and cake, don't you?'

'Of course I do!' Matt said. 'All the more for me, then.'

Jim saw Matt's eyes flick over to Hoggy's board.

'None of us have given up on it, you know that, don't you?'

'I do,' Jim said. 'I'm going to head over to see his mum and dad later today. Isn't that right, Fly?'

The dog's tail thumped.

'Wish we had more you could tell them,' Matt said. 'Losing a child, I don't see how you can ever get past that.'

'Perhaps you don't,' Jim said.

They were both quiet for a moment.

'You heard from Harry?' Matt asked, making his way over to the kettle and getting on with a task they all regarded as the first job of the day, sorting out a good mug of tea.

'Why, is something up?'

'Got a message from him that he's been up Snaizeholme since the early hours with Dave Calvert and, would you believe it, Rebecca Sowerby.'

'The pathologist?' Jim said, unable to hide the surprise in his voice.

'My thoughts exactly,' Matt said. 'Not sure what's gone on, like, but we're bound to find out soon enough, I'm sure.'

'He's not going to be in the best of moods then, is he?' Jim said.

Matt laughed again.

'When is he ever?'

'Oh, he's not that bad,' Jim said, as Matt sat down, a steaming mug of tea now in his hand. 'Bark's worse than his bite and all that.'

Fly slipped from his cushion and nuzzled Matt's free hand.

'True,' Matt said, stroking the dog. 'Though I do wonder sometimes.'

'How do you mean?'

Matt took a sip of his tea.

'I'm just saying that I'm not sure I'd like to see him angry, if you know what I mean.'

'You make him sound like the Hulk!'

'Maybe I do,' Matt said. 'Maybe I do. I'm just saying that I reckon he keeps himself in check. And I'm more than a little glad that he does. Can't imagine it's all that pretty if whatever's hidden deep down in that old bugger boils over.'

'No, perhaps you're right,' Jim said. 'Anyway, what are you on with today?'

'What day is it?'

'Wednesday,' Jim said. 'At least, I think it is.'

'You don't sound too confident about that.'

'No, it was market day yesterday, wasn't it? So, it's definitely Wednesday.'

'You're right, it was,' Matt said. 'Did you see that new butcher's stall?'

'I did,' said Jim. 'Can't see it doing all that well, can you? Not in Hawes, anyway. Competition is too strong. What's it like?'

'Expensive,' Matt said. 'All fancy-pants packaging and over-the-top recipes for its pies and sausages. I mean, I'm all for trying new things, but I'm not sure I want a beef, chilli, and chocolate sausage!'

'You're having a laugh!'

'I'm serious!' Matt said, then held up a hand and started to count through the various flavours he'd discovered. 'Beef, chilli, and chocolate; lamb and mint; lamb, rosemary, and red wine; beef and Guinness; pork, apple, and cider; vodka and Red Bull! There's even Irn Bru!'

Jim couldn't believe what he was hearing.

'Vodka and Red Bull? Irn Bru? In a sausage?'

'I know, right?' Matt said, shaking his head. 'Irn Bru!'

'Who'd buy that, then?' Jim asked, but then he saw the grin on Matt's face.

'You didn't.'

'I did.'

Jim couldn't help laughing.

'And?' he asked. 'What were they like?'

Matt placed his mug down on a nearby table, then rubbed his chin thoughtfully.

'Interesting,' he said.

'In a good way or bad?' Jim asked.

'Very good indeed, actually,' Matt said. 'Too good, if I'm honest. I ate a pound of the buggers all by myself.'

'Seriously?'

'I'm of a mind that those Irn Bru sausages are possibly dangerous,' Matt said, tapping his stomach as though it was still full. 'So dangerous, in fact, that I'm half wondering if we should get in touch with Police Scotland and have a word. We've got enough problems of our own without addictive meat products from the Highlands turning up on our doorstep!'

Jim pulled out his phone and put it to his ear.

'Hello? Yes, is that the Fort William constabulary? We've got a problem with some sausages...'

Another voice joined in the conversation and Jim and Matt turned to see Detective Inspector Gordanian Haig at the door.

'Fort William?' she said.

'Went there on a Scout Camp years ago,' Jim said. 'Well, not to the Fort as such. We camped down by a river somewhere close by, I think. But we visited the place a fair bit, for food and souvenirs.'

'Very interesting,' Gordy said. 'And you're phoning the station there to talk about sausages, are you?'

Jim stuffed his phone back into a pocket.

'If that's them on the phone now,' Gordy said, 'could you do me a favour and ask them to pop round to the Nevis Bakery for me? They do these haggis, neeps and tatties pies to die for!'

'You're kidding!' Matt said, and Jim was pretty sure that the DI was drooling.

'Do I look like a kidder?' Gordy said. 'Honestly, get yourself up there when you can, grab a pie from them, and make sure you nip into JJ's café for a breakfast.'

'I think I need to sit down,' Matt said. Then he looked over at Gordy and added, 'Didn't think you were over this way today. Something up?'

'Neither did I,' Gordy replied. 'And yes, there is. I had a call.'

'Who from?' Jim asked.

'Me,' interrupted another voice, gruff and hard enough to bring with it the promise of dark storm clouds on the brightest, cloud-free day.

Jim looked over to see Detective Chief Inspector Grimm.

'Hi, boss,' he said, then smiled and lifted his mug. 'Tea?'

CHAPTER FIVE

Harry was sitting in a corner of the office watching everyone begin their day with the usual chatter and banter that could only come with a group of people who knew each other very, very well. And they did both with a relaxed ease born of years sharing their lives, the team, not just professional work colleagues, but—and this was the bit which really surprised him—friends. Even someone as new as Police Constable Jadyn Okri joined in as though he had been with the others his whole life.

Having worked with a good number of other such teams in his time, Harry was confident that none of them had ever been quite like the one he was now responsible for in Wensleydale. A part of him wondered if some of the differences he noticed wasn't the team at all, but actually himself. Because, after closing in on nearly a year in the Dales, the person he was now had changed dramatically from who he had been back in Bristol, not that he was ever for letting on or showing it to those around him if he could help it.

Before signing up to a life in the police, Harry had been a

soldier, a Para no less, and the bonds there, between the soldiers, whatever their rank, were ferociously strong. They had to be, because the Paras were the sharp end of the Army, hard as nails fighters generally regarded as the best of the best, particularly by themselves. Which didn't always go down too well with other regiments, but that was just the way of things, really.

The Special Air Service—the SAS—drew a large number of their troopers from the ranks of the Paras, which said a lot. One of many secrets Harry carried was that he had been a good way through Selection—the process of getting into the SAS—himself, when life had changed and he'd taken another route, one which had somehow led him to where he was right now, drinking tea and having a young sheepdog nuzzle his hand.

In the police, the various teams Harry had worked with had been a rich mix of good, bad, and absolutely bloody awful. The professionalism had never been in question, most of the time, anyway, but the people? Well, Harry had excelled at not getting on with more than his fair share of them.

In the Paras, it had all been about looking out for each other, because in theatre your lives were in each other's hands. In the police, there had been a fair amount of that, but there had also been a good number of those looking out for number one. Not just jobsworths, but individuals who would happily shop you just to get ahead. Harry didn't like those people at all. And he'd never held back on telling them so, often brazenly stating that the people he worked with were not his friends. It was a distinction he liked and one he'd used almost as a protective shield. Then his life had taken a dramatic turn, he'd moved to the dales and everything about it had changed, whether he'd wanted it to or not.

So far, and discounting Graham Swift, the practically invisible Detective Superintendent Harry had to report to both as often as necessary and as little as possible, he'd not found this to be a trait in any single member of his new team. No, they weren't the Paras, and of that Harry was glad, though they did all display a very high degree of undying loyalty to each other, which could on occasion quickly become a healthy disregard for their own wellbeing if one of the others was in a bit of a scrape.

Harry leaned forward and cupped Fly's head in his large, calloused, and scarred hands, staring into the animal's deep brown eyes, the irises flecked with a rich glimmer of gold.

'Best I get the day started, don't you think?' Harry said.

Fly simply stared up at Harry, his tail whumping gently on the carpeted floor.

Harry let go of Fly's head and rose to his feet, a movement which had the immediate effect of causing the various conversations in the room to shut down, like water turned off at a tap.

Harry saw Matt glance over to catch his attention.

'You want the Action Book, boss?'

'Is there much in it we need to go through?'

Matt shrugged as Gordy pulled the book from a cabinet and opened it.

'To be honest,' Gordy said, 'most of us know what we're on with today, I think, am I right?'

By now, the rest of the team had gathered around and Harry had walked over to stand between Matt and Gordy.

Gordy's question was answered by nods.

Gordy said, 'Want me to run through what we've got on?'

'Anything urgent?'

'I don't think so,' Gordy said, shaking her head, then she directed her attention to the rest of the team. 'Right then, everyone, who's on with what today?'

Harry was unsurprised to see Police Constable Jadyn Okri's hand shoot up into the air. He was the newest member of the team, having joined a few months after Harry. He seemed to approach each moment of his life with relentless enthusiasm and displayed an unquenchable thirst to prove himself on the job. It would've been annoying if it wasn't so endearing.

'Constable Okri,' Harry said. 'You have something to say?'

'I'm heading up to Bishopdale,' Jadyn said. 'Following up on some weird reports we've had in about some apparent trespassing going on across someone's land.'

'Weird?' Harry asked. 'How's that, then?'

Jadyn went to speak, but Liz said, 'Let me guess; those weird reports are from a certain Mr Sewell and his wife, yes?'

'You know them?' Jadyn asked.

'Heard of, rather than know,' Liz replied, shaking her head. 'When did these reports come in?'

'Earlier this week,' Jadyn said. 'Why?'

'And what did the reports say, exactly?' Liz asked.

Jadyn shrugged. 'Not much,' he said. 'Just that they've seen trespassers on their land. Oh, and that they've caught evidence of it on some cameras or something.'

'So, how's that weird, then?' Harry asked, and noticed Jadyn's eyes flicker over towards Liz.

'Out with it, then!' Harry commanded.

'I...' Jadyn began.

'They're new to the area,' Liz said, as Jayden's voice

faded to nothing. 'Not sure where they're from, exactly, but they've bought a nice property with some land over in Bishopdale. A rambling place, needs a bit of work...'

'You're not exactly getting to the point, are you?' Harry sighed.

'Deer,' Liz said.

'Dear what?' said Harry.

'No, as in deer, the animal, you know, Bambi? That kind of deer. Not dear as in, *oh dear*, or *deary me*.'

'Or, *by 'eck, that's dear, lad*,' Matt added, his accent suddenly thick as molasses.

'I know what a deer is!' Harry said a little sharper than he'd meant to, but he was still tired from his early morning. 'What I don't know is what any of this has to do with PC Okri here heading out to talk to someone about trespassing and how any of that is somehow weird!'

'Let's just say they're not used to the countryside,' Liz said.

'And what's that got to do with Bambi?' Harry asked.

'They're not happy that deer are able to walk freely across their land,' Liz said. 'Not just deer, either. There've been a few incidences of sheep doing what sheep do and getting through a bit of a break in a wall here and there, or a fence. They weren't happy about that at all. Went around to see the farmer and told him they were going to get him arrested.'

Harry had no idea what to say to any of what he was hearing.

'So, if I'm hearing this right, they've moved to the countryside, but they don't actually like the countryside.'

'Oh, they like it,' Liz said, 'but only if it's contained and controlled and doesn't make a mess of their lawn.'

Harry laughed.

'Good luck with that, then,' he said, nodding over to Jadyn.

'There's also a public right of way that runs right through their land,' Jadyn said. 'And if you think they're unhappy about deer and sheep, you should hear what they have to say about the general public!'

'I don't think I really need to,' Harry began, but Jadyn wasn't done.

'They've fenced the path so that it goes around the field rather than across it. And that fence is at least six-foot high. They're justifying it by saying they're getting a specialist in to rewild the area.'

'Rewild?' Harry said, bemused. 'But this is the Dales. It's fairly wild all on its own, isn't it?'

'The parish council aren't best pleased,' Liz said. 'Because you can't just go moving a historic right of way. That's not how things work.'

'Well, looks like you've a fascinating day ahead of you then, doesn't it, PC Okri?'

'It does, that,' Jadyn said, nodding with clear enthusiasm.

Harry moved on to the rest of the team, sweeping his eyes around them like searchlights.

'What about the rest of you, then? Anything more pressing than trespassing to be dealing with?'

Jenny Blades, the other police constable on the team, said, 'I'm over to Swaledale later. Been a theft over at Marrick Priory, the outdoor centre. A load of equipment has been stolen, including some mountain bikes.'

Harry thought back to when he'd visited the Priory himself a while ago as part of another case.

'You'll be seeing Adam Bright, the manager, then?'

'I will,' Jen said.

'How's he doing?'

It was a good few months back now, but Harry doubted it was long enough to have allowed Adam to even begin to deal with what had happened after his brother, Gary, had been arrested and charged with two murders. It was also a case in which Jen herself had ended up being caught up in a little too personally, to say the least. Harry, Matt, and Jim had got to her just in time, but only just.

'Sounded fine on the phone,' Jen said, 'but that's not saying much, is it?'

'And what about yourself?' Harry asked.

He'd been keeping an eye on Jen, and she'd been doing fine, all things considered. But still, it didn't hurt to ask.

'I'm grand,' Jen said and sent a beaming smile back to Harry.

'Well, just take it steady today,' Harry said, unable to disguise the concern in his voice. Then he glanced over to PCSO Liz Coates and asked, 'You able to head over with her?'

'No problem,' Liz said. 'I was only on with a walk around today anyway. Had a few villages to visit, say hello to folks, that kind of thing. Be that whole visible police presence, like.'

'It's not necessary,' Jen protested.

'Necessary or not, it's what's happening,' Harry said. 'With Liz there, you'll be better able to both check out the theft and check up on Adam. It's not really our role, I know, but I can't help but feel that in a community like this, it's important we show that caring side, right?'

Matt coughed.

'Something the matter?' Harry asked.

'No, nothing at all,' Matt said. 'Just wondering what

you've done with the old Grimm, that's all! Caring side? You know, you've changed, boss.'

'And for the better, I'm sure,' Gordy said, smiling over at Harry.

Harry hurried on.

'Is that it, then?'

Jim mentioned then that he was going to pop in and visit Neil Hogg's.

'How are they doing?' Harry asked.

'That's what I'm going to go and find out,' Jim said. 'And to see if I can find anything else out about Neil and what he was doing.'

Harry saw Jim's eyes flicker up to Neil's board on the wall.

'Well, don't get your hopes up,' he said, concerned that Jim was still not dealing with what had happened, well, at all. 'But if you do learn something of interest, call in immediately, okay? Now, anyone else? Nowt else pressing?'

Silence from the rest of the team, though in his head all Harry could hear was the echo of his own voice using the word *nowt*.

'Good,' Harry said at last and stood up, stretching as he did so to rid himself of the weariness that had set up shop in his muscles earlier that morning. 'Then, I suppose I'll be telling you what's been going on up in Snaizeholme...'

CHAPTER SIX

HARRY FACED HIS TEAM, BUT BEHIND HIS SCARRED FACE his mind played out the tragic and bloody scene from the barn earlier that morning. He couldn't help but drop his eyes to Fly, who was now sitting at his owner's feet, curled up and asleep. The thought that someone could get a kick out of watching a creature like that be ripped apart by another, and put money on the outcome, churned Harry's gut into a violent storm.

'Early this morning,' Harry said, working hard to make sure his voice was as calm as it could be, 'I was woken up by a call from Dave Calvert.'

'Didn't know Dave knew what early morning was,' Matt said.

'I'll be honest, it was a surprise to me as well,' Harry said. 'Turns out, we never end up knowing as much about people as we think we do. Early mornings aren't just something he's happy with, but something he's positively excited about seeing, as he's big into wildlife.'

'Dave's just big, full stop,' said Jim.

'He called me from Snaizeholme,' explained Harry. 'He was up there checking up on some wildlife cameras of his when he saw something in a barn he thought I should have a look at.'

'What's there to look at in Snaizeholme?' Liz said. 'There's nowt up there but red squirrels and the wind.'

'Don't forget the rain,' added Jim. 'That place seems to always have more of it than anywhere else.'

'When I arrived, he took me to the barn,' Harry continued. 'He'd mentioned on the phone that he'd seen some blood and there was plenty of it. Sensibly, he'd not gone in for a closer look and left that to me.'

'Can't say I want to know the answer to this question,' Gordy said, 'but what exactly did you find?'

Harry sighed.

'A proper mess, to be honest. More blood, evidence of a lot of activity. And a body, though it wasn't human. Oh, and some owls who nearly gave me a heart attack.'

Harry saw confusion write itself onto every face in front of him and went on to explain.

'When I was back down south,' he said, moving to perch on a table and fold his arms, 'I dealt with more than my fair share of pretty horrendous stuff. The worst kinds of people doing the worst kinds of things, and not just to each other, either.'

'How do you mean?' Liz asked.

'A few years ago, I was part of a small team tasked with investigating illegal gambling,' Harry said. 'Everyone knows it goes on, and most of the time it's just small timers running backstreet high-stakes poker games, though we had a fair few number of illegal fights to deal with as well.'

'Bare-knuckle stuff, you mean?' asked Jadyn.

'Oh, it went further than just the knuckles,' Harry said. 'In fact, the bare-knuckle fights weren't too much of a problem because the blokes doing that generally came away from it looking worse than they actually were. Lots of blood, a few bruises, but that was about it.'

'You make it sound like it's not actually that bad,' said Jen.

'I'm not saying that at all,' Harry said, perhaps sharper than he'd meant to. 'But the damage done in a bare-knuckle fight isn't half what can be done to someone in a professional bout.'

'Seriously?' Jim said. 'Bare-knuckle is safer? How's that, then?'

'For a start, the fights are shorter,' Harry said. 'And the fighters themselves don't generally try and completely destroy their opponent and give them brain damage. They're skilled, too. It's not just some mad brawl.'

'Where's this going, boss?' Matt asked.

'Like I said, for some it went further than just bare knuckles. There was some real fringe stuff going on, and it was looking impossible to crack.'

'Fringe,' Gordy said. 'Is that a polite term for sick and twisted?'

'In this world,' Harry said, 'if someone's thought it or imagined it or dreamt it up in some insane, mad, disturbed dream, then it's probably been done.'

'Well, that's not dark at all, is it?' said Matt, shaking his head.

'Such a lovely cheery chat and so early, too,' said Gordy. 'Sets you up for the day!'

Harry ignored them both, the memories rushing at him now, a thunderous charge of things he'd witnessed over the years, all tumbling into him like jagged rocks and crushing boulders down a mountainside.

'The fights were all for money, and the fighters themselves could do well out of it, too. And the more extreme, the more dangerous the fight was, then the higher the stakes, and the more money could be made.'

'How dangerous exactly?' Liz asked. 'What the hell were these people into?'

'This is starting to sound like a dodgy straight-to-video movie from the Eighties,' Matt said. 'One of those ones that would have a moulded cover on it and have all the gory bits on the back, with a title like *Death Match Blood Fest: The Revenge* or something.'

'Maybe that's where they got their ideas from,' said Harry. 'If you've ever watched mixed martial arts, some of what I saw makes that look like a playtime scrap in a school yard.'

'Fun, then,' said Jen.

Harry shook his head.

'No, not really. Anyway, it wasn't just mad violent types trying to take each other apart with bike chains and clubs,' Harry said. 'We also stumbled onto dog fights.'

Harry saw Jim immediately reach down to scratch Fly's head.

'The fights were never in the same place twice,' explained Harry. 'They'd move them around, some in disused factories, others in warehouses, derelict houses in the middle of nowhere, forest and woodland, just anywhere that they knew would be out of sight and noise range of anyone who might spot them. And, of course, us, the police.'

'And what's that got to do with what you saw up at

Snaizeholme?' Jim asked. 'There's no one round here into anything like that, I'm sure of it.'

Harry heard the conviction in the PCSO's voice, as well as the concern that perhaps that conviction was misplaced. Everywhere had dark secrets, Harry thought, and the dales were as likely as anywhere to be home to more than a few of humanity's nastier members.

Harry went to speak, but Matt got in there first.

'That's not quite true,' he said, looking at Jim.

'How's that, then?' Harry asked. 'You mean there's been dog fights around here before?'

Harry knew better than to get his hopes up for this to be a lead, but there might still be something in what Matt was saying.

'Not dogs, no,' Matt said. 'Cocks.'

CHAPTER SEVEN

Harry didn't have to wait long at all for the childish giggles to sweep through the team. He heard a particularly loud snort and turned to stare at Gordy, shaking his head.

'Really?'

Gordy stifled her laugh, but the others were still tittering as Matt, ignoring them, continued.

'Well, when I say cocks, I'm not just referring to the animals that had to fight,' he said. 'This is a good few years ago now, like, but there were some idiots in the Young Farmers' Club.'

'Some?' Liz said.

'Don't knock it,' said Jim. 'I used to go to all the local meetups. Great fun. And we raised a lot of money for charity, too.'

'Anyway,' Matt said, dragging the conversation back to what he was saying, 'it was only a small number, like, and I think they got the idea from some movie they'd seen. So, they got a few of their old hens together and threw them into a pen to see what would happen.'

'Hens?' Jen said. 'I thought you said cocks?'

'And what did happen?' Harry asked.

'Nowt at all!' Matt said laughing. 'I mean, who the hell ever thinks that hens are going to have a good scrap? Bunch of idiots! And they'd bigged it up as well, invited a good number of folk over, friends and whatnot, and everyone got drunk, then these hens get thrown into this ring made out of a sheep pen and nothing happens! Nothing! No, I lie. One of them laid an egg.'

'Where's this going, exactly?' Harry asked.

Matt was now laughing hard, tears rolling down his cheeks.

'Hens!' he said. 'Can you imagine it? People had turned up for drink and a bit of illegal blood sport, and all they got was a few hens pecking at the ground and ignoring each other! Brilliant, or what?'

'How did you find out about it?' Harry asked.

'Someone called in a noise disturbance,' Matt said. 'Though this was all miles from anywhere, so someone not happy with what they were up to clearly just grassed on them.'

'Anything happen to the organisers?'

'Yeah, they got thick ears from their parents and were kicked out of the Young Farmers,' Matt said. 'One of them particularly so, seeing as his dad, Mr Slater, runs the local bookies.'

'Not exactly crime of the century, is it?' Jadyn said.

'No,' Harry said. 'Matt, I don't suppose you can remember the names of those involved, can you?'

'Must be twenty years ago,' Matt replied. 'But I can go

and have a chat with Mr Slater. He's not the warmest of folk, but I'm sure he'll be happy to oblige if I ask nicely.'

The hen-fighting interlude over, Harry said, 'Right, back to the barn. Now, obviously, this will be confirmed by the vet later today, once the necropsy is done, but it looks like the body we found was that of a spaniel.'

'Necropsy?' Jadyn said, the word clearly not one that sat well with him.

'It's an autopsy for animals,' Gordy said.

'Also, I found a dog collar at the crime scene,' said Harry. 'From that, I've got the name and phone number of the owner. Jim?'

'I can check it against our records,' Jim said, noting both. 'See if or when the dog was reported missing. And I'll check on other dog thefts, too.'

A few months ago now, Harry had given the PCSO responsibility for any crimes to do with domestic animals. The aim had been to help him focus and to feel like he was doing something directly related to what had happened at his parents' farm, with the theft of their sheep. But it also covered everything from dealing with lost cats to nuisance dogs and escapee rabbits. Harry assumed that if other dogs had gone missing, then there was a good chance there would be a report of it.

'What else did you find?' Matt asked. 'Sowerby was out with you as well, right?'

Harry gave a nod.

'She was. Can't say I relished calling her, but she came out and got on with the job, professional as always. We'll have her report in soon enough, I'm sure. But right now what we know is this...'

Pushing himself up from the table he'd been leaning

against, Harry turned to face a blank board and grabbed a pen. Then he started to write as he spoke.

'At some point last night, a group of people congregated in that barn in Snaizeholme to participate in a dog fight. Whether it was for money or not, right now I don't care, though that may give us a lead at some point as to the kind of people we're dealing with.'

'Those who like a bit of a flutter, you mean?' Liz suggested.

'More than a flutter, I think,' Harry said.

'I'll look into that,' said Matt. 'When I'm having my chat with Mr Slater.'

'He won't be giving up names though,' Harry said. 'Confidentiality and all that.'

'No, but he might have an idea of anyone who might bet a bit on the wild side,' Matt said.

'Anyway,' Harry continued, 'I personally can't see a fight like this being for any reason other than money, so that's what we're going to assume for now. At least two dogs were involved, that much was evidenced by the damage done on the deceased dog found at the scene. There's a good number of tyre marks heading in and out as well. Right now, though, we've not got much to go on at all. And that's always an issue with something like this. The people who do it, they're careful, secretive. They don't want to be found.'

Harry turned around to look at the team.

'I'm going to be speaking to the owner of the dog once we're done here,' he said. 'So, while I'm on with that, I need actions right now from everyone here. Because we don't want this kind of stuff on our doorstep. Whether they're local or outsiders or both, this kind of activity, well, it's insidious. It happens in the background, in whispers that few hear, but before you know it, it spreads like an infection and then you're in all kinds of trouble.'

'Surely it's just a one-off, though,' Jim said.

'Could be, but I doubt it,' Harry said. 'And I know from experience the kind of people that'll be involved are not the kind of people we want wandering up and down dale. Because if this is what they're into, then it's only the tip of the iceberg.'

For a moment, everyone fell quiet, deep in thought, their minds focusing on what Harry had said and what they could all do now.

Matt spoke first.

'I'll head up to Snaizeholme,' he said, 'have a word with the farmer, see if he's seen or heard anything, not just last night, but at other times, too. There's bound to be security cameras on account of it being a nature sanctuary. Then I'll head over to the bookmakers.'

'I forgot to ask Dave about his cameras,' Harry said. 'They might have picked something up.'

Gordy was next.

'The only way in and out of Snaizeholme is the road through Widdale,' she said. 'So, they've either come up through Hawes or along from Ribblehead way. I'll head over and start on a door-to-door.'

'We'll join you once we're done over in Swaledale,' Jen said, with a glance over at Liz. 'It's a big area to cover.'

'Farmers don't miss much,' Gordy said. 'Someone might have seen something.'

'I'll head down to the vet's,' Jadyn offered. 'Might hurry them along a bit.'

'I'll come with you,' Jim said. 'I shouldn't be too long over at Neil's parents' place. And I know Andy fairly well, thanks to living on a farm. Vets are more like friends, to be honest. They certainly visit more often than relatives, that's for sure.'

'And who's Andy?' Harry asked.

'Andrew Bell,' Jim said. 'He's the director and one of the veterinary surgeons there. They've a fairly large team, covering the whole of the dale, like, with a branch in Leyburn as well as up this way in Hawes. Nice bunch, as well. Busy, what with this being such a farming area.'

'That's everyone, then,' Harry said.

'It is indeed,' said Gordy, having noted everyone's jobs down in the Action Book.

Harry pulled out his phone.

'Best you all get on with what we've discussed,' he said. 'As yet, I don't think this case requires an office manager as such, so we'll just run that role between us; whoever's in at the time, they keep everyone else up to date should anything come in. And as soon as I hear from the pathologist, I'll let you all know.'

'What about Swift?' Matt asked.

Harry shook his head.

'Can't see him being too bothered about a dead dog, can you?'

'No, not really,' Matt agreed.

Meeting over, and after Jim had checked to confirm that the dog whose collar Harry now held had indeed been reported missing, Harry headed outside to make the call. As he went to tap in the number, Jim and Fly walked past.

'Jim,' Harry called out.

The PCSO stopped and turned to face Harry.

'Boss?'

Harry held the young man's eyes for a moment, then

said, 'I'm going to assume that I don't need to tell you to keep an objective mind with regards to visiting Neil's parents.'

'No, I mean yes, I mean,' spluttered Jim. 'I'm okay, honestly.'

Harry wasn't so sure.

'I can't have you going off on your own again,' he said, his voice a low growl, though it was one of concern more than anger. 'You remember what happened last time, the trouble you ended up in, and dragged me into as well? You've had more than enough time to reflect on just how far south that could've gone.'

Harry knew he didn't need to remind Jim, but it had to be done, and the look on his face was enough to let him know that his words had hit home.

Just a few months ago, he'd run off on some wild chase to nothing and ended up in more than a spot of bother in Darlington, and it had been Harry who'd had to go and get him out of it. Hadn't been too easy either and it'd had all the hallmarks of something that could've gone very bad indeed, but it hadn't and they'd got away with it, thanks to a healthy mix of good luck and Harry's brand of getting things done.

'I hear you, Harry,' Jim said.

'You sure you're not just saying that?'

Harry stared hard at the PCSO, almost daring him to lie.

'Yes.'

It was a firm *yes*, for sure, but Harry still wanted to drive the point home.

'You need to be able to deal with things in turn,' he said, his voice quieter, forcing Jim to move in closer to hear him, and that only made the lad more aware of just how imposing Harry could be if and when he wanted, or needed, to be. 'You can't let one case overshadow another.'

'I know.'

'I'm talking, Jim...'

'Yeah, sorry.'

Harry continued.

'It's hard, I know, but if you can't do it, then you can't be objective. And if you can't be objective, if you can't look at things from a distance, then you're no use to anyone in this job, particularly yourself. If you keep on carrying the weight of Neil's death around with you, all it's going to do is end up crushing you.'

'I understand.'

Harry leaned in even further, forcing Jim to step back a little.

'Do you, though, Jim? You sure about that?'

'Yes, I'm sure,' Jim said. 'Look, Harry, I know what you're saying, I really do. I get it. I was a dick, I'm sorry. But I'm okay now, I'm sorted. Trust me.'

'Trust you?' Harry said. 'I never said I didn't, Jim. I'm just telling you, in my own unique way, that I'm concerned. Understand?'

'I do,' Jim said.

'Well, you had certainly better do,' Harry replied. 'Now, off you go.'

Harry watched as Jim and his faithful dog, Fly turned and headed off. He was good at what he did, Harry thought, just needed a few more years of experience, that was all. Not that he wished Jim to become old and jaded, or so thick-skinned that he was never affected by any part of the job, just that a bit of maturity would help him judge things a little better. Perhaps.

Harry rubbed tiredness from his eyes and lifted his phone, making the call to the owner of the dog found at

Snaizeholme. Above him, the weather itself was clearly aware of what he was doing, as grey clouds gathered and a cold gust of wind rushed at him, sending an icy shiver through to his bones.

The call connected.

Harry spoke.

CHAPTER EIGHT

An hour or so later that morning, Harry was sitting in the kitchen of a small cottage down the dale in the pretty little village of Redmire, a place he had never actually had reason to visit before, until now. And as reasons went, it wasn't one he'd have asked for. Reporting a death of any kind was always traumatic for the ones receiving the news.

With a choice of two routes, one heading along the main road that cut through Wensleydale, from Hawes to Leyburn and following the River Ure, the other taking a left in Bainbridge and then on through Askrigg and Carperby, Harry had gone with the latter. It was a road he didn't know quite so well, so he took the opportunity to have another look, half wondering if he was, by now, used enough to the dales not to be wowed by it.

He could not have been more wrong.

Leaving Askrigg behind, though perhaps not the memories of a previous case involving the sad and rather grisly murder of singer Gareth Jones, Harry rolled on down the road, not exactly in a rush to reach his destination. The brief conversation he'd had on the phone with the dog's owner had leached sadness into his already bone-cold day, and he had no doubt at all that when he arrived he would be dealing with an owner in mourning. Though Harry had never had a pet, he'd known plenty of people in his life who had. And the loss of a pet was, to many, like losing one of the family.

The grey clouds which had sat over Hawes stayed there and as he drove along Harry enjoyed a clear sky and an empty road. This route was certainly quieter than the other, and to Harry, it was as though he'd stepped back in time a few decades, to those distant days when there weren't so many cars on the road and perhaps people were in less of a rush.

Then again, even on a busy day, the traffic in the dales had nothing on what he'd ended up becoming almost blind to down south in Bristol. Getting from one side of that small city to the other was nothing less than an exercise in not going batshit crazy, the traffic moving at a snail's pace from one junction to the next, traffic lights and crossroads and roundabouts funnelling the masses through roads designed for horse and cart, not cars and trucks and suicidal moped riders. True, a huge amount of work had been done to improve the roads, but Harry wasn't convinced any of it had been all that successful, particularly the run in along the A37 and through to Temple Meads Station. It never ceased to amaze him just how slow that road could be, how so many people could all be going in the same direction.

In his time, he'd been on the receiving end of more than enough examples of road rage, drivers frustrated by the stop-start-stop of their journey to the point that they just snapped and needed someone or something to blame. Breaking up a fight between a man in an expensive suit armed with a car jack he'd grabbed out of the boot of his car, and a van driver wielding a hefty length of wood had certainly been a highlight. Though, perhaps the most bizarre of all was the woman in her eighties with hair so pink it looked more like candyfloss than anything grown from a human skull.

On that day, a hot one in the middle of summer, the traffic had been particularly bad. But when everything came to a dead stop, it didn't take long for things to start getting out of hand. Horns were beeped, windows wound down to allow creative swearing to be aired, and as Harry had pulled himself out of his vehicle to go and see what exactly the problem was, he'd found himself faced with a sight he would probably never forget.

The woman, a Mrs Mary Hall, was eighty-three, an ex-school teacher, and an enthusiastic member of her bowls club. Widowed a decade before, she lived alone, attended church every Sunday, and took her role as a grandmother very seriously indeed, often baking so many cakes and biscuits that she had to share them with neighbours. All of this was information she had been happy to share down at the station.

On the day in question, Harry had found Mrs Mary Hall, who stood barely a hair's breadth under five feet, going at it with everything she had as she repeatedly whipped the front end of a very expensive white BMW with her walking cane. Dents were appearing all over the bonnet like welts on the palest of skin, a headlight had been smashed, its glass scattered across the road, and ignoring the pleading screams of the BMW's owner, Mrs Mary Hall had then moved away from the car to take her attack to the driver himself, a smartly dressed forty-something man with a receding hairline and a double chin that would have made a walrus jealous.

Breaking the fight up had given Harry a black eye courtesy of Mrs Mary Hall's cane. When interviewed later, Mary had been as surprised as anyone by her own reaction, blaming not just the heat and the traffic, but also the driver of the other car. When asked why she had reacted so violently, her answer had been simple, to the point, and said with the conviction of someone who absolutely believed that in this case, they were in the right.

'He was a very rude man!' she'd said, her eyes wide and firm. 'Rude!'

And that was that.

Harry couldn't remember what had then happened to either party, but it certainly brought a smile to his battered face as he drove through Carperby, a village blessed with a small green, a stone cross, and a pub, the Wheatsheaves. Even this early in the day, it looked like an inviting place to pop into, not that it was open.

Beyond Carperby, and closing in on Redmire, the fields and meadows stretched out on either side of the road, and far off on his right rose the steep slopes of Penhill, shadows clutching to its sides like weary children.

A few miles on, Harry spotted out to his left the towers of Bolton Castle, a tourist hotspot and one he'd not got around to visiting yet. His younger brother, Ben, had been though, thanks to his blossoming romance with Liz, who'd taken him there on the back of her motorbike. Harry had loved hearing just how much fun his brother had had, though couldn't quite see the attraction himself of feeding wild boars or listening to someone talk about how the longbow shaped the history of Medieval England.

At last, Harry arrived in Redmire, and after following the road around a bend into the village, he hung a left, past a small green on the right, then taken another left just after another pub, the Bolton Arms, which had looked even cosier and inviting than the Wheatsheaves in Carperby.

Parking up, Harry walked over to the front door of a small cottage and gave a sharp knock. The door opened barely a heartbeat later.

'Thought I recognised your voice on the phone,' said the man standing in the doorway. He was smaller than Harry, at least twenty years his senior, and had skin tanned by time, wind, and rain. 'That's that soldier police officer, I said to myself, and right enough, here you are, right enough.'

It took a moment for Harry to register who he was talking to.

'Mr Black, isn't it? The gamekeeper?' Harry said. 'I'm Detective Chief Inspector Harry Grimm.'

'Call me Arthur,' said Mr Black. 'Can't say I expected to be talking to you again so soon, or at all, if I'm honest, like.'

It had been a good few months since Harry had last talked to Mr Black when the man had found an abandoned car while out feeding pheasants. That particular car had been owned by best-selling thriller writer, Charlie Baker, whose body had then been found by Arthur's dog in some nearby woods.

'You coming in, then?' Arthur asked.

'Yes, if that's okay,' Harry said.

'Can't see that it matters either way,' Arthur said. 'But personally, I'd prefer to chat inside in front of the fire, rather than out here waiting for the weather to come in. And it will, sure as I'm standing here talking to you.'

Harry hesitated, not sure then if Arthur was inviting him in or not.

'Well, get yourself inside, lad!' Arthur said. 'I'll get the kettle on.'

Harry stepped inside the house as Arthur moved to one side.

'Through that door there,' Arthur said with a nod of his head to a room just off the small entrance hall. 'How do you take it?'

'Just a splash of milk,' Harry said.

'Right enough,' Arthur said, then pushed on through another door into a small kitchen, leaving Harry on his own.

Harry stood for a moment in the hall. On the wall to his right was a coat rack loaded with numerous waxed jackets and a few empty gun slips. Above the kitchen door was the stuffed head of a fox, staring at the front door as though keeping watch.

Harry moved through to the room where Arthur had directed him and found himself in a small, cosy lounge made even cosier by the fire burning in the grate. A two-seater sofa and an armchair faced the fire as though desperate to pull themselves closer towards it. To the left of the fire, shoved in a corner stood a small television, nothing fancy, and to the right a bookcase. The walls, which were painted a plain white, were mostly hidden behind numerous photographs, all of which were either of various dogs, Arthur and one of said dogs, or a girl, who Harry assumed to be Arthur's daughter, caught in freeze-frame at various stages of her life.

Harry followed the photos around the room, time-travelling through someone else's life.

'That's my daughter, Grace,' Arthur said, coming into the room and handing Harry a chipped mug of strong tea. 'Doesn't half look like her mother.'

Harry realised then, that other than the ones of Grace all

grown up, she was the only woman to feature in any of the photos on display.

'Died when Grace was a baby,' Arthur said, answering Harry's unspoken question.

'I'm sorry to hear that,' Harry said. 'Must've been tough.'

'It was,' Arthur said. 'Still is, at times, you know? But Grace, she's done alright, all things considered. Followed me into the business, you know, gamekeeping, like. Loves it. Always has. There's no money in it, but she's happy, and that's what's important, isn't it; happiness?'

'Lives locally, then?' Harry asked.

'She does,' Arthur said. 'And you'd be asking that why?'

Harry saw Arthur's eyes narrow as he stared up at him. There were questions hiding in them, and not just about Harry, either.

Harry gestured to the sofa.

'Perhaps we should sit down,' he said, changing the subject from whatever direction old Arthur's eyes were suggesting their discussion was heading in.

Arthur held Harry's gaze for a moment longer, clearly making a point, though what exactly, Harry wasn't sure, then took the armchair.

Harry lowered himself into the sofa. The cushions were soft and for a moment it felt as though the sofa was trying to swallow him. Then a furry head rose from the floor and rested on his knee and Harry found himself eye-to-eye with an old Springer Spaniel, her white and brown fur mottled with age.

'Get yourself down, Molly!' Arthur said, but Molly's only response was to lean into Harry's leg.

Harry reached over and patted the dog on her head. He heard her tail tap happily on the carpeted floor.

'Molly!' Arthur said again. 'Leave him be, will you, you daft dog!'

'It's fine,' Harry said, scratching Molly's chin. 'She's a soft one, then.'

'She's old, she's deaf, and she's a complete tart is what she is!' Arthur said. 'Molly! Just ... will you ... Honestly, that dog!'

Harry couldn't help but smile as the dog continued to stubbornly ignore her owner. Then, as though deciding at long last to do as she was told, Molly left Harry and mooched on over to the fire, where she slumped down onto her stomach and within moments was snoring.

'Used to be a proper gun dog, that one,' Arthur said. 'She'd work a hedge like you wouldn't believe, flushing birds out all over the place. And she could sniff out a downed bird like no other dog I've ever had. Soft mouthed, too; could carry a raw egg for miles in her mouth and hand it back to you uncracked.'

Harry had no idea at all what Arthur was describing, or why a dog would ever need to be 'soft-mouthed,' so he just nodded agreeably.

'She's certainly got a lovely temperament,' he said.

'That she has,' Arthur said, and Harry heard an echo of sorrow in his voice. 'But it's not Molly you're here to talk about is it?'

'No, it's not,' Harry said.

'So,' Arthur said, sitting back in his chair, 'best you get on and tell me what happened to young Jack, then, wouldn't you say?'

CHAPTER NINE

'HE WAS FOUND IN A BARN,' HARRY EXPLAINED, 'OVER IN Snaizeholme, if you know it.'

'Know it?' Arthur said. 'I've lived in the dales all my life, lad! So I know the place like the back of Grace's head! Every beck and lane and field and stile! Bit of a bleak place is Snaizeholme, like, and I've not been up there in years. Nature reserve now, isn't it? Need more of that up here, that's for sure. Protect the place, you know? Stop it getting ruined by whatever the world's got going on.'

'Currently, we're unable to say what exactly happened,' Harry said, 'but there is reason to believe that he, that Jack, was not killed by accident.'

Harry was expecting a bit of a pause then from Arthur, as he took in what he'd just said, but the old gamekeeper clearly had other ideas, as he heaved himself up and out of his chair again, face red with rage.

'And just what the hell's that supposed to mean, then, not killed by accident? What are you saying? What happened to Jack? I mean, he could be a right wee sod, that's for sure, and that's why Grace insisted I had him, but it sounds to me like you're saying he was killed on purpose, and that just doesn't sit right at all!'

'Right now, all I can say is what I've already said,' Harry replied, staying seated, knowing that he was dealing with a man who wouldn't accept such an answer. 'The death doesn't look accidental.'

'Was he shot, then, for bothering sheep? Is that it?' Arthur asked, his voice growing louder, a fire bursting to life behind his eyes. 'Young Jack shot, just like that?'

Arthur clicked his fingers in front of Harry's nose, the wind from the action gusting across his face.

'We don't think he was shot, no,' Harry said, 'and Jack's body is currently being—'

But Arthur wasn't listening.

'Because I tell you right now, lad, that's bollocks, that is! Jack was a Springer-cross, as soft and gentle as they come! Well, not as soft as Molly here, obviously, and like I said, he was a bit of a nightmare, so maybe not soft as such, like, but don't get me wrong, he was a properly lovely dog! Bothering sheep, though? No, that's not young Jack, not at all, and I'm telling you that for nowt! He was protective, of me, and that was it!'

Harry saw an anger in the man that, despite his age, was on the edge of deeply unnerving.

'Jack was one of the best dogs I've ever had! Not as a gun dog, though, just so we're clear, because he was next to bloody useless at that.'

'Really?' Harry said.

Arthur gave a nod.

'I mean, he had Springer in him for sure, but that part of his brain was clearly nowt but porridge. Whatever else was in him, though—I always reckoned on it being a bit of Alsatian, but we never knew for sure—well, that was all loyal guard dog. Trained him myself, from a pup. He wouldn't bother sheep, not in a month of Sundays, and that's a fact! And if some farmer's gone and shot him, I'll...'

Arthur's voice broke as he seethed.

'He wasn't shot,' Harry said, but Arthur was lost to himself now and momentarily deaf to Harry.

'I tell you now, lad, I'll be round there to give whoever it is a couple of barrels up the arse myself, that's for bloody sure, you hear? I'll have them! I may be old, but I'm no pushover! And while I'm thinking on it, I bet it wasn't a farmer, was it? No, it wouldn't be. I bet it's that bastard, Eric Haygarth!'

'Arthur...' Harry said, trying to get him back on track.

'WORST BLOODY GAMEKEEPER AROUND, he is! Doesn't care about animals, doesn't care about anything, just the money going into his bloody pockets. And they are bloody, that's for sure! Take the number of birds of prey he's killed, well that's criminal for a start, isn't it?'

Harry went to answer, but Arthur didn't give him a chance.

'I mean, who the hell thinks it's right to do that? Who? Birds of prey, they're rare for a start, but it's not just that, you know, it's the ethics. That man has no love of the countryside, no love of nature! And he's a jealous old bastard. Always has been. Fancied Grace's mum, you see. Never liked that she married me and never once threw an eye his way.'

'Arthur...'

'There's plenty he should be locked up for, you mark my words! Whether he's involved in what happened to Jack or not, he needs putting away, that's for sure! He's an embarrassment to all of us gamekeepers who do the job properly, caring for the animals, for the land, working with both.' Arthur was on his feet. 'Come on! Let's go arrest him now!'

'Arthur!' Harry said, his voice a little louder than he'd expected it to be, but at least it had the desired effect and grabbed the old gamekeeper's attention, stopping him from rambling on and on. 'I'm telling you, if you'll just listen for a moment, that Jack wasn't shot! That much has been confirmed by the pathologist. And we'll know more when I've spoken to the vet. Also, I can't just go around arresting people because they're not liked.'

'Wasn't shot?' Arthur said, still on his feet. 'Then, what happened to him? And what do you mean, exactly, by Jack not being killed by accident? If he wasn't shot, how else could he have been killed, then? Run over on purpose? I wouldn't put it past Eric to do that, either. Hates me, he does. Feeling's mutual, that's for sure.'

'He wasn't run over either,' Harry said.

'So, he wasn't shot and he wasn't run over, but it wasn't an accident? You're making no sense! What does that leave us with, then? Random attack by low flying military aircraft? What else could've happened to him?'

Harry went to say something but decided it was best to just leave Arthur to burn himself out.

'And, while we're on the matter of things that don't make any bloody sense at all,' Arthur continued, 'just how the hell did he end up all the way up that end of the dale in Snaize-holme in the first place? I need to know! He was my bloody dog, lad! My Jack!'

Harry rested his mug on a small coffee table in front of him, then leaned back on the sofa, in an attempt to make himself seem as unthreatening as possible and hopefully have Arthur follow suit and sit back down in his own chair as well.

After a moment or two of silence, Arthur eventually retreated back to his chair, falling back into it wearily. As he lowered himself down into it, Harry saw the old man visibly age in front of him, his movements slow and sore, not just with age, but with the feelings clearly churning around inside him at the loss of his dog.

'We checked our files this morning,' Harry said. 'You reported Jack missing back in March, yes?'

'That's right, I did,' Arthur said. 'I was out checking some squirrel traps on a local farm. I mean, I know I'm retired, but I still help out a friend here and there, you see? And those blasted little grey tree rats don't half make a mess.'

'Trapping them?' Harry said.

'Numbers have to be kept down,' Arthur said. 'They're not a native species, you see. And they carry the squirrel pox virus. Doesn't harm them at all, but it's the reason we've got hardly any red squirrels left, because it'll go through a dray of those reds like a scythe and wipe them out.'

Harry remembered then about the red squirrel sanctuary up in Snaizeholme and mentioned it to Arthur.

'And that's what makes it even more important to keep those grey numbers down,' Arthur said. 'Now, what were we talking about again? Oh, that's right, Jack, that was it. He was with me. Left him in the old Land Rover. He usually just sleeps you see, but then when I came back, the door was open and he was...'

Arthur's voice cracked then, but Harry stayed quiet, allowing the man time to gather himself.

'Anyway, he was gone,' Arthur said, rubbing his scalp, his face lined with confusion about what had happened to his precious dog. 'I always just thought he'd somehow managed to get out, you know, and then just buggered off on some damn fool dog adventure. The doors on that Landy have a habit of just popping open now and again, so he could easily have gotten out. And he did have a habit of buggering off now and again. But he'd always come back, or we'd get a phone call. Though if Eric had found him, there's no way he'd call. Jack's not the first dog he's taken, you know. I mean, there's no proof, but everyone suspects.'

Harry made a note of this Eric fellow, but continued with his questions for now.

'So, where were you, exactly?' he asked. 'When Jack went missing?'

'Over at a mate's, like I said,' Arthur replied. 'Well, not at his house. I mean, I was on his land, down in one of the woods. Just a couple of miles away from here.'

'Would you be able to give me the location? And your friend's address?'

'Of course,' Arthur said. 'You want that now? What about Eric, though? If you're heading round to his, I'll come with you, have it out with him right away, just you watch me!'

'I'll have the details before I leave,' Harry said. 'And any questioning and visiting, well, that'll be down to myself and the rest of the team. Now, did anyone know where you were at that time? Did you see anything suspicious?'

'How do you mean, suspicious?' Arthur asked. 'And yes, of course, someone knew where I was. Grace for a start, because she doesn't half keep a beady eye on me now. And Phil, the farmer whose land I was on. Went to school together, we did. Bloody hell, we're a proper pair of right old buggers now, the two of us, that's for sure. Makes his own pies, does Phil. Pork pies, like. You've not tasted anything like it, trust me.'

'They're that good?' Harry said.

'Good?' Arthur laughed. 'Of course, they're not good! They're absolutely bloody awful is what they are! Don't go near them, whatever you do. And he'll try and force one on you, I promise you that.'

Harry laughed, couldn't help himself.

Arthur lifted a hand and started to count through all the things wrong with Phil's pies.

'Too much pastry, the filling's more gristle and fat than actual meat, soggy bottoms, the jelly in them is like biting into ballistic gel, but does that stop him making them? Like hell it does! So, if he ever offers you one—and like I said, he will, you mark my words—accept it graciously, then bin it hastily. Muck, they are. The worst!'

Harry was warming to Arthur. It was impossible not to. One moment he was all thoughtful and full of grief, the next he was raging about his old friend's terrible pork pies.

'So, both Phil and Grace knew where you were,' Harry said, working to get the chat back on track. 'No one else? You've mentioned this Eric...'

Arthur shook his head. 'There's no reason for him to know what I was doing,' he said. 'But he's got a knack for making everyone's business his own. Nasty piece of work, he is.'

'You've had run-ins with him before, then?'

'Who hasn't?' Arthur said. 'He'll do anything he can to

make sure the pens he looks after, the birds on the shoots he's responsible for, grow up fat and safe, ready for the shooting season. And by that I mean, illegal traps, taking eggs from the nests of hawks and killing the parents, you name it, he's done it.'

Harry didn't like the sound of Eric at all.

'And he's never been caught?'

'No evidence,' Arthur said. 'He's not a fool, old Eric.'

'Why take eggs?'

'They're worth a bob or two on the black market,' Arthur said.

'But he didn't know where you were that day?' Harry asked.

'Can't see why he would. I'm not one for announcing my every move to all and sundry, if you know what I mean. Eric, least of all. I was on my own, Grace was away meeting with one of the shoots she runs, Phil was busy on his farm.'

Harry saw then a flicker of realisation catch the corner of Arthur's eye while he rambled on.

'You think someone stole Jack, don't you? That's what you're getting at, isn't it?'

'All I know,' Harry said, 'is that he was in your vehicle, that he was gone when you got back, and somehow, between that moment and last night, he ended up at the other end of the dale, dead in a barn.'

'But there's no way someone took him, if that's what you're suggesting,' Arthur said. 'It's, well, it's just impossible, that's what it is. Couldn't happen!'

'Why's that?' Harry asked. 'Couldn't this Eric have taken him?'

Arthur leaned forward and stared at Harry, then pointed at him with a gnarly, stubby finger with skin like tree bark.

'That dog had a bark and snarl on him that'd make Satan crap himself,' he said. 'Any stranger reaching into that old Land Rover to grab him? Anyone he didn't like, such as Eric, for example? Well, good luck to them, because they'd be losing a limb, I'd put money on that.'

Thinking about what Arthur had just said, Harry asked, 'What if he'd known them? Would it be easy to take Jack then?'

'You mean someone I know did this? Someone I know took Jack? A friend? You're having a laugh, aren't you?'

Harry said nothing, instead, letting Arthur think for a moment.

'I guess that could be it,' he said eventually. 'But that doesn't make sense either, does it? Someone I know taking Jack? No, that can't be it! It's impossible. Why would anyone I know, a friend, take Jack?'

Harry waited as Arthur wrestled with everything Harry had told him.

'You know, it just didn't seem to sit right with me,' Arthur finally said, 'someone taking Jack.'

'You'd considered it, then?' Harry asked.

Arthur nodded and sighed.

'Young Jack wandering off on his own, having a little adventure, roaming the fells? Now, that I could handle. He'd have been fine, too, I've no doubt about that. Young he may have been, but he was a resourceful beast. And I always hoped he'd just wander back one day, like he'd done nowt wrong. It's nicer thinking that, isn't it? Than any of this, right? Someone just grabbing him and doing a runner? I mean, why, Detective? What the hell for?'

'I'm afraid I can't answer that yet,' Harry said. 'But my

team and I will do everything we can to find out and arrest whoever's responsible.'

'Arrest? And what use will that be?' Arthur said, voice sharp with indignation. 'Jack was just a dog! Whatever happened to him, whoever did it, they'll get off with a slapped wrist, won't they? That's all. Nowt but a telling off, really, and that won't do, you know? It won't!'

'Everything we can do, we will,' Harry said.

'It could still be Eric, you know,' Arthur said. 'Jack could've got out and Eric, if he'd found him, well, he wouldn't have brought him back, that's for damned sure.'

'I'll be asking questions of anyone I think is relevant,' Harry said.

'And so will I!' Arthur said, rising to his feet.

For a moment it seemed to Harry that as Arthur stood he somehow darkened the room as though sucking in all the light from the very day itself.

'No, you won't,' Harry said. 'You'll leave the police to do our job because that's what we're paid to do.'

Arthur said nothing.

'You need to listen to me, Arthur,' Harry said, emphasising the point. 'We'll handle this.'

'Then let's just hope what you do is enough then, shall we?'

With little left to say, Harry concluded the conversation, finished his tea, then made his way out of the lounge. Having given Harry the address of the farm where Jack had last been seen, and that of the clearly nefarious gamekeeper, Eric Haygarth, Arthur reached past and opened the door for him, letting in the grey light of the day.

Stepping out of the house, Harry turned around to say

goodbye. His eyes were drawn to the fox head and how it stared and snarled.

'Clouding over, I see,' Arthur said.

'Looks that way,' Harry agreed.

'Off to see Phil now, I suppose?'

'I'll give him a ring first.'

'Remember what I said about those pies, now. Ghastly, they are.'

'Not sure I'll ever forget.'

'And be careful with Eric.'

'I'm never anything else.'

Farewells said and sensing the distant tang of rain in the air, Harry made his way back over to his Rav4.

'Excuse me...'

The voice was a woman's, and it seemed to catch the end of each word with a gentle rasp as it drifted past Harry. He assumed that whatever the enquiry was, that it was directed at someone else and kept walking.

'Hello? Can you just... Look, wait a moment, will you?'

Harry stopped and turned around to find himself face-to-face with someone he recognised immediately but had never actually met.

'Ms Black?'

'Yes?'

'You're Arthur's daughter, yes?'

'Of the two of us, you're at a clear advantage, here,' the woman said. 'Because I've no idea who you are at all. But I've just seen you coming out of my dad's place, and I'd like to know why, please!'

Grace was wearing a green waxed waistcoat, a red shirt rolled up to the elbows, jeans, Wellington Boots, and slung over her shoulder were a couple of worn, leather gun cases.

Her black hair was curly and cut fairly short and raggedy. If Harry was going to hazard a guess, he'd have put her in her mid-thirties, and judging by the lines at the corners of her eyes, she'd spent a good many of those years laughing.

'DCI Harry Grimm,' Harry said. 'I've just been to speak to your dad about his dog, Jack.'

'You found him? Where is he then, the little sod? What happened? He's buggered off before, you know, longest time was nigh on a week! We got him back because he just wandered into a house over in Grinton! It's been a month, I think, since he went. To be honest, I thought he was gone for good this time.'

'Ms Black...' Harry began.

'What?'

Harry took a deep breath then told Grace everything he'd just told Arthur. When he finished, Grace was quiet and she unslung the gun cases and leant them against the wing of Harry's vehicle.

'Dad's going to be heartbroken,' Grace eventually said.

'He seemed okay,' said Harry.

'King of the brave face,' said Grace. 'Not one for showing true emotion at the best of times.'

'He does angry well enough.'

'Indignation,' said Grace. 'Dad's rarely angry unless there's something unfair going on. He's like a soft, Yorkshire version of Charles Bronson in Death Wish.'

Harry smiled. Having met Arthur only briefly, he could see exactly what Grace was getting at.

'So, what now?' Grace asked. 'Do you know what happened, who took Jack?'

'The investigation is very early stages right now,' Harry said.

'But you've got a few leads, right? That's what they're called, aren't they? Or is that just what we see on the telly?'

'Like I said, early stages,' said Harry, then made to open the driver's door to the Rav4.

Grace stepped closer.

'Did dad mention Eric by any chance?'

Harry gave a nod.

'They hate each other,' Grace said. 'And with good reason.'

'And that would be?'

'They do the same job, but the way they do it? Poles apart,' Grace said.

'Explain.'

'Dad's a man of field and fell, I guess,' Grace said. 'Sees himself as a custodian, as much as anything. Really cares, you know? And I know some folk can't see how that's a thing, a gamekeeper caring about nature, but that's how it is, how it should be.'

'And this Eric, then?'

Grace was silent for a moment and Harry saw then the same look in her eyes that he'd seen in Arthur's. A small family they may be, he thought, but there was something formidable about them both. Together, he had a feeling they'd be unstoppable.

'You know, I think it's probably best if you judge for yourself, assuming of course that you'll be paying him a visit.'

'I will be, yes,' Harry said.

'Though, if there's anything I can do to help?'

'We've got everything in hand,' Harry said, 'but if we do need to talk to you, do you have a number I can get you on?'

'Bit forward, isn't it?' Grace said. 'We've only just met.'

'What?'

'You, asking for my number.'

'But I need it,' Harry said. 'In case I need to talk to you about something to do with the investigation. It's just police procedure, that's all.'

Grace grinned then, her smile broad and honest and open.

'Got a pen?'

Harry took out his notebook and wrote down Grace's number as she called it out.

'Thanks for that.'

'No problem,' Grace said. 'But if you call me over the next two or three days, I might be difficult to get hold of, on account of Jess.'

'Jess?' Harry said. 'Who's Jess?'

'Jess is my dog. Well, one of them,' Grace said. 'She's pregnant. Due to pop any day now.'

'Puppies?'

'Cockers,' said Grace. 'The dad's a champion gun dog. Jess is no slouch, either, like.'

'Well, it was good to meet you,' Harry said, climbing into his vehicle. 'And can you pass on my thanks again to your dad for his time. It's much appreciated. And we really will do all that we can to find out what happened to Jack.'

'Well, just make sure that you do,' Grace said. 'Otherwise, you'll have Dad to deal with. And me.'

And with that, she turned and strode off back towards Arthur's house, leaving Harry to wonder just what on earth he was getting dragged into now.

CHAPTER TEN

Jim arrived at Neil's parents' house half an hour after leaving the community centre in Hawes. Their house sat up in Gayle, just past the old Methodist chapel, the pristine front lawn cut in two by a flagstone path leading down to a garage, in front of which was parked a large black BMW 4x4.

Behind the garage loomed an enormous horse chestnut tree, shadows hanging from it to drape across the grass. Up in the branches, a little too high really, an old treehouse remained. With the leaves coming back after the winter, it was hard to make out, but it was there right enough, and the little boy that Jim used to be wished he could climb up there again.

Having walked from the community centre, Jim had headed down to the cobbled lane that rode past Cockett's, but had almost immediately taken a right up a steep hill to head past St Margaret's Church on his right. From there, he headed onto the footpath that crossed a collection of ancient meadows, enclosed by drystone walls, their edges dipping down into Gayle Beck as though cooling their feet.

That path formed a very small part of the Pennine Way, a walk Jim had often found himself wondering about doing, not least because it was something that had often been discussed in his youth when he was in the Scouts. But life on a farm, later combined with his current police role, meant that he just didn't have the time. But this small bit was still beautiful and he'd always loved walking the flagstone path, which connected Hawes and Gayle like an artery.

Arriving at Neil's parents' house, not really sure what he was going to say, and very aware that he had nothing else to offer them about what had happened to their son, Jim steeled himself as he rapped his knuckles sharp against the large, green door, then stepped back onto the path.

Looking up at the house, Jim's eyes drifting to an upstairs window on the left, which had been Neil's old bedroom. Over the years, it had been many things, from the inside of a spaceship or a cave, to a lonely cell at the top of a castle tower from which they'd had to escape. And escape they had done, thanks to a length of tow rope they'd pinched from the garage and tied to the radiator, the end thrown out of the window for them to climb down to the ground.

Jim was recalling the bollocking they'd both received for doing something so stupid and dangerous, when the front door opened, releasing into the day the smell of freshly baked bread and the faint sound of a radio playing somewhere in the house.

The face he saw, however, was not the one he'd expected.

'PCSO Metcalf!' said the man now standing in front of Jim. It was Mr Richard Adams, a businessman who'd moved to the area and done a fairly good job at not getting on the right side of people while supposedly trying to do exactly that. Jim wasn't exactly sure what business Mr Adams was involved in, but it clearly paid well. It was the little things that gave his income away—his shiny shoes, the watch on his wrist, those too-straight and far-too-white teeth now gleaming at him with shark-like enthusiasm.

'Mr Adams,' Jim said, as the man stepped out of the house, a woman close behind him. 'Oh, hi, Mrs Hogg. Look, if you're busy, I can come back?'

'James!' the woman said, and her eyes warming. 'No, you come right in, now. Richard was just going.' Mrs Hogg looked at Richard Adams. 'Thank you so much for popping in. It really is hugely appreciated.'

'It's the least I can do,' Adams said. 'Neil's death was a shock to the whole community. I know that I hardly knew him, but that doesn't mean I can't help. And remember what I said, if you need anything—anything at all—you just let me know. Understood?'

'Yes, absolutely,' Mrs Hogg said.

'And we'll see you both Thursday evening, for dinner, yes?'

'Of course,' Mrs Hogg said. 'It's lovely of you to ask. We haven't actually been out since Neil was...'

Jim saw Mrs Hogg's smile fracture just a little, as her voice crumbled on the words she was saying. But she quickly forced a smile and then with goodbyes said, Richard Adams turned and headed up the path.

'So, are you going to just stand there all day, or are you going to get yourself inside?'

Jim made to step up into the house, but the woman held out a hand to stop him, a frown creasing her brow. 'And enough of the "Mrs Hogg," James, you hear?'

'Sorry, yes,' Jim said. 'I mean Helen.'

'You're not twelve anymore now, are you?' Helen said. 'Alan's upstairs in his office. Can't say I know what he's doing up there, but that's probably for the best, isn't it?'

Helen then stepped to one side.

'Well, get yourself in, then! Come on!'

Jim smiled then stepped up into the house, Helen closing the door behind them and following him inside.

'Go on through,' Helen said. 'You know where you're going anyway, don't you? Used to be like a second home for you, didn't it? Still is though, I hope you know that. How are your parents? I've not seen them in a while, not since the...'

Helen's voice faded then, crushed by the word she had been about to say.

'They're good,' Jim said. 'You should give them a call sometime. See if you can get them to think and talk about something that isn't to do with farming!'

Jim then made his way on through the house, eventually reaching the kitchen, Helen's voice chasing on from behind. As he opened the door, he paused, looking up. Staring down at him from above the door and sitting on a branch attached to the wall by a wooden plinth, was an owl.

'Nice,' said Jim, nodding at the owl, trying his best to sound like he meant it.

'Oh, God, that thing gives me the shivers!' Helen said. 'Horrible thing it is. Horrible!'

'Yeah, can't say I'm a fan, if I'm honest,' Jim smiled. 'Never been entirely sure why anyone would want a stuffed animal in their house.'

'Alan says it adds class to the hallway,' said Helen, shaking her head. 'I think it's gruesome and creepy and should be thrown away. But will he let me? Not a chance of it.'

'It's all of those things,' Jim agreed. 'Where did you get it?'

'A Christmas raffle, would you believe!' Helen explained. 'The vets get donated all kinds of things to auction off. You know, one year, someone even donated a collection of naughty postcards from the Twenties! They weren't too rude, really, but still! Unsurprisingly, it was an anonymous donation.'

'And someone won them?' Jim asked.

'No idea who,' Helen said. 'Anyway, we managed to win that feathered monstrosity. I don't like the way it stares like it knows something! The money went to a good cause, a fund to help farming families with everything from financial support and housing to stress and whatnot. But why we had to keep it, I don't know. I said to give it back, let it raise even more money, but Alan wouldn't have it!' Helen shooed Jim on into the kitchen, then turned to look up the stairs. 'Alan? Alan! James is here! Alan! Get yourself down here, now! Alan!'

From upstairs, a quieter reply came back.

'Who's that, now, Pet? More visitors? Or has that rich windbag decided to stay even longer to talk even more bollocks and eat the rest of my biscuits?'

'They're not your biscuits,' Helen replied. 'They don't have your name on, do they?'

'I'm just saying, the only reason he was round here at all was so that other people would hear about it. The visit, just like all the others, had bugger-all to do with us or what happened!'

'You could've talked to him for a little longer, instead of

going back upstairs after five minutes and leaving me with him!'

'I'm busy. Things to do. People like that to ignore.'

'Well, whatever you think, he's gone and we've someone else now. And yes, I'm going to give this someone else more of my biscuits, so you'd better hurry up hadn't you, or they'll all be gone!'

Jim heard a scuffling sound from upstairs, footsteps, a door opening.

'Right, who is it, then? Who else have you let in to scoff their way through our cupboards?'

By now, Helen was in the kitchen with Jim, but still holding her conversation with the disembodied voice of her husband.

'It's James Metcalf, Alan! You know, Jim! He's here. So, are you coming down or will I never see you again, hmm?'

'Tim? Who the hell is Tim? We don't know anyone called Tim! And if it's another of those folk trying to sell me even more Internet, I'll sling him out on his ear! We've got more than enough of it already, and what we have doesn't really work, does it?'

Jim smiled as Helen shook her head and rolled her eyes.

'I'm putting the kettle on!'

Jim took a seat at an old, worn dining table at the far end of the room. He recognised the scratches on its surface like old friends.

'He does know that's not how the Internet works, doesn't he?' Jim asked.

Helen laughed.

'I've got a nice tin of biscuits,' she said, the kettle now on. 'Would you mind getting them?'

Jim stood up and made his way over to a cupboard he'd

opened more times than he could remember. From the darkness inside he removed a battered old tin, the pattern on its surface faded and worn, but still visible enough to give him a fairly good idea of what a tin of Christmas biscuits in the early Seventies had looked like.

'Helping yourself I see. Somethings just don't change, do they?'

Jim turned to see Alan Hogg walk into the kitchen, a small, slim man who'd spent a good many years working at the Wensleydale Creamery. He still worked there, as far as Jim knew.

'Just doing as I'm told,' Jim said.

'If you expect me to believe that, then—'

'Sit yourself down, Love,' Helen said, and placed in front of them two large mugs of tea.

Jim opened the tin and took out a biscuit.

'Shortbread,' he said. 'Neil's favourite.'

The words, that name, they were out of his mouth before he could even think.

'I think of him every time I make a batch,' Helen smiled, though Jim noticed how her eyes weren't exactly joining in.

Jim focused on the biscuit, then the mug of tea, turning it in his hands, before going back to the biscuit. He wanted to say something, anything, but what? His words weren't so much caught in the back of his throat as drowning in his stomach. So much so, that he felt his guts twist.

'So, Richard Adams was here, then,' he said.

Jim's only real contact with the man was last year when he and the rest of the team had to keep the peace between him and a growing group of protesters camped out on some land he owned. Somehow, he'd managed to secure planning permission for the area, which included some rather lovely woodland. Eventually, and most likely because of the growing resentment from the whole of the local community for what he wanted to do, Adams had finally backed down and shelved his plans, and the protesters had all headed home.

'Nothing gets past you, does it?' Alan said, waggling a biscuit at Jim. 'That'll be all that police training you've been doing.'

Helen stared daggers at Alan.

'He's been around a few times actually,' she said. 'Since we lost Neil, that is. It's very kind of him, really.'

Jim saw Alan roll his eyes and shake his head.

'Is it, now?' Alan said.

Helen sent a hard stare at Alan.

'Well, he's not doing it for us, is he?' Alan continued, ignoring Helen's very obvious irritation. 'He's doing it for himself. You know that as well as I do.'

'Why do you think that?' Jim asked. 'What's in it for him, exactly?'

'He's of a type,' Alan said. 'By which I mean, he's a self-serving, money-obsessed, right-wing—'

'Alan!'

'I'm only saying what I see,' he said, shrugging. 'And I wouldn't trust him as far as I could spit.'

'Well, I hope you'll be a little more polite when we're round there tomorrow evening!'

Jim saw Alan's eyes widen in an instant like he'd just had an electric shock.

'What?'

'I accepted on both of our behalf,' Helen said. 'Seeing as you had already disappeared upstairs.'

'I didn't go upstairs and disappear! Why didn't you come up and check?'

'And what would your answer have been?'

Alan went to answer but Helen didn't give him chance.

'I'll tell you, shall I? It would've been no.'

'Yes, but—'

'Yes but nothing!' Helen said. 'We're going and that's that. And when we're round there I want you to be polite.'

'I can't promise anything,' Alan said.

'Well, I think you had better try.'

'Look, just because I've got the week off, doesn't mean I have to spend my time being nice to people, does it? Particularly people like him!'

'Yes, it does,' Helen said.

For a moment, no one said a word.

'Jim,' Helen said at last, popping the tense atmosphere with her bright voice, 'it really is good to see you. Please, you must visit more often.'

'Though I'm sure you've got better things to do than visit us old duffers,' Alan said.

Jim laughed.

'It's good to see you both,' he said. 'It really is. And I'm sorry I've not been around for a while. Busy at work and the farm, you know how it is.'

'Then this must be important,' Alan said. 'So, let's have it out of you then, lad!'

Jim glanced over at Alan.

'What?'

'Whatever it is you've come round here to say,' said Alan. 'Unless of course, you're only here because you want to head up into that old treehouse like you always used to. Though you're a bit big for it now, no doubt.'

'Just a little,' Jim said.

'You'd think so, wouldn't you?' Alan said. 'But that didn't stop Neil, you know. He'd still go up there, when he visited. I think he was even up there that morning, wasn't he, Helen? When, well, you know...'

Jim saw tears glistening in Helen's eyes as she nodded.

'Never did grow up, that lad,' Alan said. 'Anyway, back to you, Jim. So, come on, what's brought you round here today, then? Out with it!'

'That's just the problem,' Jim said.

'What is?' Helen asked.

'Something to say,' Jim replied. 'No, what I mean is, I wish I had something to say, but I don't. Nothing. At all. And I should, because I promised Neil. But I've got nowt! Not a bloody thing!'

Jim took a sip from his mug and noticed that his hands were shaking.

'I'm... sorry,' he said, before either Helen or Alan had a chance to say anything. 'I just thought I'd come round, that's all, see how you are. Check in. Neil would want me to anyway, but also...'

Jim's voice stalled.

'Also, what?' Alan asked.

'I just can't shift the feeling that we've missed something,' Jim said. 'We must've done. I don't know what or where, but something, you know?'

'James...'

Helen's voice was firm, serious.

'You know what I mean though, right?' Jim said. 'We must have, or I must have, anyway. It just doesn't make sense that we don't have anything. Nothing at all!'

'It's not your fault,' Helen said. 'What happened to Neil. You're not to blame.'

Jim opened his mouth, but no words came.

'She's right, lad,' Alan said. 'We've lost Neil, and it breaks our hearts every hour of every day. But we can't have what happened, drive you to God knows what, either, if you know what I mean. You need to leave it alone, Jim.'

'I can't.'

Helen reached out and placed a hand on Jim's.

'Let it all out, lad,' Alan said. 'And then, that's enough, you hear? Enough.'

Then Jim's voice cracked as he tried to speak, and whatever words he'd been searching for crumbled to dust. A sob broke through as tears fell, and the parents of one of the best friends he'd ever had sat beside him and held him close.

A moment or so later and remembering what Harry had said to him as he'd been leaving the community centre, Jim sat back, pulling away from Alan and Helen.

'No, you're right,' he said, suddenly embarrassed, pretty sure that if Harry could see him now his face would be all storm and thunder. He pushed himself up onto his feet and away from the table.

'You're leaving so soon?' Helen asked, looking up at Jim. 'But you've only just arrived!'

'Don't complain,' Alan said. 'More biscuits for me!'

'Yes, I know,' Jim said, 'but we're all on with something up in Snaizeholme. I'd best get going, I think.'

He gave neither of Neil's parents a chance to respond as he turned and quickly walked from the kitchen and along to the front door.

'Jim...'

His hand on the doorknob, Jim twisted it and yanked the

door open. Then a hand rested on his arm and he looked around to see Alan standing close by.

'I'd best be going,' Jim said, but Alan's hand gripped his arm a little tighter, just enough to let him know that he wasn't going to be leaving just yet.

'First, you'll be listening to me,' Alan said, his eyes as keen as a hawk's.

Jim tried to pull away, to leave, but Alan held him fast, his grip firm. Then Jim felt himself guided outside by the man who pulled him to a stop just the other side of the front door.

'Now, Jim, I don't expect you came round here today for a bollocking,' Alan said, 'but that's what you're going to get, whether you like it or not.'

'I'm sorry, what?'

'A bollocking, Jim!' Alan repeated, his voice quiet, firm, and utterly serious. 'Because right now, whatever this is, whatever it is you think you're doing? Well, it's self-indulgent, isn't it? And it had better stop!'

Jim went to protest but a look from Alan was enough to stop him from saying a word.

'What happened to Neil was and is bloody awful,' Alan said, his voice shaking with sadness, hurt, and more than a little anger. 'But it's not your place to go around with the weight of it all on your shoulders, is it? No, it bloody well isn't!'

Jim again tried to speak, to say that Harry had already made it very clear where his head needed to be in all this, but Alan wasn't having any of it.

'For a start, that's for us, his parents, to bear, not you, you hear? Do you understand what I'm saying? Are you listening to me?'

Alan shook Jim's arm.

'Yes,' Jim nodded, though deep down all he felt right then was confusion.

'I don't think you are,' Alan continued, 'and you know why? It's because it's about time you grew up!'

'I don't understand...'

'Moping around the dales isn't going to help anyone, is it?' Alan said, his voice calmer now but no less firm. 'It's certainly not helping Helen and me, and I doubt very much if it's helping that team you work with, is it? And as for your parents, you must be driving them batty!'

Jim decided it was best to say nothing and to just let Alan have his say.

'Well, is it?'

'No,' Jim said, shaking his head, the whole saying-nothing thing clearly not what Alan was about right then.

'I need you to pull your head out of your arse, Jim. Can you do that for me? Because you need to. If you leave it up there too long, all you'll ever see or hear are your own problems, and that's no bloody use now, is it? And that's a rhetorical question, by the way.'

'No, you're right,' Jim said.

'I know I am!' Alan snapped back. 'If I know anything at all! Neil was and is our son. We'll do the grieving. And you, lad,' —Alan reached out and jabbed a pointed finger hard into Jim's chest— 'you will do your bloody job, understood? By which I mean, you will get on with living!'

Jim went to speak, but Alan gave him a sharp nod, a grunt, then turned and headed back into the house, pulling the door shut behind him.

Jim stood alone in front of the house, wind hooking at his clothes, his emotions confused and messy, Alan's words ringing in his ears. Self-indulgent? That had stung. And it had meant to as well. Alan had never been one for saying anything other than what he believed and the truth in his words had really hit home. Sometimes, Jim realised then, you just needed someone to point out the obvious, no matter how painful it was to hear.

Walking back down the path, and reeling somewhat from Alan's words, Jim found himself glancing up again at Neil's treehouse. He was tempted to dash up into the branches, to hide out in that secret den of leaf and twig, but all that remained up there were memories. And wallowing in them, existing in his yesterdays, wasn't life, was it?

Alan was right, Jim realised, and he admired the man for what he'd just done, what he'd said, and how he'd said it.

Jim pulled his phone from a pocket and punched in a number.

'Where are you?'

'At the portacabin the vets have at the auction mart,' Jadyn said. 'Turns out I need to head through to the main surgery in Leyburn, because that's where the necro-whatever will have been done.'

'Necropsy,' Jim said.

'Sounds like a horror movie,' said Jadyn. 'Or the name of a death metal band.'

'We'll head over together,' Jim said. 'I'll be there in ten.'

CHAPTER ELEVEN

HARRY WAS STANDING ON THE DOORSTEP OF A SMALL farmhouse, the yard behind him neat and tidy. In front of him stood a small man with rosy cheeks, no hair, and an unlit pipe clenched in his teeth. And sitting on the man's hands was an enormous pork pie.

'Well, are you going to take it, or not?'

Not, Harry thought to himself, remembering Arthur Black's advice, but at the same time reaching out to take the offered gift from Phil Thwaite, Arthur's old farming mate.

The weight of the pie shocked him. Yes, it was a large pie, far too large, in fact, for him to reach around it with both of his larger than average hands. But still, to weigh as much as it did, Harry had to wonder what exactly it contained. But that only led to even more confusion.

'It's a family size pie,' Phil said with a smile. 'Can't see the point of making them any other size. Don't last long enough, do they, small pies? Size is everything!'

'No, I suppose they don't,' Harry said, wondering what to do with it now that it was resting in his hands, and not really convinced that a pie made by someone who thought it was all about the size was ever going to taste great. He'd have to put it down somewhere soon, though, because holding it for too long would surely have him end up straining a muscle or two. 'Anyway, Mr Thwaite,' Harry said, trying to move on to the reason as to why he'd visited in the first place.

'Phil,' said Phil. 'I don't go in for all that formality rubbish. I tell you, if I met the Queen, I'd call her Liz. Not *Your Majesty*, not even *Elizabeth*. Liz. Nice and friendly, like. Best way to be, I reckon. And you are?'

'Grimm,' said Harry. 'Detective Chief Inspector Harry Grimm.'

'Harry? Really?'

'Yes, really,' Harry said. 'Why? Is that a surprise?'

He was used to people doing a double-take when he said his name, thanks to the state of his scarred face, but Harry? That was a first.

'A surprise? No, not in the slightest,' Phil said. 'It's just that... No, it doesn't matter. It's nothing. Irrelevant, actually. Forget I said anything.'

'But you didn't actually say anything,' said Harry.

'Well, that's good then, isn't it?' Phil replied. 'So, you coming in, or stopping outside?'

'Have you got something I can put this in?' Harry said, offering back to Phil the pie.

'Oh, it doesn't need to go in anything,' Phil said. 'That's the point of the pastry, you see. Protects the insides from what's outside. That's why it's so hard.'

Phil reached out and tapped the top of the pie with his knuckle. The sound was that of a mallet striking a log.

'See? Solid!' Phil announced proudly. 'Nowt bad's getting through that, is it? Bombproof!'

'I'd still rather have something to put it in,' Harry said. 'I'm not sure leaving it on my car seat is a good idea.'

Phil reached out and took the pie.

'I'll wrap it up for you,' he said. 'Just don't go forgetting it when you leave.'

'Oh, I won't,' Harry said, already planning to do exactly that.

Inside the house, Harry followed Phil along a short hall with a flagstone floor, the walls white, the skirting board a pale green, and through to the kitchen.

'It's just me on my own, like,' Phil said. 'Never married, you see. No time for it.'

Harry sat down at a small dining table. The room was, like the yard, tidy, albeit in an early 1970s way.

'Tea!'

'No, I'm fine, thanks,' Harry said, seeing as it was barely an hour since he'd had a drink with Arthur.

'It wasn't a question,' Phil said. 'Milk, sugar?'

'Er, just milk, please,' Harry said.

When Phil came over with two steaming mugs, he sat down opposite Harry and leaned back in a chair that creaked a little too loudly.

'So, Arthur sent you over to see me, then.'

'He did,' Harry said. 'I'm just here to check up on a few details. As you know, know he lost his dog, Jack, a while back.'

'Dog? Is that what he called it, now?' Phil said, rolling his eyes.

'I'm not sure I understand,' said Harry.

Phil took a gulp of the still-boiling hot tea, then leaned forward and said, 'That daft creature was more like a bear than a dog,' he said.

'How do you mean?'

'It was huge! Enormous! Bloody terrifying thing, if it hadn't been such a soft bugger to boot.'

Harry thought back to the corpse of the dog he'd found in the barn in Snaizeholme. It had seemed large, yes, but not huge. But then there had been plenty else to look at, with all the blood and damage to the poor creature. Size hadn't really been at the front of his mind at the time.

'Wasn't it a Spaniel?' Harry said. 'Well, a Spaniel-cross, anyway.'

'If that dog was a Spaniel then I'm the Pope!' Phil said. 'Oh, yes, you're right, there was a little bit of Spaniel in it, you could see that in the dog's eyes, in its colouring. But that was about it. The rest was an enormous bloody monster.'

'Arthur said something about Alsatian?'

Phil gave a nod.

'And the rest,' he said. 'By which I mean that dog must've had a wolf as a very close relative. Oh, don't get me wrong, Jack was a lovely dog.' He held his hands up. 'Paws on him like you wouldn't believe! And proper soft, too, if he knew you. But if he didn't? If you were a stranger and you crossed a line, then more fool you, because he'd have you as sure as eggs go with bacon.'

'What do you mean by crossed a line?' Harry asked.

'Arthur's doorstep uninvited, for one,' Phil said. 'Not a good idea if young Jack was around. No, not a good idea at all, that, unless you actually wanted to be eaten alive.'

'What about Arthur's vehicle?' Harry asked.

'What about it?'

'Arthur mentioned that on the day Jack disappeared, he'd left him in his Land Rover.'

'Oh, yes, that's right, when he was up sorting out those

blasted squirrels for me. The damage they cause, you wouldn't believe! Stripping trees, making a right mess! Good meat, though, squirrel.'

That last comment had Harry worrying again about the pie and its contents, but in an entirely new and unexpected way.

'So, Arthur left Jack in his Land Rover,' Harry prompted.

'And he must've got out somehow,' Phil said. 'Jack, I mean. No way else he could've gone, is there? Because that dog was better than any car alarm, that's for sure. Arthur would've heard barking first, then screaming no doubt. Jack had jaws on him like, well, like Jaws. Terrifying!'

Phil opened his arms and then clapped them against each other.

'Snap, just like that! Bite you in half, he could, I'm sure of it.'

The more Harry heard about Jack, the more he found himself thinking that whoever had taken him had known exactly what kind of dog he was: big and clearly rather terrifying when he wanted to be.

'Can you tell me anything about an Eric Haygarth?' Harry asked.

'I can tell you that the man is a bastard, that's what!' Phil said, spitting his words. 'He a suspect, then?'

'Just someone else I need to talk to, that's all. Was he around that day?'

'Eric? Eric Haygarth? Around? As in on my land and knowing what I'm doing and what's going on, on my farm?'

Harry said nothing, just waited for Phil to answer his own question.

'No bloody chance! That man is a liability! He's what my old mum would've called a bad egg. Rotten he is, from the inside. So, no, he wasn't around that day, not that I knew of anyway, because if I had known? Let's just say that he'd have been picking pellets out of his arse for days!'

Phil then mimed holding a gun in his hands.

'Boom!'

'Just so you know,' Harry said, 'shooting people is something that the police frown upon generally.'

'Oh, I wouldn't kill him,' Phil said, as though that was fine then. 'Just put some buckshot in those flabby arsed buttocks of his, know what I mean? Salt's good, you know. Just empty the pellets out and replace them with some nice big chunks of rock salt. Stings like you've sat on a wasp's nest!'

'You speaking from experience?'

'That would be telling, wouldn't it?'

Hoping to move Phil on from talking about shooting Eric, Harry asked, 'Was there anything you noticed that day at all?'

'Noticed how?' Phil asked.

'Anything out of the ordinary,' Harry explained. 'By which I mean, something that wasn't there that should've been, or something that should've been, but wasn't.'

Phil screwed up his face.

'Wasn't that should've and should've that wasn't?' Phil said. 'And what kind of sense does any of what you just said make?'

'More than enough,' Harry said.

Phil sat back and rested his chin in his hand, tapping it thoughtfully with a finger.

'Well, thinking back? No, I didn't. Which is no surprise really, seeing as I had the vet over that day checking over old Harry.'

Harry wasn't sure he'd heard Phil correctly.

'Harry?' he said. 'I think you've got me mixed up with—'

Phil's laugh cut Harry off before he had a chance to finish.

He stood up.

'Come on,' he said. 'I'll introduce you.'

Harry wasn't given a chance to ask to whom, as Phil hopped off out of the kitchen leaving him with no option but to follow.

Outside, Harry heard Phil's voice call from a barn on the other side of the yard.

'Over here! Come on!'

Harry made his way over and into the barn.

Inside, the air was thick with the sweet smell of straw and hay. The barn was gloomy, but Harry's eyes adjusted quickly and he soon spotted Phil standing over by a tall gate leading into another part of the barn, his back turned to him.

'Well, this has been very useful,' Harry said, keen to get on, 'but I think I'd best get going.'

Phil stepped back from the gate in front of him. From the darkness above the gate a huge head appeared, long and sleek and black, with a white line running from between its ears, down between its eyes, and all the way long to its nose.

'That's—'

'My Shire horse,' Phil said. 'Harry, meet Harry!'

BACK IN HIS RAV4, and now driving back up the dale and away from the largest horse he'd ever seen in his entire life, never mind stroked, Harry thought back over what he'd learned so far.

Arthur's dog, Jack, had been taken, not by chance, but

because he was the kind of dog that, judging by his reputation, would be good in a fight. And not only that, to have even stood a chance of taking the dog in the first place, those responsible for the theft would have had to have been known by the dog, well enough for him to make no fuss at all when taken.

There was mention of this Eric Haygarth chap, and Harry would be following that up, but he had a sense that was more about a deep-seated personal dislike of the man than anything else. With the day getting on now, he'd perhaps leave visiting Eric till the following day. Relevant or not, it was still something that had to be checked out.

Jack had been a large dog and fiercely loyal to his owner. A stranger, it seemed, or someone that the dog just didn't like, such as Eric Haygarth, wouldn't have stood much of a chance of getting close to him without Jack kicking off loudly and with a lot of teeth. And that told Harry something very important: whoever had taken Jack hadn't simply grabbed him by chance. No. This was planned and executed by said person or persons, who not only wanted a dog they could put in a fight, but one they could take easily and quietly. And that lead Harry to an even more chilling thought: whoever he was dealing with, they weren't just local, they knew Arthur. And they knew Jack well enough to take him and for no one to know until it was too late.

CHAPTER TWELVE

Jadyn was standing outside the portacabin at Hawes Auction Mart, wondering if the day was soon going to turn to rain. The forecast hadn't said that it would, but he'd come to realise that Wensleydale didn't always do what the meteorologists said. So even on the sunniest of days, rain could sneak down the valley and cause a surprise soaking.

The trip up Bishopsdale had been a little more eventful than he'd been expecting. What he'd thought was going to be just a gentle chat with Mr and Mrs Sewell, about how perhaps the issue of the public footpath was one to just accept as part of their new life in Wensleydale, had been anything but.

On arrival, Mr Sewell had presented Jadyn with a copy of a letter he had had his London solicitor draw up which he was then going to send to every member of the parish council. The general gist of this had been that no one was going to tell Mr and Mrs Sewell what to do, that they were going to go ahead with applying for planning permission to change the route of the public footpath regardless, and also that should any sheep stray onto their land, this would be regarded as trespassing and legal action would be taken.

Jadyn had done his best to warn them that this probably wasn't a sensible course of action, had even offered to help arrange a meeting with the parish council and local farmers, but they hadn't taken any notice. This was a pity really, because as Jadyn had left, the Sewell's driveway and front garden had suddenly become full with sheep, as one of the farmers moved a flock from one area of his farm to another.

A lot of shouting had ensued, and Mr and Mrs Sewell had endeavoured to shoo the sheep back out onto the road. Unfortunately, all this had served to do was panic the animals and send them scarpering across the garden, trampling flowers, leaping over fences and bushes, and generally causing havoc. Most notably, though, was how one of the sheep had somehow found its way not only inside the house, but upstairs and into the bathroom to drink from the toilet.

With Bishopsdale and the chaos that the Sewells seemed to be intent on fomenting at any cost, Jadyn had headed back up the dale to Hawes to crack on with the job Harry had assigned him. He'd had a quick chat with the veterinary nurse, Ellie Brown, who had been between appointments, but he'd learned nothing about what DCI Grimm had discovered early that morning, other than the location of the deceased dog.

His stomach was starting to grumble. Somehow, the day had raced ahead with itself, lunch had come around a little too quickly, and now here he was, waiting for Jim, without enough time to nip into town to grab a bite. That would have to be rectified en route, he decided, otherwise he'd have to eat one of his arms. Maybe. And when Jim finally arrived, having stopped off to pick up the police Land Rover from the marketplace, his empty stomach was rumbling a little too loudly.

'Come on, then,' Jim said, pulling up alongside, his arm leaning out of the open driver's window.

'We'll need to stop for food on the way,' Jadyn said, walking round to climb into the passenger seat.

Opening the door, he was greeted by Fly, who was curled up in the passenger footwell. He climbed in, placing a folder on top of the cubby box between the two front seats.

'You're worse than Matt,' Jim said, as they set off, Fly having rested his head on Jadyn's lap, his tail gently tapping against the floor.

'I'm still growing,' Jadyn said.

'Into what?'

'That's the mystery.'

Jim glanced down at the file Jadyn had brought with him.

'What's that, then?'

'Yours,' Jadyn said. 'You were going to check on any reports of pet theft or whatever, weren't you? So, I brought it along.'

'And?'

'I've not looked yet.'

'Look now, then.'

'Food first,' Jadyn said.

In Bainbridge, and thanks to Jadyn's stomach rumbling loud enough to be heard over the Land Rover's engine, Jim stopped at the village shop.

'So, what've you got, then?' Jim asked as Jadyn climbed back in.

'Two scotch pies,' Jadyn said. 'Fresh and hot. And a couple of bottles of water.'

The smell of the pies had Fly's attention immediately.

'Don't be feeding him,' Jim instructed, as Jadyn handed over one of the pies. 'He's already had his breakfast.'

Jadyn stared down at the dog, the animal's huge, sorrowful eyes gazing up at him, pleading for just a tiny morsel.

'He looks hungry,' Jadyn said.

'He's a dog,' Jim replied. 'He never looks anything else.'

Jim then lifted the file Jadyn had brought with him and flicked it open.

'Exciting stuff, this,' he said, flipping through the papers. 'Proper police work. An escaped rabbit, a lost cat, complaints about a barking dog. Ah...'

Jadyn saw Jim pull out one of the sheets.

'What's that?'

'Lost dog,' Jim said. 'Reported a few weeks ago. Look.'

Jadyn took the sheet of paper and quickly skimmed through it.

'You recognise the name?'

'I do,' Jim said. 'Same as the one on the dog collar Harry had this morning.'

'Says here though,' Jadyn said, reading Jim's report, 'that the dog ran off.'

'That's what the owner said. He thought it had just got out of his vehicle somehow. It happens.'

'There's a mention here of squirrels,' Jadyn noticed.

'The owner's a gamekeeper,' Jim explained. 'Retired anyway. Still helps out a few farmer friends with vermin control.'

'Squirrels are vermin?'

'Greys, yes,' Jim said.

Jadyn thought for a moment then said, 'Why would a gamekeeper's dog run off? Of all the jobs around, I would've thought that being a gamekeeper would mean having well-trained dogs.'

'Maybe it didn't run off,' Jim said. 'Could've been taken.'

'Or it could've been picked up by someone after it went walkabout,' Jadyn said.

With little else to be said on the matter, both Jadyn and Jim fell quiet as Jim shuffled further back through the file.

'There's another report here,' he said, Jadyn having now finished his pie.

'Stolen dog, you mean?'

Jim nodded.

'Six months ago.'

'What's it say?'

Jim was quiet as he read, then said, 'Not much. Alsatian, though.'

'I remember, there was this woman who lived on our street back home had one of those. She was tiny. Bought an Alsatian as protection. Daft animal was soft as anything, but the mouth on it!'

'Big, then?'

'When it yawned it was like it was about to swallow her whole.'

'Well, it's something else to check, isn't it?' Jim said. 'You never know. Might be useful.'

A few minutes later, and the pie having calmed Jadyn's stomach, he asked, 'So, how was it? Round at Neil's parents?'

Jim was quiet for a moment, then said, 'Neil's dad gave me a bollocking.'

Jadyn coughed on a mouthful of meat and pastry.

'What? Why?'

Jim shook his head but Jadyn saw a faint smile on the PCSO's face.

'Because I deserved it,' he said.

'How?'

'Neil's death,' said Jim. 'Blaming myself, I guess.'

Jadyn said nothing and finished off what he was eating. Jim had taken what had happened hard, but that was understandable, he thought. And he'd not been himself since. Not helped by the fact that the investigation had hit a wall.

'Something'll come up,' he said eventually.

'It will,' Jim agreed.

Driving on down through the dale, the weather held. Jadyn had to work hard to not allow the rumbling thrum of the engine, and the warmth of Fly now leaning against his legs, to send him off for an early afternoon nap. He thought about the dog that had gone missing, and how it had somehow ended up in a dog fight. Either it had been stolen, or it had been picked up after it had done a runner. In either case, they didn't have much to go on. Murder investigations were one thing, but missing dogs? Unless it was chipped, then—

That thought burst a bright light in Jadyn's head.

'Was it chipped?' he asked. 'The dog; did the owner have it chipped?'

'It'll say in the notes,' Jim said. 'I can't remember.'

Jadyn checked again.

'Yes,' he said. 'It was.'

'So?'

'So,' Jadyn said, 'it'll be another way to confirm that the deceased dog is this one reported missing.'

When they eventually arrived at the veterinary surgery in Leyburn, Fly was so asleep that he barely stirred when Jim pulled the vehicle to a stop alongside a huge mud-splattered motorbike loaded with shiny metal panniers, and clearly designed for trails and rough tracks as well as roads.

'Liz would love that,' said Jadyn.

'Belongs to the surgery,' Jim said. 'Means the vets can get to emergencies a lot quicker across fields and down lanes.'

'What about four-by-fours?' Jadyn asked.

'They have those, too,' Jim said, and pointed at a couple of weary-looking Land Rovers on the other side of the car park. Then he looked over at Fly and said, 'He's coming with us so put the lead on him. Can't see how I'm ever going to be happy about leaving him on his own, even at a vet, not with what's just happened.'

At the surgery, Jadyn and Jim stood quietly in reception. It was being run by a woman who Jadyn thought was about his age. Her hair was streaked green and she spoke as much to the pets coming into the building as the owners. The plastic tag on her blue uniform gave the name Pauline Haigh and she was currently talking to a very small woman with a very large dog. So large, in fact, that Jadyn was pretty sure the woman could, if she wanted to, ride it like a pony.

The reception itself was clean and bright, with chairs around the edge of the room and a coffee table piled with magazines in the centre. Shelving against one wall contained various bags of dog food and next to it was a rack of various bits and bobs for pet owners, from dog leads and chew toys to little jumpers and catnip. In one of the windows was an odd collection of items with a sign in front saying, 'All raffle donations gratefully received.' Jadyn could see how winning some of the items would be quite nice, like the bottles of wine and hampers, but he wasn't sure he'd be all that happy with the packet of socks, four-pack of baked beans, or the stuffed pigeon.

'Bit weird,' Jadyn said, pointing at the raffle prizes.

Jim laughed.

'Neil's parents were unlucky enough to win something like that at Christmas. They've got it on the wall!'

'Why?'

'Apparently, it adds class,' Jim said.

'But a stuffed bird in a vets?' Jadyn said. 'Really?'

Jim shrugged and before Jadyn could say anymore, Pauline the receptionist called them over.

'You're here to see Mr Bell, yes?' Pauline asked. 'The veterinary surgeon?' Then she spotted Jim. 'James, how are you! How's your mum and dad? What happened at your farm, that was awful, with the theft and everything. Are they okay?'

'Yes, they are, thank you, Pauline,' Jim replied. 'Is Andy about, then?'

'I was told he would be,' Jadyn added.

'He was,' Pauline said. 'But he was called out just after he spoke to you I think, but he's on his way back.'

'Emergency?' Jim asked.

'Something to do with sheep,' Pauline said with a shrug. 'But then, what isn't round here?'

'Was it serious?' Jadyn asked, making conversation, if only to take in a little more the lurid colour of Pauline's hair.

'With sheep, it's always serious,' Pauline said. 'I swear those animals all get together in the morning and decide who is going to get foot rot or fly strike or just die for no reason. You'd be mad to farm them.'

Jadyn saw Pauline's eyes dip to Fly.

'And who's this, then?' she asked, coming out from behind her desk. 'This your new dog, Jim? Kath mentioned it, but she didn't say how adorable he is!'

As she approached, Fly's tail started to wag.

'Isn't he a strong-looking boy!'

'He's a good sheepdog,' Jim said. 'Well, he will be eventually if people will stop spoiling him.'

Pauline dropped to her knees and Fly rolled onto his back for a tummy rub.

Jadyn laughed as Jim rolled his eyes.

'And you're no help,' Jim said.

'Sorry.' Pauline laughed.

'Not you, the dog!' Jim said.

The fuss over, Jadyn and Jim sat down to wait. In the reception area was a cat in a basket, the fluffiest puppy Jadyn had ever seen, and a young Staffordshire Terrier whose face seemed to be set in a permanent smile, its tongue lolling out comically.

The sound of a loud engine rattled the windows of the building and Pauline stood up to look out through a window and onto the car park.

'Officer Okri?'

Jadyn looked up to receive a wave from Pauline.

'That's Mr Bell; he's just arrived. He'll be with you in his surgery in a few minutes, okay?'

Jadyn nodded a thank you and a moment or two later they were following Pauline out of reception and down a short corridor. As they headed off, Jadyn looked back at the terrier and found himself waving to the dog who returned the gesture with a wagging tail. The owner, however, a man wearing bike leathers and the most enormous beard Jadyn had ever seen, stared back at him with narrow eyes then reached down and patted the dog's head.

'Nice dog,' Jadyn said.

The man said nothing in reply.

'Through here,' Pauline said, and Jadyn and Jim, with Fly in tow, entered a small room that smelled not exactly unpleasant, but sort of funky and medicinal, Jadyn thought. It was a smell he could put up with, yes, but not one he'd want to take home with him. Two people were in the room waiting for them. The one on the left, a tall man wearing glasses, his dark brown hair cut short, who Jadyn put a guess at being in his mid- to late-thirties, welcomed them.

'I'm Andrew Bell,' the man said. 'Director of the surgery and one of the veterinary surgeons here.'

He spoke with a soft dales accent, Jadyn noticed, as though it had been slowly eroded by time, but not enough for it to disappear completely.

'I'm Police Constable Okri,' Jadyn said.

'Good to meet you,' Andrew said, then looked at Jim. 'And hello, Jim! Fly's growing into a fine-looking dog, I see!'

'He is,' Jim said. 'Just a bit too soft if you ask me.'

'Sorry I was out,' Andrew said. 'But that's the life of a vet, I'm afraid, particularly around here. Lots of emergencies on farms, as I'm sure you both know. Particularly with all the lambs now running around and getting themselves into all kinds of trouble. I swear they're born with a death wish.'

Like the man standing beside him, Andrew was dressed in a white veterinary jacket, which fell to his knees.

'And this is Toby Halloway,' he then said, introducing the other man. 'Been with us about six months now I think. And seems to be falling in love with the dales, isn't that right? Probably helped by the fact that he gets to race around it on a motorbike, but then who am I to judge?'

Toby smiled.

'What's not to love?' he said, his voice betraying a hint of Welsh to it.

'Still, it has its darker side, though,' Jim said.

Toby nodded.

'Everywhere does.'

Toby, Jadyn observed, was a good few years younger than Andrew. He also noticed that he was carrying a physique that required dedication and a gym membership, his square shoulders sitting beneath a head of blond, wavy hair, which made him look more like a surfer.

'You're here for the necropsy,' Andrew stated.

'Yes,' Jadyn said. 'I understand you've sent your results through to the pathologist, but I was asked to come over and have a chat about it anyway.'

'First things first, though,' Toby said, then dropped to his knees and took Fly's head in his hands. 'Aren't you the strong, handsome boy, then, eh?'

Fly's tail thumped on the surgery floor.

'Don't tell him that!' Jim said. 'Last thing I need is him getting even more full of himself!'

Toby laughed and Jadyn couldn't help but join in, particularly when the dog flopped down and rolled over onto his back, paws in the air.

'He's a terror, then, I see,' Andrew said, as Toby scratched Fly's stomach, causing the dog to twist around in obvious ecstasy.

'He'll make a good sheepdog, eventually,' Jim said.

'You sure of that?' Jadyn asked, staring at Fly.

'I have to be,' Jim said. 'I can't exactly afford to get another.'

Toby gave Fly another belly scratch then stood up. Once on his feet he reached around to a desk at the side of the room and grabbed a folder.

'Here you go,' he said, handing the folder to Jadyn.

'That's the report,' said Andrew, as Jadyn opened it. 'I warn you though, it doesn't make for an enjoyable read.'

But the warning was too late in coming, and as Jadyn's eyes fell on the photographs, and as he read through what the vets had found, his hand reached down instinctively to pat Fly on his soft, warm, furry head.

CHAPTER THIRTEEN

MATT HAD SPENT MOST OF THE DAY SO FAR, LEARNING very little indeed. The trip out to Snaizeholme would have usually been an enjoyable one but knowing what had gone on only served to taint the whole experience. Having spoken with the farmer, all he'd found out was that yes, they'd heard something, vehicles on the lane, and gone out to investigate. Having had some trouble with a few idiots treating it like a small rally course at various times before, they wanted to catch them in the act.

'So, what did you see?' Matt asked.

'Nowt much,' the farmer replied. 'Just a lot of lights zipping past. We were too late.'

'Nothing else you can remember at all?'

'One of the cars was red,' the farmer had then added. 'Yes, definitely red. At least I think it was. I mean, it was late, wasn't it? Dark and all.'

Then, before Matt had left, the farmer had expressed his anger at what he'd told him, his face growing redder with every word he barked into the day.

'And you know what I'd have done? Do you? Do you know? I'd have been out there giving them a bit of what they deserve, that's what! Coming down here, doing that? It's disgusting, it is! Animals, the lot of them! And do you know what we do with bad animals? With dogs that go wild and bother sheep? We shoot them, that's what! We shoot them!'

Matt had then advised the farmer against taking any such vigilante action should he see someone else on his land, advising that it would be best to just give the police a call instead. He also asked him to call him if they saw anything suspicious going on again or remembered something they thought might be useful.

After the visit to Snaizeholme, he'd then popped in to have a quick chat with Dave and only just managed to get away before being invited in for a look through, not just a collection of badger and otter video clips, but a slide show. Matt had known Dave for a good many years, but this nature-loving side of him was quite the surprise. Not that he loved nature as such, but that he was so into it. Matt had always assumed Dave's interest in the natural world involved country sports and walks to and from the pub. But wildlife cameras? Otter spotting? Really?

Now that it was late afternoon, and after checking in with Gordy, Jen, and Liz, and knocking on a few doors himself, he was at the bookmakers in Hawes, and sitting in a little back room away from the main shop out front. The owner, Mr Slater, a man who refused to be called by his first name by anyone, and whose passion for gambling was only eclipsed by his love of always wearing a waistcoat and pocket watch—which he seemed to check every two or three minutes—was sitting on the other side of a desk. He was early-sixties, Matt thought, his skin pale from so long spent inside the premises of the bookies.

The afternoon was growing late and Matt was keen to have this little chat kept as short as possible. He wanted to get home, not just for some dinner, but to check on Joan. He wasn't over-protective—Joan made damned sure of that—however, having a wife in a wheelchair was one thing, but now that she was pregnant? That was a little different. Though he was pretty sure that Joan didn't really need him around as much as he liked to think that she did. She was still working full-time up at the secondary school in Leyburn teaching art, and every day she seemed to look healthier and healthier. Matt would never admit it out loud, but he was almost a little jealous. Almost.

'You could've called before gracing us with your presence,' Mr Slater said, checking his pocket watch, even though Matt had only just sat down.

'That I could,' Matt said, 'but everyone loves a surprise, don't they?'

'No,' Mr Slater said. 'They don't. Certainly not here, anyway. Makes people jumpy.'

'I don't see why it should,' said Matt. 'Everything you do is legitimate and above-board, isn't it?'

'Of course it is!' Mr Slater said, bristling at Matt's words. 'But that doesn't detract from the fact that the police walking in can have chins wagging.'

'About what, exactly?'

'I wouldn't know,' Mr Slater replied. 'But when they do, all kinds of nonsense usually spills out, doesn't it?'

Matt leaned back in his chair. It creaked loudly as though keen for him to get out of it, and quickly. But he stayed where he was, not offering anything yet in the way of a reason for his visit.

'Well?' Mr Slater eventually said.

'Well, what?' Matt replied.

'Your visit!' Mr Slater said. 'There's a reason, I assume?'

'Of course, there is,' Matt said.

Mr Slater stared, waiting for Matt to reveal why he was there.

'I'm a busy man, Officer Dinsdale,' Mr Slater said. 'And just so you're aware, I will be unable to give you any details as to who my customers are, or their finances.'

The smile on the man's face was just the right side of smug to have Matt wanting to reach over and rip it off like a plaster.

'And that is as I would expect,' Matt said. 'But what about your son?'

Mr Slater's smile didn't budge, but Matt noticed a twitch in the corner of his left eye. If he was a poker player, it was that kind of tell that Matt would take advantage of to clear him out.

'What about him?' Mr Slater asked. 'Haven't seen him in months.'

'Any particular reason?'

'If there is or isn't, I can hardly see that it would have anything to do with you.'

'No, you're right,' Matt said. 'It's just, I was talking with the rest of the team earlier today, and I remembered something from way back. Really had everyone laughing it did, so I just thought I'd pop in, because I realised I'd not seen him around in a long time.'

'How caring of you,' Mr Slater said. 'And what was this that you remembered? Or do I not need to ask?'

Matt smiled as warmly as he could.

'Hens,' he said.

'You popped in here to ask how our Dean is, and all because of that? It was years ago! How can that have anything to do with anything?' Mr Slater held up a hand to stop Matt from answering. 'No, don't bother, because I'll tell you how; it doesn't, does it?'

'Actually, it does,' Matt said. 'We're investigating some pretty unsavoury gambling stuff. The kind that takes part out of sight and under cover of darkness, if you know what I mean.'

'I don't.'

'So, you wouldn't know anything about any illegal activities going on locally, then?'

Mr Slater's face was turning red.

'No, I would not!' he snapped back.

'I'm not accusing you,' said Matt, remaining calm. 'I'm simply asking, that's all. Just doing my job.'

Mr Slater rose to his feet, slowly, deliberately, and checked his pocket watch.

'And I should be getting back to mine,' he said.

'In a moment, yes,' Matt agreed. 'I won't keep you much longer, I promise.'

Mr Slater stuffed his watch back into his waistcoat and sat down.

'Like I said, I have no idea at all where Dean is. And that whole thing with the hens? Not only was it years ago, but it was also the first and last time he ever did anything so stupid.'

'You're sure about that?'

'I know my son!' Mr Slater said.

'It would still be good to talk to him,' said Matt. 'And look, I know that there's a few illegal poker games here and there. I'm not an idiot. But I'm not here about any of that. And I'm not here to try and ruin your business either. It's just that this, what we're looking into now? It's not the kind of thing any of us want on our doorstep, trust me. So, if you do know anything, if you know where Dean is...'

Matt's voice drifted off. Mr Slater breathed slow and deep, then he leaned forward.

'Do you know how long this business has been here?'

Matt didn't answer.

'My dad established it, back in the fifties. I took over when he retired. And I hoped Dean would do the same.'

'Not interested?'

Mr Slater shook his head.

'No, it wasn't that. It was more that he was too interested.'

'How do you mean?'

'The hens? He genuinely thought it was a good idea. Couldn't see the problem. Thought I was blinkered, too small-town in my ambitions.'

'So, he wasn't bothered about the legalities, then?'

'Which is why he's not in the business now,' Mr Slater said. 'He'd be a liability! A pity, really. He had this natural ability with numbers. Could work odds out in a heartbeat.'

'What's he doing now, then?' Matt asked.

'Oh, he still gambles,' Mr Slater said. 'Just on a bigger scale. Stocks and shares, that kind of thing. Gone all respectable, which is quite the shock. You should see him now, with his expensive car and expensive house and expensive wife and, well, you get the picture. Expensive everything!' He gestured around the room. 'All of this? He's no time for it now. I make a good living, but the money he's made is eye-watering.'

'So, he's not betting on hens, then,' Matt asked. 'Or dogs?'

'You wouldn't catch him at a track now,' Mr Slater said.

'Oh, these aren't racing dogs, Mr Slater,' Matt said.

At this, whatever emotion there was on Mr Slater's face slipped away like ice from a cliff.

'Where? Where did this happen?'

'I can't say,' Matt said. 'But it did. Now, I'm not suggesting your Dean is involved. But there were others there, that night, correct? He wasn't the only one involved in putting it together. It would be good if I could speak to them, too.'

'But that's ancient history,' Mr Slater said. 'And it was stupid. You know that as well as I.'

'That I do,' Matt said. 'But stupid isn't always a one-off, is it? Sometimes it happens again.'

Mr Slater shook his head, rubbed his eyes.

'You know I've never been, and would never be, involved in anything like what you're talking about, don't you?'

Matt said nothing.

'The hens thing, yes, Dean was involved, but there were two others that I can recall.'

'And they were?'

'Well, one of them's dead,' Mr Slater said. 'Danny something or other, can't remember his surname. Car accident somewhere. But then he always did drive like an idiot.'

'And the other?'

'You wouldn't believe me if I told you,' Mr Slater said.

'Try me.'

'Andrew Bell,' Mr Slater said. 'The vet.'

CHAPTER FOURTEEN

Arthur Black wasn't feeling very hungry at all. But this had no bearing in the slightest on the considerable pile of food his daughter, Grace, hadn't just cooked for dinner that evening but also had ladled onto his plate at least fifteen minutes ago now.

'You alright, Dad?'

'Just not that hungry, that's all,' Arthur said.

'Hungry or not, you're eating,' Grace said. 'It's your favourite, too, isn't it? Mince and potatoes? And those carrots are from my garden.'

'It is, lass,' Arthur said. 'And it's as tasty as always.'

'Then get it down you,' Grace said, her own plate empty, the gravy mopped up with a slice of bread. 'There's pudding, too, you know. Had some rhubarb in the freezer so I made a crumble.'

Arthur shovelled a fork-load into his mouth. Yep, definitely tasty, but it didn't make swallowing any easier.

'I know you're thinking about what happened to Jack,' Grace said, 'but the police are investigating now, aren't they?

And I met that officer myself. Grimm, wasn't it? And he seemed okay.'

Arthur sat back in his chair, his cutlery resting on his plate.

'They'll not be able to do nowt, though, will they, Gracie?' he said. 'It's just a dog, isn't it? Hardly the crime of the century. They've other things to be on with, I'm sure. And what if Eric's involved, eh? What then?'

'You have to leave it to them, Dad. And please don't go doing anything stupid.'

'Me?'

'Yes, you!' Grace said. 'Everyone knows what Eric is like, but you going round there and accusing him of something isn't going to help with anything, is it?'

Arthur said nothing.

'Is it?' Grace said again, her voice firm.

'It'd help make me feel better, that's for sure.'

'You're impossible.'

'I'm old.'

'With you, those two things seem to be one and the same more and more often.'

Arthur laughed, but the sound had as much warmth as a north wind on a dark, December evening.

'Look, all I'm saying is that a dead dog isn't going to be high on the list of crimes to be investigated. It just isn't. We both know that.'

'Regardless, you still need to eat,' Grace said, standing up with her empty plate and pointing at Arthur's. 'You'll find it helps if you actually hold your cutlery.'

Arthur harumphed, leant forward, grabbed a fork, and went in for a few more mouthfuls.

'There, that's better, isn't it?' Grace said, having taken

her plate through to the kitchen. 'I'll be off then, okay? But I don't want you leaving any of that, understand? And don't think I won't be checking either.'

Arthur looked up from the table and into the eyes of his daughter. She was giving him her stern look, but it was ruined a little by the faint hint of a grin showing through.

'He was a good dog, was Jack,' Arthur said. 'How could anyone want to harm him, or any animal, like that? Just doesn't make any sense.'

'No, it doesn't,' Grace agreed. 'There's all kind of folk in this world, and more's the pity that some of them are complete bastards.'

Arthur breathed deep, shook his head.

'Anyway, you've got Molly, haven't you?' Grace said. 'And she's not going anywhere, that's for sure.'

At the mention of her name, the old dog wagged her tail. Not that Arthur could see her, seeing as she was hidden somewhere in the dark under the table.

'I'll let myself out,' Grace said, and then she headed off, leaving Arthur with Molly and his own thoughts for company.

LATER THAT EVENING and having managed in the end to eat at least half of what Grace had made him, though unable to touch the rhubarb crumble she'd left for him as well, Arthur was watching television, but thinking of Jack.

With the visit earlier from that police officer, Grimm, he'd been running through the day that Jack had gone so many times that it was now playing as an endless loop in his head. And everything he'd talked about with Grimm, and then later with Grace, had only served to deepen his belief that the police really wouldn't have time, or the inclination, to find out what had actually happened. And that if anything was going to be done at all, then it was going to be down to him to do it.

But what? That was the question bothering Arthur, because the only two people who'd known where he was at and what he was doing had been his own daughter and one of his oldest friends. There was just no way that either of them had been involved. But someone had been, hadn't they? Someone had been sniffing around, keeping an eye on him, and had known where he would be and what he'd be doing. And they'd come along and taken Jack. His Jack! Snatched him for whatever reason and now the dog was dead!

Leaning back in his chair, weariness adding a weight to his bones that made him feel like even getting up to head upstairs to bed was an impossibility, Arthur closed his eyes. A nap would do him good. He could head upstairs later, couldn't he? So, he reached forward for the remote control and went to turn the television off, when a thought struck him, and wrong or not, the thought was enough to have Arthur out of his seat and pacing.

Grace had been right because she was sensible, he knew that. But at the same time, she didn't really understand, did she? Sometimes, you just had to get on with something yourself, otherwise, a job wouldn't be done. And right now, finding out what had happened to Jack was just such a job. He could leave it to the police, of course he could, but where was the guarantee that they'd be able to do anything?

It was all about evidence, wasn't it? And sometimes—quite often, he suspected—that evidence just didn't show up or wasn't found or couldn't be used. That was life. But Arthur had his gut and it was telling him something else, letting him know that it was time to take action.

What he knew so far was that if they took Jack, then they either knew him, and thus were able to take him with no effort at all, or they had no fear of dogs and would think nothing of beating an animal into submission. Because those were the only two ways that anyone would have been able to get Jack out of the Land Rover. Drugs were also an option, he supposed. Regardless, a stranger with no idea how to handle a dog, either fairly or with a harsh hand, wouldn't have had a chance with Jack and would probably have ended up with a hand chewed off.

Right now, Arthur's gut was leading up a path that he knew he would have to explore first or he'd never get to sleep. He had to know, didn't he? He just had to! He was also aware that if he told Grace or anyone else what he was thinking, they'd have some stern words for him, that was for sure. Grace would just tell him to get to bed, and that was fair enough, but there was no way he could sleep, not unless he knew for sure.

Before he had a chance to talk some sense into himself, Arthur grabbed his phone and tapped in the number. When the call was over, he sat back and waited, Molly snoring at his feet. Anger was burning in his veins, but he was still tired, and soon he'd dropped off as well, his snoring twisting into the soft thrum of the dog's slumber.

A LITTLE OVER three-quarters of an hour later, when the knock at the front door came and woke Arthur from his nap, the old man snapped awake and was out of the lounge to answer it a little too quickly. His head spun as a dizzy spell hit him and he leaned on the wall in the hall to let the wooziness leave him. Then he opened the door.

The shadows of a dark, star-free night, of a moon hidden behind a cloud, clustered around the figure standing outside just a little too far away to make out. Arthur went to invite them in, but before he had a chance to speak, the figure stepped forward and into the light, blowing in a great plume of sickly-sweet smoke from what looked like a thick hand-rolled cigarette.

'Oh,' Arthur said in surprise, coughing on the smoke, but then the old gamekeeper's surprise turned to shock and pain and bright lights inside his head as something crashed into his face and he, in turn, crashed to the floor like an old bag of bones. As he fell, he made a grab for the jackets hanging from the wall, but his weight and momentum were too much, and the hooks they were attached to yanked free from the wall, sending brick dust into the air.

Dazed, confused, and bleeding from a smashed nose, Arthur pushed himself up onto his elbows. He saw the figure he'd opened his door to now standing above him, a tall featureless silhouette.

'You ... you hit me!' Arthur spat, rolling over now to push himself back up onto his feet. 'The hell are you thinking, coming in here and—?'

Arthur's brain burst again with bright lights and pain, as something else crashed into his skull, then he was falling, tumbling forwards through the lounge door to land in front of the fire, the embers of which still had enough about them to warm the room.

'Molly...' Arthur managed, trying to push himself back up to his feet, to defend himself. 'Get out! Now!'

Then a thick blackness swept in, swallowing Arthur whole, and the last thing he saw before he passed out, was his old dog quietly, secretly, creeping upstairs.

HARRY WAS in his flat with Ben and Liz. Dinner was over, the remains of ham, eggs, and chips still on the dining table, and they were now all in the lounge, television on, weariness taking over.

As days went, it had left a sour taste in Harry's mouth thanks to the way it had started. He'd spoken with the rest of the team and so far they had little to go on. No, they had even less than that, didn't they? Gordy, Liz, and Jen had come up with nothing from knocking on doors, not that he'd expected them to, but it was still disappointing. Jim and Jadyn's report back from the vets had added nothing to what he already knew.

After another chat with the pathologist, all he knew was what he'd already known: anyone involved in something as deeply unpleasant as dog fighting was going to make very sure that everything about it was a secret. There was that other missing dog, an Alsatian, to check up on, too. Sowerby was sending her report through first thing tomorrow, so he'd have a better understanding then of what she'd found. Blood and soil samples, they sounded good, because it was evidence that could help identify someone, but unless they were able to get a lead on finding that person or persons, then they were no use at all. And that was the problem—tracing a line from what had taken place to the door of those responsible.

Matt had met with the farmer on whose land the fight

had taken place. All he'd gathered from that was that they'd seen a red vehicle, except they weren't exactly sure that it was red at all. And Dave Calvert's cameras hadn't provided anything useful either, bar badgers running around and generally being low-riding furry hooligans. And that whole thing with the hens? Not only was it ancient history, but the fact that the local and well-respected vet had been involved as a teenager said a lot, mainly that booze had been involved, and not much sense. Still, he'd be following it up himself tomorrow for sure. No stone unturned and all that.

Harry's chats with the dog's owner, Arthur, Arthur's daughter Grace, and then Phil, hadn't really helped either, except with the realisation that whoever had taken Jack had to have been known by the dog to have been able to take him in the first place. They clearly all had it in for this Eric bloke, but personal vendettas were hardly the best evidence. Another thing to check out tomorrow, Harry thought, rubbing his eyes, stifling a yawn.

'You look tired,' Liz said, walking in from the kitchen area to plonk herself down next to Ben.

'She's right, you do,' Ben said. 'Early night, old man?'

'Less of the old man,' Harry said. 'And I'm hardly likely to leave you two young things on your own, am I? Not a chance of it! Who knows what you might get up to?'

'Nothing we've not done already,' Ben said, with a wink at Liz.

'Oh, I don't know,' Liz said, 'I'm sure we can think of something.'

Harry said nothing, just sent a stare over at Liz.

'Too much?' she said.

'A little.'

'Been a tough day, then?' Ben asked.

'I've had better,' Harry said.

'Yeah, it's not been the best,' Liz agreed.

'How's about we head out for a drink, then?' Ben asked. 'A pint down at the Fountain. That'll do you good.'

Harry liked the idea, but he wasn't in the mood.

'No,' he said. 'I'll probably grab an early night.'

'Well, now that I've said it,' Ben said, 'I think I can taste it. Liz?'

'Yeah, sounds like a good idea.'

Harry watched as Liz and Ben pulled each other out of the sofa. They were happy, enjoying each other's company, and he wasn't about to ruin that by joining them in the pub with his little black cloud.

When they were about to leave, Ben called back, 'You sure you won't join us?'

'You go on,' Harry replied. 'I'll be fine. You've a key?'

'No,' Ben said. 'I'm leaving it behind on purpose so that I have to wake you up when I get back. I know how happy that makes you.'

Then the door thumped shut and Harry was alone.

Pushing himself up out of his chair, Harry headed through to clear up the things from dinner. He liked the flat, but with Liz being around quite often now, it was starting to feel a little crowded. He'd not yet discussed it with Ben, but soon he knew they'd have to discuss moving to somewhere bigger, perhaps even Ben getting a place of his own.

Washing up done, Harry headed back to the lounge just in time to sit down and have his phone ring.

'Grimm,' he said, answering it on autopilot.

'Harry, it's Gordy.'

'A phone call at this time of night from a detective inspector is never good, is it?' Harry said.

'I'm afraid not, no,' came the reply.

Harry leaned forward, resting his elbows on his knees.

'What is it, then? What's happened?'

'It's Grace Black,' Gordy said. 'Something's happened to her dad.'

CHAPTER FIFTEEN

When, for the second time that day, Harry arrived at Arthur Black's house in Redmire, he had no recollection of the journey at all. He could remember getting into his vehicle and setting off, and he was very aware that he had now arrived, but everything in between had been erased by his mind readying itself for what now lay before him, which was a dark and no doubt usually quiet evening, blown apart by noise and light.

'Harry?'

The usually soft, almost musical lilt of Detective Inspector Haig's voice had a darker, harder edge to it and Harry's response was no different.

'What have we got?' he asked. 'Where's Arthur? How is he? Where's his daughter? Where's Grace?'

'They're in the ambulance,' Gordy said, gesturing over to the vehicle, its lights turning a still night into something more like a fairground. 'Grace found him. Air Ambulance is on its way.'

'What?' Harry said, moving towards the ambulance, which was parked outside Arthur's cottage. 'Why?'

'He's in a bad way,' Gordy said. 'Paramedics have stabilised him, but there's no way they can get him to the hospital in the ambulance in time.'

'In time? In time for what? Just what the hell happened?'

As if on cue, Harry heard the tell-tale sound of a helicopter, the blades chopping through the night sky.

Harry's eyes fell again on Arthur's cottage, the door open, police cordon tape around the scene. He also spotted Police Constables Okri and Blades.

'What about the rest of the team?' Harry asked.

'Matt's on his way,' Gordy said. 'Jim's on duty tonight.'

'And Liz has tonight off, that I do know,' Harry said, thinking back to seeing her and Ben heading out to the pub for the evening.

Harry raised a hand to Jadyn and received a professional nod back.

'Let me guess,' Harry said, 'he's the Scene Guard.'

'Of course, he is!' Gordy said. 'If there was a badge or a promotion in the police for volunteering, then he'd be first in line for it.'

'And Jen?'

'Liaising with everyone onsite,' Gordy said. 'Excellent at it, too, I might add. Has an air about her that just seems to make everyone feel more relaxed, even in a situation like this. She was first on the scene. You want to speak to her?'

'I'll just check on Arthur first,' Harry said.

At the ambulance, Harry stepped into the bright white light shining out of the open back door. Inside were two paramedics and a whole world of beeping, flashing medical instruments, nearly all of which seemed to be attached to

Arthur, who was unconscious and lying on the gurney. At his side was Grace.

'Ms Black?'

She turned and Harry caught a tear-streaked face riven with worry, and in the harsh light, her skin looked pale as milk.

'How is he?' Harry asked.

Grace shrugged, tried to speak, but her voice caught in her throat.

Harry knew he needed to speak with her, but he also knew that to try and do so now would not only prove unfruitful, it would also be deeply inappropriate.

'You stay with him,' Harry said. 'We'll speak later, okay?'

Grace gave a nod and turned back to focus on her father, then turned back to Harry, grabbing his arm.

'What is it?' Harry asked.

'He... he was here,' Grace said. 'When I came over. I saw him, I'm sure I did!'

'Who was?' Harry asked. 'Who did you see?'

'Eric,' Grace replied. 'Eric Haygarth! He was here. I saw him driving off.'

'And you're quite sure about that?'

Grace nodded.

'You definitely saw him?'

'I'd recognise him anywhere,' Grace said.

Harry paused for a moment then said, 'What was he doing?'

Grace shook her head.

'I don't know!' she said. 'But it was definitely him, his truck. He drove off when I arrived. He was here. He did this! He tried to kill Dad! It was him!'

'You don't know that,' Harry said, his voice calm, not

wishing to encourage Grace to become even more agitated and stressed than she already was.

'Of course, I bloody well do!' Grace said. 'He hated Dad, everyone knows that, and Dad hated him, but then who doesn't? I reckon he took Jack, and Dad being Dad called him and he came over and beat the shit out of him! He was here, it was him, it has to be!'

Harry was looking for something else to say when the clatter and roar of the helicopter landing broke off any chance of communication and he got himself quickly out of the way as the paramedics got to work.

Harry watched as Arthur was wheeled out of the ambulance and over to the helicopter, Grace with him all the way, holding his hand, but as they got to the helicopter, she turned to Harry and stared. Then she climbed up into the helicopter. There was a change in the tone of the engine and the helicopter lifted off, the wind from the blades kicking up dust and dirt and grass as it went.

Harry gazed up at the helicopter as it headed off into the night, then cut back around to walk over to the cottage. Jen was already on her way over to meet him. Gordy joined them.

'Hello, boss,' she said.

'What happened?' Harry asked.

'Right now, we're not sure,' Jen said, hunching her shoulders against the chill of the night. 'I've taken statements from Grace, Arthur's neighbours, and the paramedics, and we've got forensics on their way.'

'Did Grace mention seeing anyone at the house?' Harry said.

Jen shook her head.

'Nothing,' she said. 'Why?'

'So, no mention of someone called Eric Haygarth, then?'

'Eric?' said Jen. 'God, no.'

'You know of him?'

'Everyone knows about Eric,' Jen said. 'He's about as pleasant as explosive diarrhoea.'

'Nice, then.'

Jen shook her head slowly.

'Grace thinks he was here?'

'She thinks she saw his truck,' Harry said. 'Said she saw it drive off when she arrived.'

'Could be Eric, I suppose,' Jen said.

'You don't sound convinced.'

'Oh, he's a complete arsehole, that's for sure,' Jen said. 'But to do this? I just can't see it.'

'Well, it's a name to check up on,' said Harry. 'You mind giving Jim a call and see if he can find out what he can about him, where he lives, anything, really? I'd rather get on that right away than leave it.'

'We can get Jadyn to give him a call,' Jen said.

Harry looked at the cottage, to where Jadyn was standing ready and alert.

'Going to show me around, then?'

'It's a proper mess in there, to be honest.'

'How's that, then?'

'Well, you'll soon see for yourself,' Jen said. 'We've kept disturbance to a minimum, as best as we can.'

Gordy added, 'But between what actually happened to Arthur, Grace turning up and finding him, and the paramedics having to work around it all to stabilise Arthur and get him out, it's not the best.'

'I'm sure you've done what you could,' Harry said. 'Everyone would've been focusing on Arthur, getting him stable. Paramedics aren't concerned with a potential crime scene, and neither should they be, not when there's a life that needs saving. So, whatever's gone on to get us to where we are now, whatever crime, well, that's for us to work out from this point forward.'

At the cottage, Harry lifted up the cordon tape for Jen and Gordy, then followed through himself.

'And how are you, PC Okri?' he asked, as they made their way towards the cottage's front door.

'I've got a list of everyone who's been in and out of the property,' Jadyn said. 'And contact details of the neighbours.'

'Sounds like you've got it all in hand.'

'I have,' Jadyn said.

Harry noticed that, even under such stressful circumstances, the lad was keen and alert. Good. He needed him to be. Because Harry's sixth sense, one born of years in the force, was already spiking. Yes, there was always the chance that this was just a coincidence, that what had happened to Arthur had nothing to do with his dog. But in his gut, Harry suspected otherwise. He'd never been much of a fan of coincidences. And there was this Eric Haygarth Grace had spotted, too.

'Anyone mention a vehicle?' Harry asked.

'No,' Jadyn said. 'Anything in particular?'

'A truck,' Harry said. 'Grace said she saw it driving off when she arrived. Owned by Eric Haygarth.'

'I don't think anyone was out and about, to be honest,' Jadyn said. 'From what I've got here, everyone was inside, fires lit, and watching television.'

'Well, let me know if someone does mention something,' Harry instructed. 'And can you give Jim a call, as well? Ask him to find out what he can about who this Eric Haygarth is?

From what I understand, he's a gamekeeper. There can't be too many of those around.'

Jadyn gave a firm nod and was immediately on to contacting Jim.

Leaving Jadyn, and now at the open door to Arthur's cottage, Harry came to a stop.

'Let's start from the top, then, before we go in,' he said. 'What I know so far is that Grace Black called this in after finding her dad in his house in a pretty bad way.'

'She did,' Jen said.

'And whether or not this Eric Haygarth was here, we should soon find out, with Jim on that now. But why was she here? I saw her when I was over here earlier today to chat with Arthur, so she was obviously visiting him then. Why again?'

'Well, it's nowt suspicious, that's for sure,' Jen said, reading now from her own notebook. 'She has dinner with him every Wednesday. Apparently, he was off his food, after meeting with you about his dog, so she'd come round to check up on him.'

'I got the impression they were pretty close,' Harry said.

'They are,' said Jen. 'Brought her up on his own.'

Harry remembered Arthur telling him exactly that when he'd visited earlier in the day.

'So, what did she find?' Harry asked. 'When she arrived, I mean.'

'A mess, is what,' Jen said. 'The place had been really kicked about. She wasn't sure what had happened, and her only concern was her dad, which is fair enough, considering the state he was in.'

'How was he when she found him?'

'Unconscious on the floor in the lounge,' Jen said. 'Blood

everywhere. She was half-covered in it herself when I arrived. Ambulance turned up a couple of minutes after me. You'll see what I mean when we get inside, anyway.'

'What about Arthur's injuries?'

'He's been fairly knocked around,' Jen said. 'I spoke with the paramedics. He's got fractured ribs, head and facial wounds, possible spine and neck injuries. Bloody lucky that Grace was round here at all, I think,' she added. 'If she hadn't come over, then I don't see how he'd have survived it. Doubt whoever it was, planned for him to, to be honest. It was vicious.'

Harry knew exactly what Jen was getting at. It said something, not just about the injuries but their intent. Whoever had done this and attacked Arthur, perhaps just injuring him hadn't been their intention at all.

'What made them stop, then?' Harry asked. 'If you're in the middle of that bloodlust, it's hard to pull yourself back.'

'Maybe this Eric bloke Grace mentioned,' Gordy suggested.

'Unless it was him that did it in the first place,' Harry said. 'And he heard or saw Grace turn up and bolted sharpish.'

Harry could still make out the juddering sound of the helicopter far off in the blackness.

Jen gestured to the door.

'After you,' she said.

Harry, PPE now on, stepped into the house.

CHAPTER SIXTEEN

'BLOODY HELL...'

'Yeah, you could say that,' Jen said. 'Bit of a mess, isn't it?'

Earlier when he'd visited, the cottage had been tidy, a place for everything and everything in its place. And Arthur had obviously been happy and comfy and more than a little proud of the place, not so much as a house, but as a home. That much was clear from the numerous photos that lined the walls. Except now, they didn't line the walls and were instead scattered across the floor, broken and smashed.

Standing in the small hallway, two doors leading off to both the kitchen and the lounge, and the narrow stairs leading up to the first floor, Harry did his best to think back to how the cottage had looked earlier, on the off-chance that something had stuck in his mind then, to help him spot something out of the ordinary now.

Obviously, everything he was viewing right now was out of the ordinary, but he always maintained that police work generally boiled down to the simplest of observations. Either finding something that shouldn't be there, or noticing something that should be there, but wasn't. People made mistakes, no matter how careful. And Harry's purpose in life was to find those mistakes, build a case, make an arrest. Not that this was ever easy, particularly when things were as much of a mess as they were in Arthur's cottage.

The small hallway was where the carnage began, waxed jackets and gun slips strewn across the floor, the hooks they had been hung on ripped from the wall. Harry saw spots of blood spatter on the wall by the stairs. He knelt down for a closer look, then glanced over his shoulder at the front door.

'What are you thinking?' Jen asked.

'Arthur was attacked here,' Harry said, then he stood up and stared at the blood. 'But how is that there, then?'

'How do you mean?' Gordy asked.

'Give me a minute,' Harry said then he looked through to the kitchen and stepped carefully from the hall into the room itself. As he went he made sure to avoid treading on any of the smashed photographs and crockery on the floor. Cupboard doors were open, plates and boxes and tins and cutlery were scattered and broken. And there was a smell to the place as well, wasn't there? It was faint, and it hadn't been there before, he was sure of that. But it was hard to work out what it was, with everything else that had happened, the fact that the kitchen bin had been kicked over, and that there was a fresh wind blowing in freely through the front door. Then Harry saw that the window in the back door was broken, the door itself swinging free, only adding to the draft.

'That definitely looks like a break-in, doesn't it?' Jen said. 'And they fairly went through the cupboards, though goodness knows what they thought they'd find.'

'"Looks like" is the key phrase there,' Harry said, making

his way over to the door for a closer look. 'We won't know for sure until forensics gets here.'

Jen pointed at the floor in front of the door, where Harry was now standing.

'Glass is on the inside though,' she said. 'Whoever did this must've smashed it to get to the key and open the door.'

Harry's voice grumbled in his throat. He crouched down for a closer look.

'What do you think?' Gordy asked.

'I think,' said Harry, staring at the broken glass, 'that Arthur would've heard the break-in, so why do any of this in the first place?'

'How do you mean?' Jen asked.

'Break-ins are sneaky affairs,' said Harry. 'Generally done when a house is empty, and somewhere like Arthur's place here? Well, it's not like it's a huge place that you can go sneaking around without anyone hearing, is it? And smashing through this glass here, well, that wouldn't exactly have been quiet.'

'Fair point,' Gordy said.

'And if it was a break-in,' Harry continued, 'as that broken glass and open door there is clearly meant to make us believe, then what were they after and why did they come here when the house was occupied?'

'Maybe they thought it was empty?' Jen said.

'What time is it?' Harry asked, standing back up.

Gordy glanced at her watch.

'Just coming up to eleven-thirty,' she said.

'When was Grace here? When did she arrive?'

Jen checked her notebook.

'Said she was here around ten, though she's not completely sure.'

'See what I mean?' Harry said. 'Already, none of this makes any sense. If you're going to break into somewhere, you do it in the dead of night. And you usually make sure no one's around. If Grace was here when she says she was, then all of this happened when Arthur was clearly still up and about. Otherwise, why would Grace have bothered coming over? I can't see her making the trip just to wake her dad up, can you?'

'What are you saying?' Jen asked.

'I don't know yet,' Harry said, and moved from the kitchen and back into the hall to head through to the lounge. The blood caught his eye again. 'This...'

'This, what?' Gordy said.

Harry looked at the blood, then at the door through to the kitchen, then at the front door to the house.

Harry pointed to the step outside the front door.

'Gordy? Can you stand there for a moment please?'

Gordy moved and Harry came to stand in front of her. He stared at her for a moment, turned to look at the blood, grumbled under his breath, then turned to stand in front of the door through to the kitchen. Again, he looked at the blood.

'Jen?'

'Boss?'

'Come stand here, in the kitchen, in front of me, will you?'

Jen did as instructed.

'Right then,' Harry said, his mind whirring away now. 'We're supposed to think that someone broke in through that door, yes? All that broken glass, that's what it's there to make us think, isn't it?'

Jen and Gordy both agreed.

'But see this blood spatter here?' Harry said, gesturing down to the red drops on the wall. 'If it's Arthur's, then how did it get here?'

'Whoever broke in attacked him,' Jen said.

'Attack me now, then,' Harry said.

'What?'

'I don't mean for real, obviously, but come at me like you've broken in. I've come out here to investigate, and here we are. What would you do?'

Jen looked shocked.

'How the hell should I know?'

'Come on, Jen,' Harry said. 'You're a burglar. Someone's found you out, so what are you going to do?'

Jen stared at Harry, at Gordy, looked around the kitchen.

'I'd run,' she said.

'I've seen you,' Harry said. 'I know who you are now. And you're angry and desperate, maybe you've got some alcohol in you, drugs, who knows? But you can't just leave, not now. So, what do you do?'

'Hit you?' Jen suggested, clearly not comfortable at all with even the thought of imparting violence on another.

'Pretend to do exactly that,' Harry said. 'Throw a punch, anything!'

Jen hesitated.

'Just do it, Jen! Come on!'

Jen raised her arm and threw it at Harry, who stepped back.

'Come at me again!'

Jen did exactly that, following Harry out into the hall.

'What's this leading to what, exactly?' Gordy asked from outside the house, peering in through the front door.

'Look where I am,' Harry said. 'I'm backed up into this

corner. I'm nowhere near that blood. Even if I'd tripped, if Jen had lamped me one hard enough to end up on the floor, I'd still be over here, wouldn't I? Not there.'

Harry gave neither Gordy nor Jen time to reply, instead, going to stand in front of Gordy.

'So, what about if you attacked me?' he asked, staring at the detective inspector.

'Tempting, but no,' Gordy said. 'I wouldn't want to hurt a precious lamb like you now, would I?'

Harry laughed at that.

'Do what Jen did,' Harry said. 'Come at me!'

'Well, if you insist.'

'Get on with it!'

Gordy faked a lunge at Harry, who stepped back.

'Keep coming,' Harry instructed. 'Come on! Attack me!'

Gordy stepped into the house. As she did so, her hands raised in an attempt to look threatening, Harry lowered himself to the carpet, leaned back, and looked at the wall.

'See?' he said, and pointed at the blood spatter.

'See what, exactly?' Jen asked. 'I can't see anything.'

'The blood,' Harry said. 'It's here, isn't it? It's not over there, where I was after you attacked me from the kitchen. But when Gordy came at me from the front door, look where I've ended up...'

Harry pushed himself back up onto his feet.

'Whoever did this,' he said, 'and I know we'll need the report from forensics to confirm it, but that broken glass and the smashed door, that's staged. It's a red herring.'

'The attacker came through the front door, then?' Gordy said.

'They did,' Harry said, 'and you know what that means, don't you?'

'What?' asked Jen. 'That Arthur knew them and let them in?'

'Possibly, yes,' Harry said. 'Or they came out here with no other motive than to do him harm, by which I mean, enough to kill him.'

With that bombshell dropped, Harry remembered something. 'Molly!' he said. 'Where is she?'

'Who's Molly?' Gordy asked.

'Arthur's dog.'

'I thought that was Jack,' said Jen.

Harry shook his head.

'Molly is an old thing,' he said. 'She was here this afternoon. Didn't Grace mention her? Molly's the dog that found the body of that Charlie Baker chap a few months back.'

'The author?' Gordy said. 'How could I forget?'

Harry remembered then that Gordy had been a huge fan, and had even attended a launch event of Charlie's in a local bookshop a day or so before he'd wound up dead, his head obliterated by a shotgun blast.

'Grace didn't mention another dog,' said Jen. 'What with the state her dad was in, I don't think there was much else on her mind, to be honest.'

'No, that's understandable,' Harry said. 'But I still want that dog found sharpish. Can't have Arthur losing another.'

'Might she have got out?' Gordy said.

'God, I hope not,' Harry said. 'Two dogs gone would be too much for Arthur I think. He looked at Jen. 'And you're sure you've not seen her?'

'Absolutely,' Jen said. 'Could whoever did this have taken her?'

'I doubt it,' said Harry. 'Too much hassle taking a dog with you. Which is another thing that doesn't sit right with all this—breaking into a house that has a dog! No one does that! And if they do, they kill the dog. But she's not here, is she? So, where, then?'

'Some people are pretty stupid,' Gordy said. 'We've all met them.'

'And arrested them,' said Harry. 'But even so, none of this strikes me as stupid. It's deliberate. Glaringly so. So, where's Molly?'

Harry was about to head into the lounge when he glanced up the stairs.

'Jen?'

'I'll go and check,' she said, reading his thoughts.

'She might be injured,' Harry said. 'Be careful.'

Jen headed upstairs and Harry moved into the lounge, Gordy with him.

'What an absolute bloody mess,' Harry said, taking in the destruction. 'Really went to town, didn't they?'

'Makes you wonder what goes on in the minds of some people, doesn't it?' Gordy said. 'Assuming anything is going on in the mind of the kind of person who does this.'

'Oh, something was definitely going on in their mind,' Harry said. 'We just need to work out what, exactly.'

The room, which earlier had been a small, cosy haven filled with happy memories of a father and daughter, was now a smashed and broken mess. Cushions from the sofa had been cut, their guts spilling fluff onto the floor, which itself was strewn with photos from the wall, broken glass and shattered frames. A small coffee table was on its back, legs broken. The television had been kicked onto the floor. The only thing which was undisturbed was the fire, still smouldering in the grate.

Harry saw blood and felt the temperature of his start to rise.

'Grace found Arthur just over there,' Gordy said, pointing at a spot on the floor where a dark stain of blood was clearly visible on the carpet. 'But judging by the spatter, he was certainly kicked around a fair bit beforehand.'

Jen appeared in the doorway. In her arms was Molly, the dog resting its head on her shoulder.

'Where was she?' Harry asked, then he saw that the dog was bleeding.

'Under one of the beds,' Jen said. 'Poor thing's terrified.'

'And lucky to be alive,' Harry said, walking over to see what was beneath the blood.

Molly whimpered as Harry touched near the blood, but it was clearly out of fear rather than pain, as the dog didn't flinch at all.

'I think that's Arthur's blood,' Harry said. 'Either that, or it's from whoever did all of this.

Harry stroked the old dog's head and Molly's tail wagged just a little. Then he gave the animal a quick check over, feeling her legs and down body. As he did so, her tail just wagged harder.

'Yeah, she's okay,' he said, his voice quiet.

'You sound surprised as much as relieved,' Gordy said.

'I am,' Harry replied. 'Come on, let's get some fresh air.'

Outside, Harry checked in with Jadyn, who'd not heard anything back yet from Jim about Eric Haygarth, and instructed him to call forensics, then moved away from the house and stood back to stare at the building, his thoughts a jumble. Jen and Gordy joined him.

'There are three things here that don't make a blind bit of sense,' Harry finally said, lifting his right hand and counting them off as he spoke. 'When it was done, how it was done, why it was done.'

Jen crouched down, placing Molly on the ground. The dog sat down, then just slumped and lay on her side on the grass.

'We need a sample of that blood,' Harry said, nodding at Jen. 'Go and see if you can find any scissors in Arthur's kitchen, then we can snip some off and bag it.'

Jen headed off.

'You're right, by the way,' Gordy said, as Jen entered the house. 'About this. Doesn't smell right at all, does it?'

'No, it doesn't,' Harry replied. 'It smells rotten, if you ask me. Every single bit of it has a stink on it that turns my stomach.'

'Looks like we're going to be busy then, doesn't it?'

'Yes,' Harry said. 'It does. Which means we'll need everyone together tomorrow morning to sort out what we do next.'

'I'll let them know,' Gordy said.

CHAPTER SEVENTEEN

A WHILE LATER AND HAVING JUST DRIVEN DOWN A DARK lane that seemed to lead only into thicker darkness, Harry was standing outside the kind of cottage he thought would look rather good on the cover of a horror novel. It was small, squashed almost, as though hunkering down out of the wind, and around it hung trees seemingly weighed down with silent horrors only they had witnessed.

The work over at Arthur's cottage had continued into, as Gordy would say, *the wee small hours*, and he'd stayed around until forensics had done their bit. This time, Rebecca Sowerby had been accompanied by the rest of her team, and they had done a thorough job as always. A clean-up team would be out in a day or so to put the house back into as good an order as possible. Once it was all done, and with Jim having found Eric Haygarth's address for him, Harry had then set off over the fells from Redmire and down into Swaledale. Driving through Reeth, he'd then headed on up into Arkengarthdale.

With the blanket of night still thick, despite the fact that the light of morning would very soon be swooping in, Harry had been unable to see much of the scenery. What he had noticed, however, was that for a good deal of the journey, the road was not lined with the usual drystone walls, but instead cut its way through open moorland. This sense of rolling, hidden vistas gave the journey, draped as it was in thin threads of moonlight hanging like threads from a vast torn blanket above, an eerie sense of creeping openness.

It was difficult for Harry to put his finger on what exactly made him feel ill at ease. He knew that it surely had much to do with what had happened over the past twenty-four hours. However, as his headlights mined their way ahead, silently carving a flickering tunnel into the darkness for him to drive through, he found it impossible to shake the feeling that out there, beyond the safety of the light, and right at the edge of the night, something wasn't just hiding, but watching. The moors were a place of ancient whispers and Harry wondered if he wound down his window, would he hear something calling to him, and just the thought of it raked his skin with a harsh chill.

Having arrived at his destination a few moments ago, Harry was now standing outside his vehicle, staring up at the dark windows of the building, wondering why and how the usually sweet air of Wensleydale was, in this place, considerably less pleasant. He couldn't quite put a name to what it was he could smell exactly, but it was as though the air was stale, like the breath of a tomb.

Harry closed the driver's door behind him and wandered along the front of the cottage, looking for the truck Grace had mentioned, though what kind he wasn't sure. Jim had provided him with an address and a phone number, but there had been no answer when he'd called, so ignoring the fact that it had been gone midnight, he'd travelled over regardless. If Mr Eric Haygarth was in and fast asleep and thus not answering, he would soon find out.

Though the cottage had no garden to the front, to the side was a brick shed and beyond that, an overgrown garden cast in a deep gloom that Harry suspected would be there in the middle of the brightest day as much as it was right then, when the night was at its thickest.

Harry found no vehicle, though tyre tracks were visible at the front of the house, which was not so much a drive as a rutted farm track suffering from a rapidly expanding population of potholes.

Walking up to the door, Harry gave a hard rap against the weathered wood with his knuckles. If Eric Haygarth was in, Harry was prepared for him to be not entirely happy at being woken at such an hour. He'd experienced it too many times before, bleary-eyed members of the public bellowing at him about the time of night and of course, they were asleep and what else did he expect, knocking at their door at such an ungodly hour. But a lead was a lead, and that meant that he had to check up on what Grace had said. Leaving it till the morning wasn't an option, not with the seriousness of what had happened to Arthur.

Nothing stirred from Harry's knock and the cottage remained still and quiet and dark. He tried again, this time with the heel of his fist, his banging on the door enough to wake the neighbours, had there been any. But there weren't, because this was a lonely cottage just far enough away from the nearby hamlet of Arkle Town, the closest collection of other dwellings to be ignored.

Harry tried once again, this time the pounding of his fist bringing with it the sound of something inside falling to the floor. But still, nothing. Not a sound, not a hint of another living being inside the cottage.

With no justifiable cause to break into the house to make absolutely sure that Eric Haygarth wasn't ignoring him, or hiding in a cupboard, or both, Harry turned to head back to his vehicle. A shiver down his spine caused him to pause, and he turned back around to stare at the cottage. The windows of the building stared back, dead eyes in a broken face.

Reaching over into his vehicle's glove compartment, Harry removed a torch, then wandered back over to the cottage. He shone the bright beam into the windows to the left and right of the front door and saw nothing that looked in any way suspicious. The rooms were little more than a simply furnished lounge and dining room, although the table in the dining room was somewhat hidden beneath boxes of goodness knew what. Harry then walked to the side of the house and slipped through a small gate between the house and the brick shed.

Wading through the thick tufts of grass and weeds of the garden, Harry crept down the side of the house until he was around the back. Beyond the garden, the beam of his torch fell on a thick wall of trees, the brown-grey of their trunks skeletal against the night.

At the back of the house, Harry peered in through a large window to the right of a door, the smaller window to its left being frosted and offering Harry no view of what lay beyond. The glass was clue enough though and Harry assumed it was a downstairs bathroom.

Through the larger window, Harry stared into what he knew was a kitchen, but the room seemed to have more in common with a medieval butcher than anything to do with the twenty-first century.

Sweeping his torch slowly around the room on the other side of the glass, Harry saw the carcasses of a number of animals hanging from hooks attached to the ceiling. Most were rabbits and hares, though he also caught sight of a few pigeons and a couple of crows. There were also what looked like three very large chest freezers in the room. With the amount of death Harry could see, he was surprised he couldn't smell it outside. On one of the walls, Harry saw the taxidermied head of a fox and hanging from a hook to its side was a leather apron.

Harry didn't know what to think. This eerily silent cottage and gamekeeper's home was certainly strange. The fact that the owner was not around didn't necessarily tie in with Grace saying she'd seen Eric Haygarth leave her dad's house earlier that night. For all Harry knew, the man was out doing whatever it was that gamekeepers did. And as for what he could see on the other side of the window? Well, a game-keeper's life involved shooting and trapping, so that would explain the animals on the hooks; probably just there waiting to be butchered. Though he didn't really see why anyone would want to eat a crow.

Making his way back around to the front of the house, Harry decided to try the door of the brick shed. There was a padlock on the door, and he almost walked on, but then noticed that although the lock looked snapped shut, it actually wasn't. Perhaps the key had been lost, Harry thought, as he slipped the padlock off the door then opened the latch.

Bringing the beam of his torch around and into the shed's interior, Harry jumped back as the beam picked out sharp, bared teeth. Swearing under his breath, his heart racing now, Harry calmed himself down and looked again. Facing him, he saw a table in the centre of the space. Against the walls were rolls of wire mesh and various hand tools. On the table itself, was the oddest creation Harry had ever seen. Skeletal legs held up a body comprising wire mesh moulded into the shape of an animal's body. Attached to this was a skull, the bone a pure white, the teeth sharp and shining in the light of his torch.

He'd been right about his horror movie observation when he'd arrived at the place earlier. He stepped further into the shed, curiosity causing him to reach up and test the sharpness of the skull's teeth. Around the room were various other animals, all at different stages of preservation, from squirrels to buzzards to what Harry assumed was a fox on the table. There was even an owl, the beauty of the animal preserved with astonishing attention to detail, reminding Harry of his encounter back at the barn.

After a couple more minutes taking in the contents of the shed, Harry reversed out through the door, but his eyes fell again on the strange and somewhat horrifying creation on the table. At first sight, he'd thought it to be a fox, but as he stared at it now, taking in the size of the thing, the large skull, he realised then that there was just no way that this, whatever it actually was, could be a fox. No. And then the realisation hit him. If it wasn't a fox, then the only other thing it could be was a dog.

With the skull of the dead animal staring at him, Harry left the shed, replaced the padlock, then made his way back to his vehicle, more than a little creeped out by what he'd seen. Okay, so he was no wiser as to whether or not Eric Haygarth had indeed been the man Grace had seen over at her dad's. That he wasn't home was strange, but certainly wasn't an admission of guilt. He'd also discovered that Eric was a fan of taxidermy, the shed showing various stages of the process. And that, Harry realised, would explain the state of the kitchen, the freezers. However, it was the skeletal dog that bothered him the most. All the other animals he understood were easy to come by, but a dog? Was it Eric's? Had he skinned and was now in the process of preserving his own dog? Or was it someone else's? And if so, how the hell had he come by it?

Heading back down Arkengarthdale towards Reeth, Harry tried to pull together what he had so far from what had been found at the barn in Snaizeholme, what had happened at Arthur's, and now his little visit into another ancient dale. But with the hours of the early morning crashing in on him, all that did was give him a headache.

Rubbing his eyes, and focusing on the road ahead, Harry let his mind wander. Sleep would help, he decided, so he focused on getting home without incident. And perhaps, come tomorrow, which was already today, some answers would start to surface.

CHAPTER EIGHTEEN

THANKS TO A SECOND NIGHT OF VERY LITTLE SLEEP AND having allowed himself an overly generous four hours kip to try and make up for it—just enough to ensure he was almost human for the rest of the day—Harry woke mid- to late-morning to a smell in his bedroom he really wasn't used to—that of an animal, and one that clearly had a flatulence problem. He lay there trying to work out just what the hell it could be, for a moment concerned that a fox had broken in to have a good rummage around in the clothes basket—not a good idea—when a faint, sonorous snore slipped into his day.

Rolling over onto his side, Harry saw on the floor of his room at the foot of his bed the curled-up form of Arthur's old dog, Molly. Her bed was made up of one of his old jumpers and a few cushions from the lounge, and was, judging by the sounds of contentment coming from the old animal, perfectly adequate.

The late night over at Arthur's had soon become an early morning, with the arrival of Sowerby and her team. When they'd finished up and collected everything they'd deemed relevant, Harry had been able to send Jadyn, Jen, and Gordy home, before he'd then trundled over to Eric's place. But that had still left him with Molly. So, with no other option, he'd taken the old dog home with him and sent a message through to Grace to let her know. She had been very grateful and had said that if she wasn't able to come over and pick her up, then a friend of hers would, someone who was looking after her own dog for her while she was with her dad.

Harry swung himself out of bed and headed to the bathroom for a shower. As he walked past Molly, the dog didn't move. He crouched down just low enough to scratch the dog's head, at which point she rolled onto her back to show him her stomach.

'So, you're awake after all,' Harry said, and gave the dog a scratch.

Molly let out a long, satisfied breath and just stayed as she was, on her back as Harry continued on his way. And she was in the same position when he returned. It was only when Harry was in the kitchen and opening a tin of food for her that he'd taken from Arthur's house, along with a lead and some bags for the one job anyone without a dog looked at with utter bafflement and disgust, that Molly moved from her makeshift bed. The smell of the food was to Harry's mind much akin to that of the worst kind of bowel disorder.

'That got you moving, then, I see,' Harry said, placing a cereal bowl filled with dog food on the floor next to another filled with water, dog bowls being the one thing he'd not grabbed from Arthur's.

Molly tucked into it with gusto, farted, then made her quiet and assured way back to Harry's bedroom. Harry cut her off at the pass, pulled on his jacket, and took the dog outside for a quick walk on the way to the office. It was clear that the dog wasn't in the mood for much in the way of exercise, and once she'd relieved herself in as public a place as possible—right in front of Hawes Market Hall—and with Harry having to avoid the stares of people as he'd picked it up, she'd then just turned back the way they had come. Somehow, Harry had managed to drag her in the opposite direction and along to the office. Every few steps she'd stopped and stared at him, her eyes clearly telling him, *No, I don't want to go any further.* The whole experience had him wondering once again, what the joys were in owning a dog.

Once at the office, Molly settled down in a corner by a radiator while Harry waited for the rest of the team to arrive. When they did, and despite the weariness he saw in their eyes, everyone was restless, clearly itching to get on with the day ahead.

'Grace is going to pick her up when she can,' Harry explained to Jim, as Fly stared at Molly. 'I've said to not worry. She's not exactly a bother.'

'Not so sure Fly would agree with you there,' Jim said, as his dog edged closer to Molly, eventually coming to sit right next to her as though in the hope she might want to play. Then he gave up on that, lay down, and closed his eyes.

'You sure he's going to be alright with her being here?' Harry asked. 'I know he looks like he is, seeing as he's now asleep, but I just want to make sure. I can take her back to the flat if you want.'

'Oh, he's fine,' Jim said, as Fly pushed himself back up into a sit, yawned, then lifted a paw and rested it on Molly's head. 'I think he's a bit confused to have another dog somewhere he probably classes as his.'

'What's he doing now, then?' Harry asked, as Fly started to massage the crown of Molly's comatose head with his paw.

'He just wants her to play,' said Jim. 'Not that there's going to be much of that going on, by the looks of things. How was she last night?'

'A bit whiffy, if you know what I mean,' Harry said. 'That old dog creates smells you can actually see.'

Jim smiled at that.

'Other than that, though,' Harry continued, 'she was no bother at all really. Didn't even stir when Ben got up this morning to head to work.'

There were two reasons for this, Harry thought to himself. The first was that Molly was deaf and could sleep through anything. The other, and this was one reason he wasn't about to tell the rest of team, was where Molly had slept.

Having arrived home, Harry had done his best to set out a little bed in the lounge area of the flat for the dog, a mix of cushions and a blanket or two. Molly had settled down, but as soon as Harry had headed off to bed, she'd upped and followed. He'd done his best to get her to stay, but each time she just followed, so with little choice, and no energy to argue the point, Harry had moved the makeshift bed onto the floor of his bedroom. And there Molly had stayed, without complaint. He'd had to keep the window open the whole night, not that it had made much difference to the rich and varied collection of smells Molly had managed to produce.

'I'll take her for a walk once we're done,' Jim said.

'No, you won't,' Liz said, jumping in. 'Last thing that old dog needs is young Fly bothering her. I'll take her.'

'Fight it out between yourselves,' Harry said, then he clapped his hands together to bring a start to the meeting.

'Right then, before we start putting anything up on the board, I think it's probably best if I run through what's been going on. That way we'll all be clear on what's what, because, as of last night, it looks like what happened over in Snaizeholme is even more serious than what we initially thought.'

Harry was about to explain why when he was cut off by the sound of the office door being pushed open.

'Detective Superintendent Swift,' Harry said, looking over to see his superior officer now standing in the office. 'I didn't know you were due to visit us today.'

'I wasn't,' Swift replied curtly and took a seat behind the rest of the team.

'Well, it's good to have you here,' Harry said, lost for anything else to say, and amazing himself with his own politeness.

'Pretend I'm not even here,' Swift said and smiled, if what his face was then doing could be called such. Because to Harry, the man looked like he was in pain, as though the act of trying to look relaxed and happy was something his face just wasn't keen on attempting.

'Okay then,' Harry said, focusing on his team. 'As you'll all recall, this time yesterday, what we thought we were dealing with was illegal dogfighting. For all we knew, it was a one-off, but it was on our turf as it were, it involved the death of a dog belonging to a retired gamekeeper down dale in Redmire, and the last thing any of us want is that kind of activity becoming common. But as of last night, we are now investigating what I believe to be a credible link between what happened up in Snaizeholme, and the attempted murder of the dog's owner, Arthur Black.'

'That's quite the jump,' Swift said.

'I don't think it is,' Harry replied.

'But a dog fight is a very different affair to attempted murder.'

'Arthur's dog was killed in the fight,' Harry said. 'I met with Arthur yesterday and then last night he was attacked in his own home and is now in hospital and lucky to be alive, if you ask me. In fact, if his daughter hadn't decided to pop round to see him, then I think there's a good chance this would now be a murder investigation. This was no random attack.'

Harry waited for Swift to say something, but the man simply folded his arms and stared back. Harry then gave a nod to Jadyn.

'Let's get on with filling that board up then, shall we, Constable Okri?'

Jadyn was on his feet in a heartbeat, pens at the ready.

'In addition to what we already know about the dog fight, and what we saw at Arthur's house,' Harry said, 'we've heard back from the pathologist with her report, photos and so on from what happened at the barn. And we'll be hearing later on today about what's been found at the house.'

'And is any of it much use?' Swift asked.

'Unsurprisingly, we've not got much to go on,' Harry said. 'But that's to be expected. People attending something like this don't usually hang around or make a point of leaving anything behind that can be traced to them.'

'Except a dog,' said Swift.

'And so far, that's only led us to the owner,' Harry said.

'So, it's a dead-end, then,' Swift grumbled.

'That's not what I said,' Harry replied. 'Although we have nothing like DNA, for example, except for that of Arthur's dog, what we do have is some evidence from outside the barn.'

'And the red vehicle the farmer saw,' Jadyn added, giving a thumbs up to Matt.

'Yes, and that,' Harry said.

'A red vehicle?' Swift said. 'Well, that narrows it down, doesn't it?'

Harry ignored the comment.

'As you know, there were plenty of footprints inside the barn, but these are all fairly scuffed up and of little use. However, there were a good number of fresh tracks from various vehicles, and Sowerby took casts of these, soil samples, and so on.'

'And she's found something useful?' Matt asked.

'Potentially, yes,' Harry said. 'Assuming that we find our way to tracking down potential suspects.'

'So, what have we got?' Gordy asked.

'In the tyre impressions from one of the vehicles Sowerby found traces of cement dust and tiling adhesive.'

'How did that get there, then?' Jadyn asked.

'Tyres are very good at trapping dirt and dust,' Gordy said. 'Even after hundreds of miles, they'll still have traces of surfaces they've not touched for days. A tyre lasts for thousands of miles so it takes a good while for them to wear away.'

'So that means, then,' Jadyn said, 'that the owner of one of the vehicles drove it somewhere where it came into contact with those two substances?'

'Exactly,' Harry said. 'And I know that right now that doesn't seem like much, but it could be more than enough to link someone to that barn a couple of nights ago. But only if we can track down who was there and get our hands on a vehicle.'

'But we can't exactly start searching for everyone in the dales who's bought cement and tiling adhesive, can we?' said

Jim. 'That's impossible! Even if we do know that one of the vehicles is red.'

'Can I just point out that the farmer wasn't exactly sure about that?' Matt said.

'You're right, Jim,' Harry said. 'We can't really do that, but what we can do is look at building projects in the area, that kind of thing.'

'How so?'

'Well, it's not like we're in a city where there are potentially hundreds happening at any one time, is it? Whoever was there, they'll have travelled a fair distance, I'm sure, but I can't see them wanting to be further than an hour away, and even then, I think that would be pushing it.'

'Why?' Liz asked.

'Because criminals are inherently lazy,' Swift said, answering for Harry. 'Nine times out of ten crime is an excuse to make a lot of money from not much work. Otherwise, what's the point?'

'So, you don't think they'll have travelled far, then?' asked Jadyn.

'I very much doubt it,' continued Swift, continuing to answer for Harry. 'I'm not saying that I think they're local, as in from Hawes or Gayle or whatever, but I think Grimm is right on this point. They won't have travelled too far to take part in a dog fight in the middle of the night.'

'Let's narrow it down, then,' Harry suggested, surprised Swift had so readily agreed with him. 'Let's stick to Wensleydale itself and the surrounding area. Then, if we find nothing, we can widen the search.'

'That's still quite a large area, though,' said Matt. 'It'll take us a fair while to cover it all.'

'It is, yes,' Harry said, 'and it will. But Sowerby also found something else. Granite dust.'

'Granite?' Liz said. 'I'm assuming you mean for worktops in expensive kitchens, that kind of thing, rather than just lumps of the stuff?'

Harry nodded. 'I do. Which means we can narrow things down a bit further then, can't we?'

'It's still a large net to be casting,' Gordy said. 'But you're right, it's something. Particularly when we have nothing else.'

'Nothing else *yet*,' Harry corrected. 'What happened in that barn will be high stakes stuff. We're not talking a few hundred quid changing hands, but thousands. That's half the thrill. It's not just the violence, but the winning, and the fear of losing.'

Jim raised his hand.

'We got something through last night from Andrew Bell, the vet,' he said. 'A toxicology report. It's pretty detailed.'

'And?'

'Arthur's dog had quite a cocktail of stuff in its veins,' Jim said. 'None of the substances are illegal, because they have legitimate uses, but apparently, they are commonly found in connection with illegal dogfighting operations.'

'And how do you know this?' Swift asked.

'I read the report and I looked it up,' Jim said, turning around to face the DSup. 'I was on duty last night. The report came in, so I did a bit of research.'

'Well done,' Swift said.

'So, what did the dog have in it, then?' Harry asked.

'There's quite a list,' Jim said. 'But you're talking vitamin supplements to help the blood carry more oxygen and decrease lactic acid, stimulants to help it fight for longer and with more aggression, anti-inflammatory agents, steroids.'

'You sure that report isn't about that cyclist bloke, Lance Armstrong?' Jen said.

'There's a lot of crossover from sports into dogfighting,' Jim replied. 'It's pretty shocking.'

'That poor animal,' Liz said.

No one disagreed.

'The vet also found the chip,' Jim continued. 'That confirmed that it was indeed Jack, Arthur's dog. I know we knew that anyway, but it's worth knowing I think.'

'And that cocktail of drugs supports what I've just said about this being high stakes,' Harry said. 'It's not cheap to pump a dog full of that stuff.'

'But how is any of this linked to what you're telling me is an attempted murder?' Swift asked. 'All you've done so far is talk about a dead dog pumped full of drugs and a wild goose chase of hopefully finding a vehicle, which may or may not be red, either on a building site or at a house undergoing some home improvements!'

Harry levelled his gaze at Swift.

'Like I said, we're waiting on the pathologist about what was found at the crime scene last night, but I tell you now, it was no break-in. It was not a random attack or the act of someone caught in the act.'

'And you know this how?' Swift asked.

'Because that's what the evidence shows,' came another voice new to the discussion.

Harry looked up to see the pathologist standing at the office door.

'Well,' he said, 'this is a surprise.'

'A pleasant one, I hope,' Sowerby replied.

Harry didn't know what to say to that, so said nothing as

Sowerby made her way deeper into the room to join the rest of the team.

'Now,' she said, taking a seat, 'before we go any further, I just need to know one thing...'

'And what's that?' Harry asked.

'Am I too late for a bacon butty?'

CHAPTER NINETEEN

THE UNANNOUNCED ARRIVAL OF DETECTIVE
Superintendent Graham Swift was one thing, but having the
pathologist turn up as well? It wasn't exactly too much for
Harry to deal with, but it was certainly something he
could've done without. So, taking advantage of Sowerby's
announced requirement for food, he quickly sent an enthusiastic Detective Sergeant Dinsdale off to the top end of town
to grab a round of bacon butties from the Penny Garth Café.

'And take this,' Harry said, handing the DS his card. 'My
shout.'

'You sure, boss?'

'Very,' Harry said. 'Just make sure mine's double bacon,
okay?'

With Matt gone and the meeting paused for a moment,
Harry had a little time to chat with both Swift and Sowerby
about what was going on and to find out why they were there
in the first place. He may not have been the biggest fan of
having everything planned out in the minutest of detail,

often preferring to go with gut instinct, but a heads-up now and again would certainly be appreciated.

'I don't always announce my visits ahead of time,' Swift said, staring up at Grimm, and having just informed the DCI that he was there merely to observe. 'I think it's important that I see a team in the rough as it were. If I gave you a date and a time of a visit, I would never be entirely sure that you weren't in some way performing for me, running through a well-rehearsed and polished sequence of points and actions.'

Harry wanted to laugh at that, but somehow managed not to.

'You do know this team, don't you, sir?' he asked. 'Because I'm not sure that performing is one of their key skills, if you know what I mean. And certainly not in any polished fashion, that's for sure.'

'No, I'm not sure that I do know what you mean,' Swift said.

Harry thought for a moment as to how best to put what he was about to say next, and in such a way as to not offend, then just gave up and went with it.

'This isn't a bloody circus, sir!' he said. 'They're not here to put on a show and do backflips and somersaults just because a superior officer has come over to watch them work!'

Swift said nothing, just stared, lips so thin they were little more than thin red lines.

'That isn't what I'm suggesting, Grimm,' he eventually said, and Harry noticed a twitch of annoyance in the man's eyes. 'At all.'

'Well, to be frank, sir, I'm not sure a single one of them gives a rat's arse about what you, or I, or anyone else thinks of their performance, if that's what you want to call what they do. All they actually care about is doing a good job, for the community in which they live. And I, for one, think that's exactly what they should care about, don't you?'

Swift opened his mouth to speak, but Harry didn't give him the opportunity.

'I've worked with too many people who have, for whatever reason, spent more of their working life trying to prove themselves to people like you and me, than actually getting on with the job in hand.'

'Well, it's important to be aware of what your colleagues think,' Swift said, but Harry wasn't listening.

'But this lot?' he said, gesturing at the team, who were all busy in their own conversations over mugs of tea. 'They're not like that, thank God. Not a single one of them. Even our newest and keenest member, PC Okri. He's enthusiastic, I'll give him that, a little too enthusiastic at times maybe, but he's not trying to show off or make sure I see what he's doing. He's just trying to do the best job that he can.'

'Sounds like things could very easily get a little sloppy with an attitude like that,' Swift said, clearly not giving up his viewpoint or showing any indication of considering Harry's own. 'Police officers need to be kept on their toes, Grimm, otherwise, how can we, as a force, improve?'

'By giving the people in it the space and support to do their job, to ask questions, use their initiative, and to learn from their mistakes,' said Harry, working hard to stay calm in the face of Swift's mean-spirited and suspicious small-mindedness. 'If they're being kept on their toes, if they're always worried about being pulled up on something that didn't go well, or something they did that didn't quite follow this policy or that procedure, then what chance have they got?'

'Well, policies and procedures are there for a reason, Grimm. You know that as well as I do. And though I am loathed to remind you why you're here in the first place, I suggest you cast your mind back to that right now!'

The breath Harry then sucked in was long and deep enough to rid the room of all its oxygen. Then, with a voice as still and calm as the eye of a storm, he said, 'You leave them be, sir. They're a good team. Arguably the best I've ever worked with. They don't need spying on. They don't need box-ticking exercises. They just need to be allowed to get on with what they do best, and that's the job they're all doing right now.'

Then, as if on cue, Detective Sergeant Matt Dinsdale bounced through the office door and dropped a heavy carrier bag onto a table.

'Right then, everyone!' he bellowed, as though announcing the best news he'd ever had to impart in his life. 'Get that lot inside you before it goes cold!'

Both Swift and Grimm stopped talking and in the momentary pause in the discussion, as the team tucked into Matt's delivery, Sowerby stepped forwards and spoke.

'You're actually both right, you know,' she said. 'A team needs to be given the space to breathe, but it needs policies and procedures as a solid foundation to build on.'

Harry watched his team as Matt dished out white, grease-spotted paper bags, then walked over and took one for himself and another for Sowerby.

'I'll be honest,' Harry said, handing Sowerby her bacon butty, 'it's a little early for these kinds of professional development discussions. Just so long as we don't stray into person development plan territory, then I think I can just about handle it.'

'PDPs are essential, Grimm,' Swift began, but Harry wasn't listening and the DSup's voice faded, as did whatever point he was about to make. The man had bowed out of ordering a butty and instead stood there nibbling on a Rich Tea biscuit. Harry thought how that said an awful lot about the man in front of him.

'I really needed this,' Sowerby said, biting into her butty.

'Be warned, though,' Harry advised, tucking into his own. 'They're addictive. Before you know it, you've had one every day for the past month and put on a stone.'

'Not sure I care right now,' Sowerby said.

'Next time I'll get them to throw an egg in as well for you,' Harry said.

He couldn't help but notice that over the past few months, he and Sowerby's usually frosty working relationship had thawed a little. And now here she was, eating an unhealthy breakfast with his team. Did they have this effect on everyone? he thought. Then he saw Swift finishing off his bland biscuit and thought, perhaps not. Which was a shame, really.

'I stayed over at my mum's in Askrigg,' Sowerby said. 'In case you're wondering why I'm here. Which I'm sure you are. You've that look in your eye.'

'Look?' Harry said. 'I don't have a look.'

'Oh, you do,' Sowerby said. 'You have quite a few, actually. And most of them seem designed to put someone ill at ease.'

Deciding to not follow that observation up, and remembering that the pathologist's larger than life mother was also the district surgeon, he said, 'What made you stay over, then?'

'Exhaustion mainly,' Sowerby said, finishing off her food. 'And I'd been meaning to come over for a visit anyway. So I brought some work with me before I came over. I'll be around over the weekend, trying to catch up on some bits and bobs, and to have a bit of a rest. And mum's a great cook. Always likes to feed me up.'

'Fair enough,' Harry said.

'When I woke up this morning I thought that I may as well come down here and go through our findings with you first-hand. Hope that's okay. I didn't want to interrupt your meeting, but there was no point in me just walking around the marketplace until you were finished.'

'Not a problem at all,' Harry said. 'And to be honest, with how this is all developing already, getting your thoughts can only be a good thing.'

'I hope so,' Sowerby said. 'You sound concerned.'

'I am,' Harry nodded. 'A dog fight, that's one thing. But when something escalates like this, and so quickly?' He shook his head. 'I don't want to think about where it all might lead.'

'Could be you're joining up all the wrong dots, though,' suggested Swift, his appetite clearly sated by the solitary biscuit. 'It does happen. We've all done it.'

'Maybe,' Harry said, his eyes falling to where Molly was fast asleep on the floor. 'But then that would mean what happened last night was just a coincidence. And if that's the case, then we've got a problem.'

'Have we?' Swift said. 'And what's that?'

'He doesn't believe in coincidences,' Sowerby said, then looked up at Grimm. 'And neither do I.'

Harry took centre stage again, over by the board, the

movement enough to get the attention of the rest of the team. They all fell quiet and took their seats.

'Jadyn?' he said.

'Yes, boss?'

'Get your pens ready. You're going to need them.'

CHAPTER TWENTY

WITH THE MEETING OVER, AND EVERYONE SET WITH
their tasks, Harry popped back home to drop off Molly, on
the way giving Ben a quick call to tell him to give the dog a
run that evening if he wasn't back in time. Then he nipped
back into the office just to make sure everyone was clear with
what they were doing before he headed off to see Arthur and
Grace. Sowerby and Swift had already gone by the time he
returned, and everyone else was in the process of leaving to
make the most of what was left of the day. They'd found
several local construction sites to check up on, so that was
something. And then there was the case of the mysterious
missing Eric Haygarth, which Harry had given to Matt.

'And take someone with you,' Harry said. 'Just in case.'

'Just in case of what?' Matt asked.

'Because this Eric bloke is the kind of person who enjoys
stuffing dogs,' Harry replied. 'Although I'm sure there's a
perfectly reasonable explanation for it, I'm not entirely
convinced that someone who does that shouldn't be someone
we're wary of.'

'I actually rather like a bit of taxidermy,' Matt said.

'If only I could stand here and say I was surprised.'

'I'll take Liz,' Matt suggested. 'She's just popped out but will be back in a few minutes.'

'Worth starting at his house, I suppose,' Harry suggested. 'I know he wasn't there last night, but he might have gone home, you never know. Whatever, it's all a bit odd that Grace saw him and now he's vanished. See what you can find, knock on some doors, the usual.'

'Police work always boils down to this, doesn't it?' Matt said. 'You can have all that fancy science stuff, forensics, even the occasional exciting car chase and shoot-out at an abandoned warehouse, but most times, it's all down to knocking on doors.'

'I can agree with most of what you said,' Harry said.

Matt looked at Harry, an eyebrow raised in question.

'Most, boss? How do you mean?'

'Well, for a start, you've never had an exciting car chase and shoot out,' Harry said. 'And my advice is, you don't want to, either.'

'You mean it's not like it is in the movies? All near-misses and jumping through the air and shooting the bad guys?'

'Not even in the slightest,' said Harry.

With Matt tasked, and happy with what the rest of the team were on with, Harry was soon behind the wheel of his Rav4 and heading down dale, this time all the way through to Northallerton, the hospital where Arthur had been taken. Grace was still there with him. She hadn't left his side. And with it now being the afternoon, Harry was concerned that her exhaustion was soon going to be an issue. He also needed to speak with the doctors who had dealt with Arthur, just in case they had any insight into what had happened after patching him up.

The journey over to the hospital was probably very beautiful and full of the most striking scenery, as was pretty much every journey in the dales, but Harry remembered none of it. His mind was only on the investigation, what had happened to Arthur's dog and then to Arthur himself. He couldn't think of a connection, but he would, and when he did, the person responsible was going to be in a very bad place indeed.

Once at the hospital, Harry quickly found his way to where Arthur was recovering, only to find Grace standing outside the ward waiting for him.

'You really didn't have to visit,' Grace said as Harry walked over.

'There are a lot of things in my life I've not had to do but have done anyway,' Harry replied. 'Too many, probably.'

'Why am I not surprised?'

'So, how is he?' Harry asked.

'Asleep,' Grace said. 'And stable. So, that's something.'

'It is,' Harry agreed. 'And I know I hardly know him, but your dad strikes me as someone strong enough to come through this.'

Grace nodded, a weak smile on her face and a tiredness in her eyes that betrayed the fact she'd clearly had no sleep other than the worst kind in a hospital waiting room.

'Fancy getting a coffee?' Harry asked. 'I passed a café on the way up here. Looked okay, too.'

'Sounds good,' Grace said.

'I just need to chat with the doctors who've been sorting out your dad,' Harry said. 'Here...'

Harry handed Grace some cash from his wallet.

'I'm not that kind of girl,' Grace said, and Harry was impressed that her sense of humour somehow still managed to break through her tiredness and stress.

'Grab us both a drink and a snack and I'll be down in five,' Harry said.

Grace walked off and Harry pushed through to the ward Arthur was on. At the reception desk, a quick chat and a show of his ID was enough to have a doctor to him within minutes.

'I'm Doctor Kelly,' said the woman in front of Harry. It was clear from her body language that she was in a hurry and that this distraction was one that, although she understood, she didn't necessarily have the time for. She was tall, dark-haired, and had bright, piercing eyes.

'I won't keep you long,' Harry said. 'I was just wondering if you were able to tell me anything about Mr Black's injuries, how he is, that kind of thing.'

'Well, he took a hell of a beating, that's for sure,' Doctor Kelly said. 'Though, it looked considerably worse than it was. That doesn't detract from the fact that he's bouncing back very quickly. He's clearly made of tough stuff. His daughter told me he was attacked in his own home?'

'That's correct,' Harry said.

'What actually happened to him? Was it a burglar?'

'Right now we don't know all that much, but we're investigating a number of lines of enquiry.'

'I understand,' said the doctor. 'You know, you police, you talk a little like us doctors. You're very good at saying just enough without giving too much away.'

'And we'll only give something away if and when we

know, as well as we can anyway, that we've got the facts straight.'

'Exactly that,' Doctor Kelly said.

Harry noticed that the doctor's expression had changed a little, as though she was thinking about something and not sure what to say.

'Something bothering you?' Harry asked.

'The injuries,' the doctor said with a nod. 'I'm trying to work out the sense of them.'

'How do you mean?'

'He's been hit and punched and kicked everywhere,' she explained. 'The attack was thorough, there's no doubt about that. But it doesn't strike me as something someone would do if they were discovered mid-robbery and they wanted to just put him out of action and run away before the police arrived.'

'A fair point,' Harry agreed. 'What else?'

'He's bruised everywhere,' the doctor said. 'He was unconscious when he was brought in, but I think that was more shock from the attack than anything, his body just shutting down to protect itself and repair.'

'I'm not sure I follow,' Harry said.

'It's like the attack was restrained,' the doctor said. 'I know that sounds a bit mad, seeing as he was actually beaten up, and quite badly, but it could've been a lot worse.'

'Any broken bones?'

'None!' the doctor said, clearly surprised by the fact that she was giving such an answer. 'You see what I mean? There's plenty of bruises, scratches, and cuts, a few burns from being on the carpet, but he's actually okay, all things considered.'

'Like you said, he's tough,' Harry said.

'Particularly so, considering his age,' the doctor agreed. 'But I can't help thinking it could've been a lot worse.'

'He was lucky, then.'

'Well, I wouldn't go that far,' said the doctor. 'No one who's been kicked and punched like that is in any way, shape, or form lucky. He's in a lot of pain and we need to keep him in for observation, but he'll be out in a day or so I should think.'

'That soon?'

'Yes,' the doctor said.

'What do you mean by what you said about the attack being restrained,' Harry asked. 'In what way? I saw him, and that didn't look like whoever did it held back.'

'I'm not sure,' the doctor said. 'You're the detective, after all, not me. But the injuries, they're wild, all over the place, and really he should be in a lot worse state than he is. And yet...'

The doctor's voice hung in the air.

'What?' Harry asked.

'Maybe the attack was supposed to, I don't know, seriously injure him at least, maybe even kill him, but the attacker either didn't want to or couldn't go through with it. Does that sound crazy?'

Harry shook his head.

'It's harder than you'd think to beat someone to death, to kill another person. Much easier to shoot someone because there's a distance to it.'

'Is that the voice of experience I hear?'

Harry said nothing, and he could tell from the look on the doctor's face that that was more than enough.

'Guns aren't easy to come by though, are they?' the doctor said.

'Well, they can be, if you know the right people,' Harry said. 'Which suggests that whoever did this didn't, if you get my meaning.'

'Perhaps he was lucky after all, then,' the doctor said.

'He was,' Harry said, then he thanked the doctor for her time and headed off to meet with Grace in the café.

CHAPTER TWENTY-ONE

'I got us both an Americano,' Grace said, as Harry walked over to sit down opposite her at a small, round table with two chairs and the smallest laminated menu he had ever seen. 'With an extra shot and milk.' She pointed to a plate. 'And a couple of brownies.'

'A couple?' Harry said. 'But there's only one.'

'I already ate mine,' Grace said. 'And I was about to start on yours. Barely eaten all day. I'm starving.'

'Then you have that one as well.' Harry smiled, picking up his coffee.

'I couldn't.'

'Oh, I think you could.'

Grace hesitated, then took the second brownie.

'Just so you know,' Harry said, 'Molly is doing just fine. Made herself right at home, I have to say.'

'I'm sure she has,' Grace said. 'She's a lovely dog. Thirteen years old now, soon be fourteen. Just seems to keep on going somehow. Watch out for your underwear, though. She's a fan of knickers and pants, especially.'

'What?' Harry said, choking on his coffee. 'Why?'

'It's disgusting, I know,' Grace said, brushing a crumb from her mouth. 'But she has a habit of stealing them, then burying them around the house.'

'And why does she do that?' Harry asked. Then holding up a hand to stop Grace from answering, added, 'Actually, I don't need to know. I'll use my imagination.'

'Maybe she thinks they're food,' Grace said. 'Dogs will eat anything, you know.'

The conversation died for a moment as Harry and Grace sat together, both of them trying to feel a little more human from the caffeine, and in Grace's case, the cake.

'The doctor says he's doing well,' Harry said.

'They're keeping him in for observation,' said Grace. 'But he'll be able to come home in a day or so. He was lucky. Could've been a lot worse.'

'That's what the doctor said,' Harry said, his voice trailing off.

Grace leaned forward and stared at Harry.

'There's something you're not saying, isn't there? What is it?'

Harry paused, then told Grace what the doctor had said about the injuries.

'What does that actually mean, then?' Grace asked.

'I'm not really sure,' said Harry. 'But it's like someone went over to your dad's to do considerably more harm than they actually ended up doing in the end. Like they bottled it as soon as they started.'

'You mean they meant to kill him but couldn't?'

Harry nodded, then said, 'Maybe not kill him, but certainly put him more out of action than he is.'

'But who would want to kill Dad or injure him like that?'

Grace said, slumping back, rubbing her eyes, then looking up again at Harry. 'This kind of thing just doesn't happen around here! It doesn't make any sense!'

'These things rarely do.'

'You've met him, right? Who would want to harm him that badly? What the hell has Dad done to anyone to deserve this? What?'

Grace's voice, which had been so calm, was breaking now as her emotions broke through.

'Well, it's got nothing to do with deserving it, that's for sure,' Harry said, 'because he didn't. And as to who did it and why? That's what we're working on. All of us. The whole team. I can assure you of that, Grace.'

A warm smile crept briefly onto Grace's face.

'You know, that's the first time you've actually used my name,' she said.

'Can't be,' Harry said.

'It's been Ms Black or nothing at all, up to now.'

'I hadn't noticed.'

'I had.'

Harry wasn't sure what to say next, so he went for something that had nothing to do with what had happened to Arthur.

'You said you had some puppies.'

'I will have very soon, yes,' Grace said. 'The mum's due to pop any day now. I've a friend just checking in on her while I'm here. No reports of any new arrivals yet.'

'Well, that should be exciting,' Harry said.

'Oh, it is,' Grace said. 'Do you want one, then?'

Harry laughed, shook his head.

'Good God, no. I've not got the time!' he said.

'That's just an excuse,' Grace said.

'There's a big difference between what I said and an excuse.'

'Tell you what,' Grace suggested, leaning forward onto her elbows. 'When they arrive, why don't you pop over and see if I can't change your mind?'

'Not a chance of it,' Harry said.

'Just come over and have a look! What harm is there in that?'

'No harm, I know,' Harry said. 'But the answer's still no.'

'What are you so afraid of?' Grace asked.

'Me? I'm not afraid of anything!' Harry said, suddenly on the back foot and not used to it at all. Which would explain why I responded in such an uncharacteristic way, he thought. So, he added, 'I just don't have the time, that's all. For a pup. And anyway, can you see a dog wanting to live with me? Wouldn't be fair on the poor thing.'

Grace leaned back.

'Well, we'll see, shall we?'

Harry smiled, shook his head gently, then took another gulp of the coffee.

'See?' he said, changing the subject clumsily. 'Told you the café was okay. Not bad this, is it?'

Grace placed her cup on the table between them and then once again leaned forward on her elbows.

'I know you're avoiding the questions you want to ask,' she said. 'But you really don't need to. I'm fine. Dad'll pull through. So, ask away. Please.'

Grace, Harry could tell, was someone who didn't beat around the bush. He liked that a lot. Saved a lot of faffing about.

'First of all,' he began, 'can you think of anyone who might want to do this to your dad, to harm him in some way?

Have you heard him arguing with anyone? Has he talked about anything that has had him upset or angry?'

'Eric Haygarth, like I said,' Grace said. 'I saw him there. Have you spoken to him yet?'

'I have my officers on that today,' Harry said, wondering how Matt and Liz were getting on with finding the so-far elusive Mr Haygarth.

'He can be a right bugger to track down,' Grace said. 'Too used to keeping himself to himself, always hiding, making sure no one finds out what he's up to. It's like he's part rodent. Has kind of a ratty face, too. All pinched and just not nice to look at, at all.'

Grace used a hand to mime having a pointy face, then her face dropped.

'Oh, I didn't mean...' she said, stumbling over her words. 'I'm not saying I judge someone on how they look, it's just that... I... well...'

Harry smiled.

'I know what you're trying to say.'

'I'm sorry,' Grace said, looking a little embarrassed.

'Don't be,' said Harry. 'Every time I see my scars I'm reminded that I'm alive. Others weren't so lucky. Anyway, I'm sure we'll find him.'

Grace ate some brownie.

'So, other than Eric, anyone else?' Harry asked.

Grace thought for a moment then shook her head.

'No one,' she said. 'Dad wasn't one for enemies. The opposite, really. He's well-liked, up and down the dale. Prides himself on it.'

'Phil said that Jack was a bit of a monster.'

At this, Grace's weary face broke into a laugh. It was a

bright sound, Harry thought, the kind that should be available on prescription.

'He didn't give you one of his pies, did he?'

'Yes, he did actually,' Harry said.

'Please tell me you've thrown it away!'

'Not yet.'

'Just don't eat it, that's all,' Grace said. 'Though if you manage to get past that pastry without a little help from a freshly sharpened chainsaw, then you'll have done better than most.'

'Your dad warned me before I went over,' Harry said.

'How was Phil?' Grace asked.

'Seemed fine to me,' Harry said. 'Quite a character, isn't he? Introduced me to another Harry.'

'His Shire horse?' Grace said, shaking her head in disbelief. 'He's prouder of that beast than he is of anything else in his life! And you said he described Jack as a monster?'

'A bear actually, not a monster,' Harry said.

'Pretty accurate description,' Grace said. 'He was a big dog. Soft and friendly though. Well, not with everyone.'

'Not a fan of strangers,' Harry said.

'Not at all,' Grace said. 'Which means whoever took him, well, he knew them for sure, didn't he?'

'Possibly,' Harry agreed.

'So, it has to be Eric, doesn't it?' Grace said. 'That's the only explanation!'

Harry knew full well that there was never only one explanation for anything.

'Where did he get the dog?' Harry asked.

'Local breeder,' Grace said. 'Just outside Hawes, over in Hardraw.'

'You mean someone bred him on purpose?'

Grace shook her head.

'One of their guard dogs got a bit frisky with one of their bitches. There was a storm last year and it got out and they found it all cuddled up with this beautiful Springer. They were mortified. And because of what happened, they had this litter of pups they had to get rid of, so Dad took one. Well, he paid for it, but you know what I mean.'

'Nothing's free,' Harry said.

'And if it is, there's always a catch,' Grace agreed.

Harry took down the name of the breeder, then realised he'd seen the name before. It was the same one Jim had found in those files, the one who'd had a dog stolen a while back.

'Something up?' Grace asked.

Harry shook his head and put his notebook away.

Grace checked her watch then said, 'Dad should be awake now. Nurses told me he was going to be given something to eat around now.'

'Eating? Well, that's something, isn't it?' Harry said.

Grace stood up and Harry followed, as she led them back up to the ward where Arthur was being kept.

When Harry came to stand beside Arthur's bed, the bruises on the man's face, the bandages, the beep-beep-beep of the monitors he was attached to, didn't exactly fill him with confidence, regardless of what Doctor Kelly had said. That was, until the old man himself spoke.

'And I thought I looked bad.'

Harry smiled and sat down on a nearby chair.

'I'm sorry if this is too soon,' Harry said.

'Don't be,' Arthur replied. 'And it isn't. But I don't know what use I'll be to you, if I'm honest.'

'How do you mean?' Harry asked.

Arthur pointed at his face, the bruises on it as purple as the ripest plums.

'Because I've no idea who did this, that's why!' Arthur said, wincing a little with pain. 'Whoever it was, they came in wearing a balaclava, would you believe? Pulled right down over their head, like this!' He then pretended to pull on an invisible balaclava. 'How cowardly is that? Couldn't even give me a proper hiding either, could they? Here I am, still alive and kicking! Well, not kicking, maybe, but I'm alive! Let them try again though, and I'll be ready for them. I'll give them a taste of their own medicine, see how they like that!'

Harry couldn't help but admire the fire in Arthur's belly.

'What actually happened that evening?' Harry asked.

'This happened,' Arthur said, his voice gruff and weary.

'Dad...' Grace said, admonishing him gently.

'Well, Grace here was round, weren't you? Trying to get me to eat, which usually isn't a problem, but I wasn't hungry, not after you'd been round.'

'It was a lot to take in,' Harry said.

'And I got to thinking about it all,' Arthur continued. 'After you'd gone, and when Grace left. And I thought I'd just get on with it myself, you see? Because the police are too busy, aren't they? To be bothering about a dog.'

Harry saw shock rake itself across Grace's face.

'What are you on about, Dad? What the hell did you do?'

'What anyone would do if they thought they knew who killed their dog,' Arthur replied, folding his arms. 'I called them.'

'You what?'

Grace's voice jumped two pitches at least.

'You called them? Who did you call, Dad? Who?'

'Eric, who else?' Arthur said. 'Told him that I knew what

he'd done and that he'd better come over and explain himself. Had a right go at him I did. Of course, he said he had no idea what I was talking about, but I didn't believe him. Why should I? He's a lying, mean old bastard, is Eric, and I wasn't having it!'

'Then what happened?' Harry asked.

'You're looking at it,' Arthur replied. 'I fell asleep waiting, was woken up by a knock at the door. Next thing I know, old balaclava head is trying to kill me.'

Grace turned to Harry.

'See? It's Eric! It must be! Dad called him—and the stupidity of that we'll ignore for the moment—and he came over to sort Dad out once and for all!'

Harry was quiet for a moment, then asked, 'What do you remember about your attacker? Did they tell you who they were, why they were there? Or is there something about them that you remember? It doesn't matter how small; anything is useful at this stage.'

'What does any of that matter?' Grace asked. 'Dad called Eric and then someone attacked him! Eric attacked him!'

'I'm not so sure,' Harry said. 'Why would he do any of this? Why wear a balaclava? Why beat up your dad? And if he came out with the intent to kill, but at the last minute chickened out, like the doctor suggests, why wear a balaclava in the first place?'

'So Dad wouldn't recognise him!' Grace said.

'Why would that matter if he was going to kill him? But he didn't, did he?' Harry said, then looked back over at Arthur. 'So, can you remember anything else? Anything out of the ordinary, maybe?'

Arthur fell quiet for a moment. So quiet, in fact, that Harry was sure the old man had fallen asleep.

Grace gave Arthur a gentle nudge.

'What?'

'Dad?'

'Gracie?'

'You were telling us about your attacker.'

'Us? Who's us?'

'DCI Grimm here, and me,' Grace said.

'Grimm? That detective fellow? He's here as well? You've seen his face, right? Poor bloke, suffering that. Suits his name and personality though, doesn't it? Though I think he's more bark than bite. Most of the time anyway.'

'Dad...'

'What?'

Harry said, 'I'm right here, Arthur.'

Arthur turned his head and his eyes fell on Harry.

'Oh, there you are, yes!'

Arthur's forgetfulness was to be expected, Harry thought. He'd been through hell and back, so his body was in the thick of repairing itself, with a little help from the NHS.

'He was wearing a balaclava,' Arthur said.

'Yes, you've told us that,' Grace said. 'Was there anything else?'

'Pulled right over his head it was!'

'So, it was definitely a man, then?' Harry asked, making a note of this new bit of information immediately.

'Yes,' Arthur said. 'Definitely a man. At least I think it was. Like I said, he was wearing a balaclava, I'm very sure about that. And I'm also pretty sure it was a man. Oh, and there was this smell, wasn't there? Yes, a smell. Bought it in with him. A proper stink.'

Harry jumped at this new information. 'Smell? What smell?'

'A smell!' Arthur repeated. 'And it was certainly one that I've never had in my house, that's for sure. Or ever want again.'

'Can you describe it?'

'Rank, it was,' Arthur said. 'Came into the house before he did, when I opened the door, like. Sort of sweet, like a cheap cigar, only worse, much worse. Remember potpourri? That, only not, if you get my meaning. Stank the place out good and proper.'

Harry had no idea what Arthur was on about, then his tiredness shifted just enough for him to remember something from his visit to the house the night before, after Arthur had been taken to hospital, and Sowerby's information from that morning.

'You're right,' he said, thinking back, sifting through the memories and images of Arthur's cottage. 'There was a smell. I noticed it myself, couldn't work out what it was at the time, what with everything else to take in.'

'Can't see how a smell's useful though,' said Arthur.

'You'd be surprised,' Harry said. 'That description you've just given? I know what it was.'

'Even this still works,' he said, tapping his nose and winking at his daughter.

'So, what was it, then?' Grace asked.

Harry looked over.

'Cannabis,' he said. 'I think that whoever attacked your dad, that's what they smelled of. And forensics found a couple of spliffs, one in the house, the other on the road outside. For the smell to be strong enough to still be around when I was there says a lot.'

'Really?' Grace said. 'Why? In what way?'

'The stuff most people smoke, weed, well it has a smell,

yes, but it doesn't hang around a place in the same way as the stronger stuff, does.'

'You mean skunk, right?' Grace said. 'That's what you think the smell was?'

Harry frowned.

'Don't look at me like that!' Grace said, raising an eyebrow. 'I've smoked! Who hasn't?'

'Me for one,' Harry said. 'Never did as a kid. Wasn't about to touch the stuff when I was in the Paras. And I can't say I've ever been tempted to since, now that I'm doing this.'

'That's not really a surprise,' said Grace, and Harry saw a sly smile spend the briefest of moments on her face.

It suited her, he thought. He'd certainly met people where a smile made them look like they were in pain. But a smile on Grace's face just seemed to make sense, like it belonged there.

'It's only ever been weed, though,' Grace continued. 'That's all I've ever had myself. Never tried anything stronger. Not sure I'd want to either.'

'Skunk isn't as easy to come by, not usually anyway,' Harry explained.

'None of this proves that it wasn't Eric who did this.'

'None of it proves that he did, either, which is what we have to bear in mind.'

'So, how did Eric or whoever it was that did this to Dad get hold of it then?'

'There's always a way,' Harry said. 'Some grow it themselves. Usually in the loft or in a cellar. Hydroponics.'

'Sounds technical.' Arthur yawned.

'Or you just find a dealer,' said Harry, the scars on his face moving a little as he remembered something from a good few months ago now, when he'd bumped into a few teenagers down by Gayle Beck. He'd been walking along the path, from the church in Hawes, up to Gayle.

'I'm assuming that's a smile on your face,' said Grace.

'Oh, it is,' Harry said, then stood up. 'There's a phone call or two I need to make...'

CHAPTER TWENTY-TWO

LEAVING GRACE WITH HER DAD AND HAVING MADE SURE she was sorted for a lift back up the dale to home, Harry headed off. The phone call he'd made had been through to the office in Hawes and had been picked up by Jadyn.

'Reedy?' Jadyn said. 'I've heard the name enough times, but never actually dealt with him.'

'Oh, he's a delight,' Harry said. 'You're in for a treat.'

'By treat, do you mean like when my mum would bring home a Viennetta Slice?'

'A what now?'

Jadyn was silent for a moment and Harry could sense the constable's disbelief down the line.

'You know, ice cream, loads of thin layers of chocolate,' Jadyn said. 'Proper tasty. You can get a mint one, too. And salted caramel!'

'If it's all the same with you, I don't think I will.'

'You're missing out,' Jadyn said.

'I'll take the risk.'

The last time Harry had anything to do with Reedy was

when he'd been trying to find one of his, for want of a better word, colleagues. Reedy had a reputation for dealing but was slimy and wily enough to never have anything actually traced back to him. Yet. Harry was keen to see that change. Whether this was the moment, Harry wasn't sure, but it was a good place to start to try and find a lead on the smell both he and Arthur had noticed the night before.

'Anyone there with you?' Harry asked.

'Jen,' Jadyn replied. 'Gordy's away to some meeting or something. Not sure what it was about, but she says she'll be over tomorrow.'

'What about the others?' Harry asked, deciding to give no time at all to wondering what Swift was up to.

'Jim's over in Hardraw,' Jadyn explained.

'Never been,' Harry said, recognising the name from his chat with Grace. 'Not as such anyway. I've driven through it. Blink and you miss it, right?'

'There's a famous waterfall,' Jadyn said. 'Up behind the Green Dragon Inn. Worth a trip, especially after a storm. And,' he added, 'it's where Kevin Costner swam naked across a pool in Robin Hood: Prince of Thieves.'

'That's really... fascinating,' Harry said.

'I know, right?' Jadyn replied, not catching Harry's sarcasm at all. 'Anyway, Jim's checking up on that other stolen dog. They're dog breeders, it turns out.'

'Indeed they are,' said Harry. 'That dog from the barn, the one that belonged to Arthur Black? It was one of theirs.'

'Well, they had one of their dogs stolen a few months ago,' said Jadyn. 'Oh, and Matt and Liz are still trying to track down that Eric Haygarth bloke, as per your instruction. Though he seems to have disappeared, which is a bit odd.'

Harry was quietly reassured by Jadyn's report, though

not by Eric's vanishing act since he was someone they really needed to speak to. As for the brief discussion about ice cream desserts, he'd be forgetting that as quickly as possible.

'I need you and Jen to find Reedy for me,' Harry instructed. 'Bring him in for a little chat.'

'He's a suspect?'

'He's someone of importance, that's for sure,' Harry said. 'And when you've got a hold of him, let me know. I'll meet you at the office.'

'Sure thing, boss,' Jadyn said before ending the call.

With Jadyn and Jen tasked with tracking down Reedy, Harry made another call, this time through to the veterinary surgery in Hawes.

'I'd like to speak with Andrew Bell, please,' Harry asked.

'Can I ask who's calling?' the receptionist replied.

'DCI Harry Grimm.'

'He's over at a farm West Burton way.'

'Can you give me the address?'

Harry heard a faint rustling of paper.

'Yes, here it is...'

Having taken the address, Harry then asked for a message to be given to Andrew.

'He might not get it,' the receptionist replied. 'Doesn't usually pick up when he's out on a job, not until it's finished anyway.'

'Well, if you can just let him know that I'm on my way, that would be much appreciated.'

And with that, Harry made one final call through to Jim, to tell him what he'd learned about Arthur's dog, Jack, and then he was on his way.

The journey was easy, the roads not too busy, and after passing the strange Temple Folly just a couple of miles on the other side of West Witton, he'd then hung a left towards his destination. The road was surprisingly flat for the dales, with lush green meadows on either side. Coming into West Burton, his satnav had directed him to take a hard left, up and over a bridge, to follow a lane that looked as though it was only ever used by the kind of transport which required either hooves or off-road tyres.

A couple of minutes later, he was at his destination, and he turned off the lane and into a farmyard, parking up in front of a house with brightly flowered window boxes. Further along from the house, Harry saw a large barn and various other outbuildings. In front of the house were parked a Land Rover, an estate car that looked like it was close to being scrapped, and a huge motorbike, the kind that gave the impression it would happily race up a mountain at a hundred miles an hour with no effort at all.

Harry climbed out of his own vehicle and went to knock at the farmhouse door. It was opened a couple of minutes later by a man wearing Wellington boots, green corduroy trousers with holes in the knees, and a chequered shirt, rolled up at the sleeves. He was a little shorter than Harry, barrel-chested, and had cheeks on him the colour of a ripe apple. In his hand was a tray laden with mugs of tea and a packet of chocolate digestives.

'Now then,' the man said, and handed Harry the tray. 'Hold this, will you while I just fetch the rest.'

Harry had no chance to answer as the man turned around and walked back into the house, returning a moment later with a large plate piled high with sandwiches.

'Away then,' the man said, and pushed on past Harry and headed up to the barn.

Catching up, Harry introduced himself.

'Oh, yes, I know who you are,' the man said. 'I'm Jeff.'

'Good to meet you,' Harry said. 'The vet got my message, then?'

'Message? What message?'

'You said you know who I am.'

'Of course, I do!' Jeff said. 'Seen you around, haven't I? Nowt's kept much of a secret around the dales. And a new face is always noticed.'

'Mine more than most,' Harry said.

'You could say that,' Jeff said. 'So, it's the vet you're wanting to see, then? He's up here. He'll no doubt have his arm up past his elbow in a cow. Calving season, you see. Had a difficult one earlier, which was why he was called. Then another started getting awkward as well, so he's on with that now. Busy time for us, as you can imagine.'

Harry listened, said nothing, and followed on behind Jeff into the large barn. Inside the air was ripe with the smell of manure, straw, animal feed, and the animals themselves. Harry was led to a stall inside which a man was, as Jeff had warned, up beyond his elbow inside a cow. The animal was moaning and the man, who Harry assumed to be the vet, Andrew Bell, was sweating and swearing.

'You stay here,' Jeff instructed, placing the plate of sandwiches on a weary-looking picnic table placed outside the stall.

The vet saw Harry.

'What've you done now, Jeff?' he asked, nodding over at Harry.

'Nowt,' Jeff replied. 'He's here for you. Probably caught you speeding on that idiotic bike of yours.'

'It's not idiotic.'

'It bloody well is!' Jeff replied. 'Would you get on a horse with an engine?'

'What?'

'A horse, with an engine,' Jeff said. 'No, of course, you wouldn't. Why? No brains and too fast, that's why. And that's what that thing is. Get rid. Sharpish.'

The vet strained again, clearly trying to heave something out from inside the cow, which Harry assumed to be a calf.

'Your argument makes no sense at all,' the vet said. 'Horse with an engine? What are you on about?'

Jeff glanced back at Harry.

'You agree with me, don't you, Grimm?'

Jeff, Harry realised, wasn't one for airs and graces, or for taking time to get to know someone, and was already speaking to him like he'd known him for years.

'Well...' Harry said.

'See?' Jeff said, turning back to the vet, giving Harry no chance to say anything more. 'Everyone thinks that machine will kill you. Even the detective here!'

'Here we go!' the vet said, and Harry saw two legs appear as the vet pulled his arm out from inside the cow. 'Come on, lass. Come on!'

A few moments and a lot of straining and swearing and mooing later, a calf flopped out onto the straw-covered floor.

'Bloody hell,' Harry said.

'Quite a sight, isn't it?' Jeff said. 'Big bugger as well, that one. No wonder it was a struggle. You okay, Andy?'

The vet walked over, one arm covered in all kinds of stuff Harry didn't really want to think about. He then washed himself clean and held out the same hand to Harry.

'Pleased to meet you,' he said.

Harry shook the extended hand, doing his best to ignore where it had just been.

'You mind if we have a quick chat when we're done?' Harry asked.

'Not a problem at all,' Andy replied. 'First things first, though, eh?'

Then he reached over and with the hand that had, only minutes ago, been deep inside a cow, grabbed a sandwich.

CHAPTER TWENTY-THREE

Having headed out from Hawes, and now just rolling over the start of Hardraw, Jim had pulled through a gate and across a cattle grid, and rolled onto the grounds of a large house with impressive outbuildings. It was an expensive property, that much was clear, so breeding dogs was obviously good money. A large 'Beware: Guard Dogs!' sign stood as a welcome at the gate.

He was welcomed at the house by a woman with a blonde perm so huge it was as though a sun-drenched cloud had decided to take a holiday on her head. She was wearing jeans and a black long-sleeved top and was rubbing her right arm nervously, Jim noticed.

'You must be the PCSO,' she said, her accent hard to place, because it wasn't really there at all. Sort of a general English accent, Jim thought, as though it wasn't really from anywhere. Or, if it was, it was trying to disguise it. 'PCSO Metcalf, yes?'

She was smiling, and Jim couldn't help but notice that she seemed almost too pleased to see him. Relieved even, not that he could think of a reason as to why she should be. It unnerved him a little.

'Mrs Peacock?' Jim said. 'Yes, that's me, PCSO Metcalf. Call me James though. Much more friendly that way I think. I really appreciate you taking the time to see me.'

'It's not a problem at all,' Mrs Peacock said, her smile still wide as she invited Jim inside. 'And call me Jan.'

Inside, the hallway was decorated with numerous awards for breeding dogs, and even more photographs of said dogs. A wooden staircase swept upstairs. Jim was led through to a lounge on the right.

'Can I get you anything?'

'No, I'm fine, thanks,' Jim said.

Jan looked at a clock above the fireplace.

'It's about time for afternoon tea, wouldn't you say?'

'Honestly, I'm fine.'

'Well, I was just get something anyway,' Jan said, and before Jim could protest, he was left alone in the lounge.

The room was, for want of a better word, polite, Jim thought. It had a white leather three-piece suite, a glass-topped coffee table, and a nice marble-effect fire surround, with a large mirror hung above. The walls were white and were decorated with a few photographs on canvas, the kind Jim had seen for sale in Darlington. There wasn't much personality to the room. It gave nothing away about the owners. And maybe that was the point.

A few minutes later, Jim heard the sound of tinkling crockery and turned to see Jan enter the room pushing a trolley.

'I was going to bring through just a pot of tea,' Jan said, 'but then I thought, why not have some nice cake, too? I baked it yesterday. I have to do something to keep busy, don't

I? I can't just sit here reading all the time or staring at the wall or watching the television.'

Jim smiled, found himself looking for a television and not seeing one.

'Oh, it's up there,' Jan said.

'What is?'

'The television. That mirror above the fire? It's a television. Far too expensive if you ask me. Not my money though.'

On the trolley, Jim saw a large sponge cake with jam and butter icing in the middle. There was also a little plate of jam tarts. A couple of minutes later, a large slice of it was on a plate and in his hand, a mug of tea on the coffee table in front of him.

'So, how can I help?' Jan asked, sitting down opposite. Again, she was rubbing her arm.

Jim couldn't answer immediately as his mouth was full of cake.

'Good, isn't it?' Jan said.

Jim gave a nod, swallowed.

'Very,' he said, reaching for his tea. 'You're a great baker.'

Jan beamed.

'Thank you so much for saying so!'

'I mean it,' Jim said. 'It's delicious.'

Jim took another bite then noticed Jan was just watching him eat, but not taking anything herself. Suddenly feeling a little self-conscious, he said, 'I just need to talk to you about the dog you reported stolen.'

'That was months ago, now,' Jan said. 'Last October I think. My husband said I shouldn't have bothered really. These things happen, don't they?'

'They do, but they shouldn't,' Jim said.

'And nothing came of it in the end, did it? The dog was never found.'

'What kind of dogs do you breed?' Jim asked.

'Springer Spaniels,' Jan said. 'Such a lovely breed. Lots of fun. Lots of energy. All pedigree, too. Sometimes I find it very difficult to let them go, but I have to. Can't have a house filled with dogs, now, can I? But they are such good company.'

'And the dog you reported stolen was an Alsatian, yes?'

'We don't breed those,' Jan said. 'He was a guard dog. We've always had them. Better than any burglar alarm, that's for sure. Always had a couple of them around. Obviously, we've only got one now. But we'll get another I think. Dogs need company.'

'But this one was stolen, though,' Jim said. 'And it can't be easy to steal a guard dog. Can you tell me anything about the night it happened?'

'We were out,' Jan said. 'I was just down at the Green Dragon, you know? A quiet drink and a bite to eat, that kind of thing. A little treat for myself, really. And when I came back, he was gone.'

'Any sign of a break-in?'

'None that I can remember,' Jan said. 'We just came home to find him missing.'

'I'm just not seeing how a guard dog gets stolen,' Jim said.

'Well, you see, the problem with Haystacks—that was his name on account of him being massive,' Jan said. 'The problem was, well, you see... he was a bit rubbish.'

'How do you mean, rubbish?' Jim asked.

'Oh, he looked the part alright,' Jan said. 'Massive paws, huge jaws and teeth, and he'd make a proper racket, too, if you came up to him.'

'Doesn't exactly sound rubbish,' Jim said. 'Sounds terrifying.'

'But then he'd just roll on his back and beg for a tummy rub!' Jan said. 'Honestly, he was just a big softy. A really lovely dog. All bark and no bollocks, as my husband would say.'

Jim laughed at that.

'You don't think he escaped, then?'

'This place is all done out to stop dogs escaping,' Jan said. 'And Haystacks wasn't one for going anywhere under his own initiative. Liked the easy life. Good living. Someone came in, took him, and left. It's the only explanation. There's a lot of money in stolen dogs, you know. And puppy farms. It's awful.'

'Haystacks was chipped though?'

'A chip can be cut out,' Jan said.

'You said you had another? Where was it that night?'

'Sick,' Jan said. 'Had to leave it in its run.'

'Anything serious?'

'Threw up everywhere,' Jan said. 'Probably ate something it shouldn't have. As dogs do.'

'Is your husband around at all?' Jim asked. 'It would be useful to talk to him as well.'

Jan's smile took on a nervousness as she shook her head.

'No, he's out,' she said. 'You're fine, I mean he'll be back very soon. You don't have to rush off, do you? I can answer any questions, I'm sure, until he gets home.'

Jim looked at his notebook, reading what he'd written down after Harry had briefly called him earlier.

'I believe you sold a dog to a Mr Arthur Black,' he said. 'A gamekeeper over in Redmire.'

'I'll have to check our records,' Jan said.

'It wasn't a Springer Spaniel though,' Jim said. 'It was a cross, I think.'

Jan stood up and walked over to a window that overlooked the drive, then was back to her seat.

'We only breed Springers,' she said. 'You must be mistaken.'

'No, I'm definitely not,' Jim said. 'The owner told us he bought it from you.'

'Oh, yes, I remember now,' Jan said. 'Sorry, I was a little confused. We of course only breed Springers, but yes, there was a little accident a couple of years ago now, when Haystacks got one of our prize bitches pregnant.'

'And you sold the pups?'

'Yes,' Jan said. 'We couldn't keep them. And obviously, we couldn't sell them for what we'd get for the purebreds, could we? But they were still worth something. Lovely looking things they were, too.'

Jim checked his notes. As leads went, this was turning out to not be one at all. One stolen dog and some pups. That was it. He'd hoped for more. If he were honest, he'd hoped to find something that would have him making an arrest, really show Grimm that he could get on with the job in hand, but that clearly wasn't going to happen.

'Well, I'd best be off,' Jim said, cake and tea now finished.

'Are you sure you don't want anything else?' Jan asked.

'No, I'm fine, thanks,' Jim said. 'Honestly. Good cake though.'

Jim stood and made to head to the door.

'Please, I'm sure there are some other questions you need to ask, yes?' Jan said. 'I'll fetch you another tea. How's that sound?'

'Very kind,' Jim said, and as he went to say goodbye and head for the front door, he heard a vehicle pull up outside.

'That'll be him,' Jan said, and Jim noticed she was rubbing her arm again, only this time a little more vigorously. 'My husband. Thank you for staying. You've no idea...'

The front door opened and in walked a man wearing a scowl borrowed from a rock face. It was a craggy thing, with deep-set eyes, which turned to stare at Jim.

'What the hell do you want?'

'Mr Peacock, I'm PCSO James Metcalf,' Jim began, but the man strode over and cut him off with a stare and a fat finger jabbed in his chest.

'Did I ask who you were? No. I didn't. I don't need to, do I? I can see who you are. I asked what the hell do you want, so why don't you answer that instead?'

Mr Peacock's accent was, like Jan's, almost without an accent, but one thing it did have was anger, the kind that never really goes away, like it was fuelled constantly from something deeply unpleasant inside its owner. A furnace of barely controlled fury.

'I just needed to ask a few questions about the dog you reported stolen,' Jim said, keeping his voice calm.

Mr Peacock snapped around to growl at Jan.

'That was months ago! Why's he really here?'

'It's about the dog, about Haystacks,' Jan said, and Jim saw her back away a little from her husband. 'He rang earlier, asked to come over.'

'And you just said yes, did you? Didn't think of checking with me?'

'You weren't here.'

'No, I wasn't,' Mr Peacock said. 'And if I'm not here, you

shouldn't be inviting anyone around, should you? And don't answer that. You don't need to. The answer's *No*.'

'Mr Peacock,' Jim said, 'it would be useful if you could answer a few of my questions as well. It won't take long, I'm sure. DCI Grimm requested that I...'

Mr Peacock snapped away from his wife and loomed over Jim.

'DCI what now?'

'Grimm,' Jim said.

'Was I speaking to you?'

'Yes,' Jim said. 'You asked—'

'I asked nothing,' Mr Peacock cut back, then looked at Jan. 'DCI Grimm, is it? That's who you were calling?'

'The police, this police officer, he called me,' she said, and Jim noticed a desperate edge to her voice. 'I didn't call them. Why would I?'

'Exactly,' Mr Peacock said, moving closer to his wife. 'Why would you?' Then he turned to face Jim and added, 'Why haven't you buggered off yet?'

Jan tugged at her husband's shirt.

'You can't talk to the police like that! You can't!'

'Police? Ha!' Mr Peacock laughed. 'He's not real police, are you, mate? No, you're just a PCSO. A plastic copper is what he is, isn't that right?'

Jim was stuck for a response.

Mr Peacock laughed again, then turned around and opened the front door.

'Go on,' he said, using his other hand to firmly guide Jim out of the house. 'Do yourself a favour and fuck off quietly now and run back to your DCI like a good little PCSO.'

Then, with a firm shove, Jim was outside and the door was slammed shut.

Jim waited for a moment, trying to work out what had just happened and what he should do next. He listened, expecting to hear a row, but there was no sound from the other side of the door.

Raising his hand to knock on the door, Jim nearly toppled backwards when the door was yanked open and Mr Peacock stepped in to fill the space.

'Are you fucking deaf, mate, is that it?'

Jim was rapidly going off Mr Peacock and for the life of him couldn't think of a reason to explain why Jan, with her enormous hair and fantastic baking, was with him in the first place.

'I just need to ask you a few questions,' Jim said, sounding to himself like a broken record.

'Oh, right, is that all?' Mr Peacock said. 'Some questions, is that it?'

'Yes, that's it,' Jim replied.

Mr Peacock grinned. 'You should've said so! Well, why don't you just step a bit closer, then, so we can have a proper chat?'

'That would be great,' Jim said.

'Come on then,' Mr Peacock said, and invited Jim back into the house with a wave of his hand.

Jim stepped forward, and as he was about to move into the house once again, Mr Peacock stepped back and heaved the door directly into him. Before Jim could react, the door crashed into his face, knocking him backwards and onto the ground. He looked up to see the door open once again.

'You alright there, mate?' Mr Peacock said. 'Sorry about that. Wind must've caught it, isn't that right, Love?'

Jim saw Jan peer around the side of her husband. She mouthed, 'Sorry,' Then said, 'Yes, the wind. It must've been.

It's happened to me before, hasn't it? Quite a few times, actually.'

Climbing to his feet, Jim noticed that as Jan had spoken she hadn't been looking at her husband at all. Instead, she had been staring at him, especially when she'd said *quite a few times.*

With one last stare at Mr Peacock, Jim turned around and headed back to his vehicle.

Back in Hawes, Jim parked up and headed into the office at the community centre. Matt was in one of their cars in the car park and offered a wave, which Jim returned. In the office, he found Liz, who had popped in to grab something from the fridge.

'Matt remembered he had a couple of sausage rolls in here,' she said. 'And we're both a bit peckish.'

'You've not found that Eric bloke yet, then?'

Liz shook her head.

'No sign yet. Seems like the kind of person who, if he doesn't want to be found, won't be. But we've not given up.' She went to leave, but then turned back and said, 'You look a little miffed. It doesn't suit you. Something happen?'

'Mr Peacock happened,' Jim said.

'How do you mean?'

'Slammed a door in my face, claimed it was the wind.'

'You mean he assaulted a police officer?' Liz said.

'No,' Jim said. 'Not a police officer. A plastic copper. So it doesn't count, does it?'

'Plastic what now?' Liz asked.

Jim slumped down into a chair.

'Nothing,' he said. 'Ignore me.'

A few minutes later, and with Liz back outside and off with Matt to try and track down Eric Haygarth, Jim thought back to his encounter with Jan and her husband. Jan had been jumpy from the moment he'd arrived, and there was that rubbing of her arm. Then there was the way she'd stared at him when she'd spoken about the door slamming into her supposedly because of the wind. As for her husband, well, he was like an advert for hostility, wasn't he? Something clearly wasn't right.

Then something else floated to the top of Jim's mind. When Jan had told him about being out the night that the dog was stolen, she'd started by saying how they were both out, but then she had only talked about herself being at the pub for a drink and a meal. A treat she'd called it, hadn't she? So, where had her husband been that night?

Whether or not it had anything to do with the case they were investigating, Jim didn't know. But what he did know was that he'd be speaking to Grimm about it. And although that on its own made him smile, what really made him grin was the thought of Harry meeting Mr Peacock face to face. That, Jim thought, would be something he'd be tempted to sell tickets to.

CHAPTER TWENTY-FOUR

HARRY WALKED OUT OF THE BARN WITH ANDREW BELL, who was carrying a large, battered black leather bag, to where the motorbike was parked.

'How long have you been riding?' Harry asked.

'Ever since I was a kid,' Andy replied. 'Gets under your skin, I think. Can't stop myself. You?'

'Never tried it,' Harry said. 'Don't trust myself.'

The bike was a fair size and Harry was amazed that it was possible to ride the thing at any speed. It just looked too large and too heavy.

'They make a lot of sense for the surgery in a place like the dales,' Andrew said. 'And you'd be amazed how much kit we can carry in those paniers they have.'

'No, I can see that,' Harry said. 'We've got one ourselves. Not as posh as this, but we have it for the same reason.'

'Is this about the necropsy?' Andy asked. 'I gave all the details on that to a couple of your officers yesterday morning.'

'That you did,' Grimm said. 'I've not had a chance to

catch up with them on that yet, as we've been rather caught up in what's happened since.'

'That doesn't sound too good.'

'It isn't,' Harry said. 'The owner of the dog you examined? He was attacked last night in his own home.'

'Seriously? That's awful. Why?'

'That's what we're trying to find out.'

Andrew frowned and stretched, and Harry heard bones pop.

'That poor dog had been fairly torn apart,' he said. 'And the toxicology report certainly came up with a few interesting things.'

'Such as?'

'There was a fair cocktail of stuff in its veins,' Andy explained. 'None of the substances are illegal, because they all have legitimate uses, but I was quite surprised by it all so I did a little bit of digging.'

'And what did you find?'

'I phoned around to a few friends in the business, as it were,' said Andrew. 'And Toby's worked at the races as a vet, so he recognised it for what it all was. He was due to be out here today but had to head off on another job. Ours is a busy life in the dales, you know.'

'Toby?'

'One of our vets,' Andrew said. 'Helped out with the necropsy, met your two officers.'

'So, what was it all, then?' Harry asked, having already heard the rundown from Jim earlier, but wanting to hear it from the horse's mouth, as it were.

'Everything that dog had in its veins, all those drugs? They're commonly found in connection with illegal dogfighting.'

'And you're sure about that?'

'I'm a vet,' Andy said. 'I know vet stuff. And Toby confirmed it too, having dealt with some dodgy types at the races before. There's a lot of stuff coming over from the world of sport into dog fighting, you see, which is quite interesting.'

'Interesting is one way to describe it,' Harry agreed. 'Though I reckon terrifying is more accurate.'

'It's not cheap though,' Andy continued.

'Well, there's good money to be made in a dog fight,' Harry said, shaking his head. 'And if people are going to win big, then they're usually happy to invest.'

As they'd been chatting, the vet had got changed out of his mucky gear from helping the cow give birth and into his biking leathers, then had a quick check through his case. Harry saw all kinds of medical equipment in the vet's bag, bandages and dressings, drugs and syringes, and a small, battered wooden case with the words 'Humane Killer' scratched into the lid.

"Always have to make sure I've got everything,' he said. 'Can't be leaving any of this stuff lying around.'

'Humane Killer?' Harry asked.

'It's a pistol,' Andy said, lifting out the wooden case and opening it to show Harry. 'Single shot. Most vets have them. Fully licensed, obviously. It's a last resort, really, but I'd rather have it than not, just in case.'

'You carry it around with you, then?'

'Good God, no!' Andy said. 'It's kept secure back at the surgery, signed in and out. I just had a job to do on the way over. Never pleasant, but sometimes, there's just nothing you can do, so...'

Harry gave an understanding nod as Andy finished getting changed.

'But you didn't come out here just to ask me about the report on the dog, did you?' Andy asked.

Harry shook his head.

'I'm sure you understand that as part of this investigation, we need to check up on various details, bits of information that come to light.'

Andy's shoulders seemed to sag a little.

'Let me guess,' he said. 'My history has caught up with me, right?'

'You could say that, yes.' Harry nodded. 'And you'll understand my concern. A vet who back in his younger days set up a cockfight? That's set a few alarm bells ringing, for sure.'

'It was hens,' Andy said, correcting Harry. 'Not cocks. And that's the bit you need to remember.'

'Why's that, then?'

'Because that was all me! I swapped them, didn't I!'

'Not sure that I understand.'

For a moment, Andy seemed to check every scratch on his motorbike helmet.

'Not everyone in farming is good at husbandry,' he said. 'Or even gives a damn about the animals in their care. You know, I've seen people kick dogs, drive tractors into bulls, set illegal traps, just ignore the pain their animals are in. It's sickening. No ethics at all. Makes you wonder why they're in it at all if they hate it that much, doesn't it?'

'And yet you set up a cockfight,' Harry said. 'And for money, too, if I'm right.'

The vet walked a few steps away, then turned back to face Harry.

'I knew that if I didn't get involved, animals would get hurt. I had to stop that.'

'How?'

'Like I said, I switched the cocks for hens,' Andy said. 'I knew everyone would be too drunk to notice, to begin with, and when they finally did, it was too late. I did it to teach them a lesson.'

'A lesson?' Harry repeated. 'How?'

'Make a fool of them all, you see? Cocks will fight because they're territorial. Hens though, they will have a flap at each other, but generally, they'll just mooch around, pecking the ground. So, in went the hens, and a minute or two later, everyone's laughing.'

'What happened to the hens?'

'They were fine,' Andy said. 'I took them back home.'

'Home?'

'They were my hens. I had a hen coop in the garden as a teenager. Used to sell the eggs for a bit of pocket money.'

'There were three of you who set the fight up though, weren't there?' Harry said.

'I didn't actually set anything up,' Andrew said. 'I volunteered to get involved so that I could do what I did.'

'You could've just reported it,' Harry suggested.

'I could have, yes, but I didn't.'

'How did they react?'

Andy shrugged. 'Can't really remember, if I'm honest. I know Dean got it bad from his dad because of it all, his reputation and all that, you know?'

'Mr Slater?'

'Yes, that's him,' Andy said. 'And Danny, well, he's dead now, isn't he? So it doesn't really matter. Car accident when he was twenty-one. Absolutely horrendous.'

'You were all kicked out of Young Farmers.'

'Not really a surprise, is it?' Andy said. 'But as I've

explained, my involvement all along was to make sure that no animals were hurt. We have a responsibility, don't we—humanity I mean?'

'In what way?'

'To animals,' Andy said. 'They're in our care, aren't they? That's why I became a vet. We're powerful, dangerously so, if you think about it, and it's down to us as individuals to exercise that power with care.'

Harry, not knowing quite what to say to this somewhat preachy moment from the vet, checked his watch.

'Long day?' Andy asked.

'Long week,' Harry said, keeping a yawn down, but only just. 'Thanks for your time. Much appreciated.'

'Anytime,' Andy said. 'So, you think there's a local dogfighting ring running then, do you?'

'Looks that way, yes,' Harry said. 'And the sooner I put a stop to it the better.'

'It's amazing what people will do for profit,' Andy said.

'You're not wrong,' Harry agreed.

'Just think of the money made in boxing, cage fighting. It's madness, really, isn't it?'

'That's my worry,' Harry said. 'That this madness is just the start of something much worse. People get a taste for it and before you know it things are out of control. It starts with dogs, but then some bright spark thinks, why stop there?'

'Terrifying,' Andy said, pulling on his helmet. 'Well, if you need any help, just give me a call.'

'Thank you,' Harry said.

Andy handed Harry a small business card.

'That's the surgery address on the front, but my home address is written on the back. You can't miss the place thanks to the scaffolding I've got up everywhere!'

Harry thanked the vet then watched as he climbed onto his motorbike and started the engine. The deep thrum of it filled the air and then he was off, the thick-treaded knobbly tyres biting into the track outside the house and sending out a spray of small stones as he raced off.

Back in his vehicle, Harry checked his phone. There was one message from Jadyn to tell him that, so far, they'd not been able to find either Reedy or Eric.

Harry knew that a long evening lay ahead. He was exhausted, but with so much on his mind, getting to sleep would be almost impossible. And even when he did, when his body finally gave in to it, he knew it would be the kind of sleep that only made you feel all the worse for having it.

Harry rang Ben to let him know he was on his way home only to be told that Molly had seemingly spent the entire day asleep not on the makeshift bed he'd prepared for her on the floor, but on his actual bed instead. Then he headed out of the farm and back up the dale, and with every mile closer to home, dark fingers of evening drew closer over the fells, pulling with them the blanket of night.

CHAPTER TWENTY-FIVE

THE NIGHT WAS A RESTLESS ONE FOR HARRY, DISTURBED not only by all the thoughts running around in his head, but the endless snoring and farting of the dog at the foot of his bed. He'd also been woken up in the early hours by the dog, of all things, sleepwalking. He'd found her in the corner of his room, trying to bury an invisible bone.

With some gentle coaxing, he'd managed to get her back into her bed, only to watch her jump up onto his and settle down. He'd not had the heart to put her back down on the floor, so had just left her where she was.

Grace had called during the evening to say she'd be over the next day to pick Molly up. Harry didn't want to admit that he actually rather liked having the smelly old hound around.

Having made his way down to the office, Molly shuffling along at his side, Harry had walked in to find that PC Okri had, being the officer on duty, had a somewhat eventful evening, to say the least. It was very clear that the whole thing had been very exciting, judging by the enthusiasm with which he was telling everyone about it.

'A break-in?' Harry said, as the young constable stood in front of him, beaming. 'Where?'

'Up in Gayle,' Jadyn said. 'Mr and Mrs Hogg.'

'Not Neil's parents, surely,' Harry said.

Jim came over and stood with Jadyn.

'Yeah, I'm afraid so,' he said. 'I popped in to see them this morning on my way over, just to check in on them, see how they are.'

'And?'

'Oh, they're fine,' Jim said. 'Well, I say fine. Helen is being very practical about it all, thankful that nothing was taken and that the mess was really only in Neil's room. Alan, though? He's not exactly taken it well.'

'How do you mean?'

'He's still at the righteous indignation stage,' Jim said. 'And I can't see him breaking out of it any time soon, mainly because I think he just enjoys having something to rage at.'

'That's understandable,' Harry said. 'Most of us would be the same under the circumstances.'

'Well, yes and no,' said Jim.

Harry frowned.

'I don't like the sound of that.'

'He thinks he knows who did it,' Jadyn explained. 'Well, not did it as such, but is responsible, if you see what I mean.'

'Which I don't.'

Harry was already beginning to wish he'd stayed in bed, dog farts and all.

'They were out last night, Alan and Helen,' Jim said. 'With Richard Adams.'

'Really?' Harry said, somewhat surprised that particular name was mentioned. 'Why?'

'He invited them over,' Jim said. 'I was there when it happened when I popped round the other day. Apparently, he's been around a few times since they lost Neil. Alan reckons he's only doing it to make himself look good in the community.'

Harry remembered Richard Adams very well indeed. He'd met many of his kind before, all teeth and gums, expensive watches and flashy vehicles. Usually spoke only about themselves, their business, or both, like one had no meaning without the other, and that by telling you about it all, your own life was given meaning, too.

'But what's any of that got to do with anything else?' Harry asked.

'Alan can't stand the man,' Jim said. 'Doesn't trust him. Only went out because Helen wanted to, I'm assuming. And as far as Alan is concerned, the only person who knew they were out that night was Mr Adams.'

'And he's jumped to the conclusion that he invited them out so that someone could break into their house?' Harry said. 'You know, saying that out loud doesn't make it sound any less crazy. Why would he? What possible motive is there?'

'He's already been around there accusing him,' said Jadyn. 'I don't think he's too bothered about a motive, just wants someone to blame.'

'But there's no reason for any link between the two at all, is there?' Harry said.

'None at all.' Jim shook his head. 'It's a break-in, just an opportunistic crime, by the looks of things. Alan will calm down eventually, I'm sure.'

'He won't do anything stupid, will he?' Harry asked. 'I mean, I know he already has done, but do we need to bring him in for a chat before a certain Mr Adams reports him for harassment?'

Jim shook his head. 'Helen has him under control. All she had to do was threaten to stop baking and he went off in a huff.'

Harry thought back over what Jim and Jadyn had told him.

'You said it was Neil's room that was turned over.'

'Nowt much was taken though,' Jim said. 'It's the only modern room in the house. Neil lived over in Darlington, but he was always popping back home so his mum kept his room nice, and he had some of his stuff there.'

'What was taken?'

'Tech basically. A record deck, amp, and speakers, an old laptop. Oh, and some tins of Helen's biscuits from the kitchen, which is what's upset Alan more than anything, I think. There was a bit of damage, but insurance will cover it. The back door, some broken pictures, that kind of thing.'

'And that owl,' Jadyn added. 'Mr Hogg seemed more upset about that than anything else, didn't he?'

'Owl?' Harry asked, remembering the ones he'd encountered out at the barn.

'Oh, it's nothing,' Jim said. 'Just this stuffed thing Alan won at a Christmas raffle at the vets. It was all smashed up in the break-in. Think whoever broke in must've knocked it off the wall and stamped on it just for the hell of it. Helen's thrilled. She hated the thing.'

'You can win one too, if you want,' Jadyn said. 'Well, not an owl, a pigeon I think it was. They've another raffle going at the vets, you see.'

'A stuffed pigeon?' Harry said. 'Hold me back...'

'You know what they say, boss,' Jadyn said. 'You have to be in it to win it!'

'Thanks for those excellent words of wisdom, Constable,' Harry said. 'Now, is there anything else I need to know about this break-in, or are we done at winning stuffed pigeons?'

'I don't think so, no,' Jadyn said. 'It was all dealt with last night and I'll be going up there again this morning.'

Harry looked over at Jim.

'You think there's a connection at all, then?'

'With Neil's murder? No,' he said, shaking his head. 'I was out there with Jadyn last night. Whoever it was, they were in and out pretty quickly by the looks of it. They didn't turn the place over or take much in the grand scheme of things.'

'Probably someone just looking for something to sell,' Jadyn said. 'Most burglaries are like that. In and out in minutes, just grab something that you can get a few quid for, then leg it.'

'And if you can smash up a stuffed bird on the way, all the better,' Jim said.

Which was enough of a signal for Harry to leave the conversation and go have a word with the rest of the team. Gordy met him halfway. And rather than a mug of tea, she was sipping from a glass half-filled with orange-coloured liquid, the rest of the glass seemingly filled with an odd foam, some of which was now coating her top lip like the worst kind of fake moustache.

'And just what the hell is that?' Harry asked, gesturing at the glass. 'Some kind of health drink or pick-me-up full of vitamins and wishful thinking?'

'This?' Gordy said. 'It's heaven in a glass is what it is!'

'You'll see from my expression that I'm not exactly convinced.'

Gordy stared at Harry.

'But you always look like that.'

'Exactly.'

'It's Creamola Foam,' Gordy explained, taking another foam-laden sip. 'Had it as a kid up in the Highlands. Went out of production years ago, but now it's back!' She took another sip then said, 'You want some?'

'Again, look at my face,' Harry said.

'You don't know what you're missing.'

'I'll take that risk.'

Gordy finished her drink, then said, 'If you don't mind me saying so, you don't look great.'

'You, on the other hand,' Harry replied, 'and Crapola Foam or whatever it was called aside, are positively beaming. Things going well with Anna, then?'

It was a few months now since Gordy had somehow ended up on a blind date with Anna, the local vicar who lived over in Askrigg. And so far, things certainly seemed to be going well for them both.

'They are for sure,' Gordy said. 'Though I can't say I ever thought I'd find myself falling for a woman of the cloth. And it's Creamola, not Crapola.'

'Potato po-tah-to,' Harry said. 'And falling for, is it? So, it's love then, is it, Detective Inspector?'

Gordy blushed.

'Well, it's early days yet for all of that, isn't it?'

'Oh, I don't know,' said Harry. 'If you find something good, I say run with it.'

'You know, Grimm, I'm beginning to get the impression that under that gruff exterior, you're just a big softy.'

'That's a secret between you and me,' Harry said. 'So, what are you on with today, then?'

'Well, I'm going to coordinate things here for you so you can meet with the pathologist.'

Harry did a double-take.

'Don't look so concerned,' Gordy said. 'She called in before you arrived, asked me to tell you she'd like to meet up and go through things with you. I accepted on your behalf.'

'So, I've a meeting, then?'

'You have indeed,' Gordy said. 'Ten-thirty, round at her mum's. Here's the address.'

Harry took the piece of notepaper Gordy handed to him, checking his watch at the same time.

'So, everything's under control here, then, is it?'

'Everything,' Gordy said. 'We've got plenty to be going on with, what with needing to find two missing people, namely this Reedy fellow and Mr Eric Haygarth. There's the break-in to deal with as well, and plenty of everything else.'

'So, I don't need to worry, then.'

'Well, you're meeting the pathologist,' Gordy said. 'That's enough for anyone to be worried about, isn't it?'

'What about Molly there?' Harry asked, looking over at the old dog who was now rolled on her back in the corner of the room, up close to a radiator, and judging by the soft snoring, sound asleep. 'Grace said she'd be over at some point to pick her up, but I'm not sure when exactly.'

'Oh, she'll be fine,' Gordy said. 'I'll keep an eye on her. Not that she's much bother.'

Harry hesitated.

'You've an hour,' Gordy said. 'So be off with you, man! That's more than enough time to get yourself back home, have the shower you obviously forgot to bother with, eat something, and then get over there.'

Harry hesitated.

'Something up?'

'No, not really,' Harry said. 'It's just that, well, it takes a bit of getting used to, all of this.'

'What?'

'People you work with actually helping you out,' Harry said.

'We're a team, remember?' Gordy said. 'Now be off with you. Go on!'

Harry walked over to the door, then turned around for a glance at the team. They were unlike any other group of people he'd ever worked with before. And for all their oddities, their strangeness, he wondered just what it was that he'd done right in his life to end up in the dales with them in the first place.

Then he was out the door and tabbing back along to his flat to make himself some way closer to being a presentable human being. Not so much for Sowerby, but the idea of turning up dishevelled and potentially bumping into her force-of-nature mother looking like he did? The thought of it was too terrifying to contemplate, even for him.

CHAPTER TWENTY-SIX

Harry pulled through the gate and onto the gravel drive of a house on the outskirts of Askrigg. The road, if he'd have kept going, would have taken him over the tops and onto open moorland, then down into Swaledale. It was a beautiful drive, and one Harry would take sometimes just for the fun of it. But today there wasn't the time, so he parked up and headed over to the front door. He reached up to knock as the door opened in front of him.

'There you are!'

The woman in front of him was wearing a waxed jacket, which she filled out to the corners, and Wellington boots, and was armed with a large garden scythe.

'Morning, Margaret,' Harry said, as the pathologist's mother, Divisional Surgeon Margaret Shaw, greeted him like some ruddy-cheeked and well-fed dales version of Death.

'Here to help me with the garden?'

'I don't think so.'

'Pity.' Margaret shrugged. 'I've been putting off getting

out there and it's a jungle now. Can't get the mower out into it so I'm on with this thing!'

She thrust the scythe forwards as though brandishing it ready for battle.

'Looks lethal,' Harry said, not wanting to get too close.

'Oh, it is,' Margaret agreed. 'Razor-sharp, too. You'll be wanting our Rebecca then, yes?'

'She in?'

Margaret turned around and leaned back in the house before bellowing out her daughter's name.

'Why don't you head on in,' she then said. 'Make yourself at home. If you go on down the hall, you'll get to the kitchen. Make a coffee or something, there's a good lad.'

Harry stepped into the house and Margaret, without another word, headed off into the day, clearly on a mission.

Heading down the hall, Harry found himself in the kind of kitchen he only ever usually saw in the lifestyle magazines found in doctor's waiting rooms. The ceiling was beamed, the cupboards, dining table, and chairs all a light oak, and instead of a normal, everyday cooker, the house was fed from a huge, green, cast iron Aga.

On seeing that the kettle was a stove-top one rather than electric, Harry decided against making a coffee, somewhat afraid of a kitchen as posh as this one, and instead just sat down at the dining table.

Rebecca Sowerby entered the room and for once wasn't wearing PPE.

'You've not put the kettle on!'

'I was going to,' Harry lied. 'And then I didn't.'

Rebecca grabbed the kettle from an iron skillet on the side, filled it, then heaved up one of the heavy covers on the oven and plonked it down on the hot plate underneath.

'French press okay?'

'French what?'

'You know,' Sowerby said. 'This.'

From a cupboard, she removed a large cafetière and a couple of mugs.

'Oh, you mean a plunger.'

'I don't think that I do.'

'Anyway, it's a yes,' Harry said.

Sowerby then proceeded to put a jug of milk on the table, along with the two mugs, a pot of sugar, a couple of small plates, and a cake tin.

'You saw Mum, then,' she said.

'Going out to either attack the garden or collect souls by the looks of things,' Harry said. 'I'm not sure which.'

Sowerby laughed and brought over the now-full cafetière and poured.

'She terrifies me with that scythe. I'm amazed she's not severed a limb. Sugar?'

Harry shook his head.

'Just some milk, thanks.'

'Open the tin,' Sowerby instructed. 'Mum always has biscuits. I think she bakes in her sleep.'

Harry opened the tin and reached in for a crumbly, buttery slice of shortbread.

'Tasty,' he said, through the crumbs.

'And she wonders why she can't lose weight,' Sowerby said, taking one for herself.

'Nice place she's got here,' Harry said.

'It's far too big for her,' said Sowerby. 'But she refuses to downsize. Loves the place too much. Too many memories, I think. Doesn't want to let them go.'

Harry sipped his coffee. Through the window, he could see up onto the fells beyond the garden.

'With a view like that, who can blame her?'

'Views are two a penny around here,' Sowerby said. 'But yes, you're right, it is lovely, isn't it?'

For a couple of minutes, Harry and Sowerby sat sipping their coffee and nibbling biscuits, both of them staring out into the dales.

'So, you asked me over for a chat, then,' Harry said.

'That I did,' Sowerby agreed. 'And thanks for coming.'

'Certainly beats chatting over a crime scene,' Harry said, reaching for another biscuit.

'It does,' said Sowerby. 'And I just thought it might be worth us chatting through everything somewhere more comfortable. And, if you don't mind me saying so, without Swift around.'

Harry laughed at that. 'You've known him longer than I.'

'That's not necessarily a good thing. Anyway, you've worked closely with him, haven't you? Is he always like that?'

'Like what?'

'Oh, I don't know,' Sowerby said. 'Like he's spent his life chewing thistles and just generally disapproving of the whole world?'

'Good description. Accurate.'

'I don't think he likes you.'

'I don't think he really likes anyone,' Harry said. 'But I've worked with worse.'

Sowerby stood up and went over to a large dresser against the wall, returning with a file, which she rested on the table then opened as she sat back down.

'So, what have we got, then?' Harry asked.

'Let's start from the beginning,' Sowerby said. 'The barn, the dog.'

She laid out some photos, not just of the barn, but of tyre treads, blood spatter, and the body of Arthur's dog, Jack.

'Not much to go on, is it?' Harry said.

'Well,' Sowerby said, 'we think that at least half a dozen vehicles were there that night, judging by the tracks, including four-by-fours, a motorbike, and also a trailer.'

'A trailer?' Harry said.

Sowerby nodded. 'There was evidence of other dogs at the site, saliva, hair, that kind of thing. Maybe they'd planned other fights but were disturbed by your friend Dave turning up?'

'Possibly,' Harry said. 'Which makes it even more important that we put a stop to it sooner rather than later. What else?'

'There's the tiling adhesive and granite dust,' Sowerby said. 'We've also got some shoe imprints, but they're not that great, if I'm honest. Might be useful though, you never know.'

Sowerby laughed then.

'Something funny?'

'I was just thinking, it's a shame we can't interview owls.'

'Is it? Why?'

'There was that one sitting there watching me the whole time I was in the barn, remember?' Sowerby said. 'Beautiful thing. It probably saw everything.'

'Not sure an owl in the witness stand would hold up in court,' Harry said. 'So, what about Arthur's house, then?'

Sowerby brought out another stack of photos and her notes.

'I'm pretty certain the attacker came in through the front door,' she said, 'and the violence started here.'

She pointed at a photograph of some blood on the wall near the floor.

'Exactly what I thought,' Harry said.

'We've identified two types of DNA from the blood we found. One is the victim's, the other must be the attacker.'

At this, Harry almost lit up.

'So, if we actually manage to find a suspect...'

'We can crosscheck,' Sowerby said.

'Well, the two we've got are both still missing,' Harry said. 'But fingers crossed and all that. They can't hide forever.'

'Two suspects?'

Harry nodded.

'That's interesting.'

'Is it? Why?'

Sowerby didn't answer the question, instead, saying, 'There's no evidence of a break-in at the back of the house. The glass was broken from the inside, as you suspected, the door then opened and most of it collected and put inside on the kitchen floor.'

'Why anyone would think that would work is beyond me,' Harry said.

'We also found some traces of ash in the carpet and on the furniture,' Sowerby said. 'We also found the stubby ends of a couple of joints. One inside the house, one on the opposite side of the road.'

'Fingerprints?' Harry asked.

Sowerby shook her head. 'No fingerprints, but we did get some DNA.'

Harry sat back, folded his arms, and stared at the ceiling.

'You okay?'

'Frustrated,' Harry said. 'It's not like we've got much, is it? Certainly not enough to really have any good leads. And where do we go from any of this?'

'I haven't finished yet,' Sowerby said.

Harry sat up and leaned forward.

'Go on...'

'I went out for another look at the barn, just to make sure I'd covered everything. And I found this.'

'What?'

Sowerby passed a photo over to Harry.

Harry drew it close, staring at it.

'What am I looking at exactly?'

'That's the stub from a betting slip,' Sowerby said. 'Says it's from the bookmakers in Hawes. No way we would have missed it first time round.'

Harry looked up from the photo.

'So, you think someone's been out to the barn since your first visit, then?'

'Looks like it,' Sowerby said.

'But what, if anything, does that tell us?' Harry asked, rubbing his eyes, as though doing so would help him to see things a little more clearly.

'Remember what I said about the joints?' Sowerby said. 'Well, we found traces of the same cannabis on this, too. And it matches what was found at the house.'

'You sure?'

Sowerby gave a nod.

'So, that means we've definitely got a clear link, then, between the barn and the house,' Harry said. 'Not just the dog, either. Someone was definitely at both crime scenes.'

'Well, yes and no,' Sowerby said.

'How do you mean, yes and no?'

'Well, we managed to get some traces of DNA from that ticket stub,' Sowerby explained, 'thanks to whoever had handled it having a cut or something. And you know what?'

'No, I don't, but I'm hoping you'll tell me.'

'It doesn't match the DNA we found on the joint from the house, but it does match the one found outside on the road.'

'You're losing me,' Harry said, rubbing his eyes.

Sowerby went back to the photos.

'We have DNA from blood at the house where the attack happened, and evidence of cannabis being smoked thanks to those two joints,' she said. 'We also have the cannabis trace and the DNA from the betting slip. However, the DNA we pulled from the betting slip doesn't match the DNA from the blood at the house.'

'My head's starting to hurt,' Harry said.

Sowerby sat forward.

'What I think we have here are two different people.'

And then, for Harry, it clicked.

'Someone was watching the house!' he said. 'The same person who left this stub at the barn.'

'Exactly,' Sowerby said.

'So that means we've got more than one person involved, doesn't it?' Harry said.

'I'm afraid it does, yes,' said Sowerby.

'Bollocks,' Harry snarled.

'Yeah, I thought you might say that.'

CHAPTER TWENTY-SEVEN

When Eric arrived home, he knew immediately that something was wrong. Well, everything was wrong, wasn't it? That was why he'd been away for two nights, sleeping rough, and had only now just arrived home, because he was cold, starving, and really just wanted to have a good wash and use a toilet that wasn't a hole in the ground or a tree.

He was also hungover and shouldn't have been driving. But it wasn't like there was much on the roads even at the busiest of times, not around Swaledale and Arkengarthdale, that was for sure. And most of his driving had been off-road, following tracks through moorland and meadow, just to find places to hunker down and hide, away from prying eyes, and to give him a chance to get his head together.

But now that he was back home, he was wondering if he should just have stayed away and never come back. Ever. Trouble was, where would he go? He'd lived here all his life. As far as he was concerned, there was nowhere else on Earth like it and certainly nowhere that he would be able to call home.

The first thing he'd noticed had been the tyre tracks leading up to his house. The only person with any cause at all to drive out here was himself, so whoever this was, they weren't welcome. Or invited.

Then he'd seen the footprints outside the house and that had just made him angry. Driving up a lane he could forgive, because people took wrong turnings, holidaymakers were nosy, and usually, when they saw his home close up, they quickly turned around and buggered off. But whoever this was, they'd either got too nosy for their own good, or driven out here on purpose for a snoop.

Eric, fighting back a yawn, his head thumping, stumbled along, following the footprints. His mouth tasted like he'd spent the past few hours just wandering around licking road-kill, and his entire body was doing its best to tell him in every possible way it could that he'd consumed far too much whisky.

When Eric came to his front door, he didn't stop to let himself in. Instead, he continued down along the front of the house and through the gate to head round to the back of the building, his anger and his worry only adding to his thumping head.

At the back of his house, Eric checked to see if any attempt had been made to break in, but the lock was fine and no windows were broken, so that was something. But it didn't make him feel any better, not after what he'd seen over at old Arthur's place.

Eric then turned and made his way back around to the front of the house, heading past his shed, which was when he noticed a scuffling on the ground in front of the door. So, he thought, they'd been in there, too, had they?

Opening the door, Eric peered into the gloom, his most recent piece of work staring back at him. He stepped inside to check if anything had been touched or disturbed, but found nothing out of place or missing, so that was something. And nothing had been damaged either, which was good.

Not everyone understood what it was that he did, viewing it as ghoulish and weird and creepy. But to Eric, taxidermy had never been that. To him, it was a way of preserving something beautiful that would, if left, just rot. And what a waste that was. Also, it was a nice little earner. Particularly with the rarer stuff. Yes, he was supposed to have a licence to sell, but then he'd have to explain where he was getting the carcasses. And he was fairly sure that, '*I shot them*,' wouldn't stand up too well in a court of law.

Leaving the shed, Eric headed back around to the front of the house and let himself inside. Bed beckoned, but he needed a drink of water and to clean his teeth. So, he grabbed a glass from the kitchen, then headed on through to the downstairs bathroom.

A few minutes later, once upstairs, having closed his curtains to the last moments of the bright light of day, Eric very slowly laid himself down on his bed, then closed his eyes. He opened them again almost immediately, as everything started to spin and he was sure he was going to throw up. So, instead, he just lay there for a while, staring at the ceiling, trying to get his head around what had happened.

What had set it all off had been that phone call from Arthur Blake, Mr Perfect Gamekeeper. God, that man had been a royal pain his whole life, constantly criticising his work, spreading rumours. So, what if most of those rumours were true? That didn't matter. It was the fact that he just couldn't keep himself to himself, could he? No. Not a bit of it.

And his damned old-fashioned views on how the job should be done, how a gamekeeper should work, raise birds, deal with vermin and the like? The man was evangelical about it, and if he ever had the chance to point the finger, then he would. But that phone call? That had been something else, hadn't it? Accusing him like that, like he'd already decided he was guilty. He'd said on the phone about how he wanted to have it out with him right then, which is why Eric had headed on over. There was going to be no discussion, no asking for proof, just an argument between two old men who'd hated each other for decades.

Eric had been up for it, that much he knew. He'd driven over there in a rage, ready and willing to have it out with the old man, to not just give him a piece of his mind, but a damn good leathering as well. But then, when he'd turned up, the door had been open. And that had taken Eric rather by surprise, mainly because he'd been looking forward to crashing his fist into the door himself and yelling Arthur's name nice and loud so everyone would know why he was there and who he'd come to see.

He'd stepped into the house. Well, of course, he had! The door was open and at that moment he was sure Arthur had left it open for him and was probably in the lounge waiting with his unfounded accusations and holier-than-thou attitude. And Eric wasn't one for holding back. No chance of that! So, in he'd strode, ready to tell that old bastard exactly what he thought of him and his accusations.

Then he'd seen it, or them, hadn't he? At first, he'd not been exactly sure what he had been looking at. A person, yes, standing in the lounge over something else on the floor. And whatever it was on the floor, they had been kicking it, hadn't they? Really going at it, too. In a moment of madness, Eric had wondered if Arthur had just been getting himself ready for a bit of scrap by practising on a sack or pillow or something, but then he'd heard a groan, at about the same time as he'd seen the blood.

It had been Arthur on the floor and someone had been beating the old man half to death, or at least that was what it had looked like. There'd certainly been a lot of flailing of arms and legs. Who it was, Eric hadn't the faintest idea, and he hadn't hung around to find out, either. Particularly after the attacker had turned to stare at him through the eye holes of a balaclava.

Of course, he could have gone in there and attempted a rescue, but the way Arthur was getting smashed about, it had been pretty clear that he wouldn't have stood a chance himself. And what was the point in getting himself beaten up anyway? So, he'd bolted, like a rabbit with a ferret on its tail, racing out of the house and over to his truck to head off into the night. And as he'd speeded off, he'd caught sight of Arthur's daughter, Grace, heading over to the house, staring at his vehicle as he'd disappeared into the night.

As he'd driven away, Eric's mind had done a real number on him, and after a stop for fuel and a couple of bottles of cheap booze, along with a good amount of chocolate and crisps, he'd ended up in a panic that had him just driving around the dales for a good few hours. Eventually, tiredness had got to him, so he'd headed down into a small dell, turned off his lights, then cracked open the whisky.

As he'd sat there in the dark, drinking himself further and further into a blurry haze, he'd thought about calling the police, about checking up on Grace, but when had anyone ever done anything nice for him? So, he'd given up on that idea, sure that whatever had been going on had nothing to do with him. It was just an unlucky coincidence that he'd been there at all. And knowing Arthur, he'd be fine anyway, the tough old sod. More's the pity.

But now, as he lay there in his bed on a late afternoon, wishing the night to arrive quickly, a creeping dread began to rake at him. Closing his eyes, the sickening spinning now having eased a little, Eric thought back to the footprints around his house, to the fact that someone had been into his shed and seen his work.

No one ever visited him, did they? Not a soul. Ever. And yet, on the night when he'd been called by old Arthur, gone over to have it out with him, and found him being kicked around, someone had been around his house in the dark. But who? That's what he wanted to know. At least, he thought he did. Perhaps ignorance was best.

If it had been the police, then that was because Arthur's daughter had told them she'd seen him, so he'd need to think of something, wouldn't he? An alibi? Yes, that was it. And if it wasn't the police then... then he'd deal with that if it happened. It couldn't have been the person attacking Arthur, could it? Not unless they knew him, knew where he lived. Now that was a thought he could've done without. But at that moment he was too tired to care, so he closed his eyes and allowed the world to drift to nothing.

CHAPTER TWENTY-EIGHT

'So, now what?' Matt asked. 'Where else is there for us to look?'

The day was getting on now, with early afternoon threatening to become late in the day with no success as yet in what they'd set out to do. Matt's stomach was already giving him warning that food would soon be on the agenda. He'd also promised Joan that he'd be back in good time to cook her favourite: cheesy mashed potato with mince and peas. It wasn't exactly high living, but it was certainly living comfortably, and he loved her all the more for it. With a baby on the way as well, life, as far as Matt was concerned, just couldn't get much better.

'Haven't the foggiest,' Liz yawned. 'He'll have squirrelled himself away into some dark hole somewhere. We'll just have to wait for him to come out.'

'What if he doesn't, though?' Matt asked.

'He will,' Liz said, but she was lacking conviction.

'You don't sound convinced.'

'I'm not.'

Neither Matt nor Liz spoke for a few moments, contenting themselves with their private thoughts.

'So, how's Ben, then?' Matt asked, breaking the silence first if only so that he didn't have to listen to his own brain.

'He's okay,' Liz said, a little too non-committal for Matt.

'And Harry's fine with it all?'

'Why, has he said something?'

Matt shook his head. 'No, not at all! It's just, you know, one of his team, dating his brother...'

'It's not illegal,' Liz said.

'You sure?'

'Very.'

Matt wanted to ask more questions, but Liz got in first before he had a chance.

'How long is it now? Before you become a dad?'

'Two,' Matt replied. 'At least I think it is. Could be three. It's definitely not four. Is it?' He counted off on his fingers, then said, 'I'm sticking with two.'

'And do you know what it is?'

'Yes,' Matt said. 'It's a baby. And do you know how I know that?'

'I'm all ears.'

Matt made a big flourish with his hands, as though revealing something truly incredible.

'Science!' he said.

Liz laughed.

'Well, that's reassuring.'

'We don't know if it's a boy or a girl, if that's what you mean,' Matt said. 'Joan preferred to not know. Said she wanted to meet them for the first time in every possible way. Also, she doesn't think it's fair if we know more about it than it knows about us when it arrives in the world.'

'That's quite nice, actually,' Liz said.

'No it isn't!' Matt exclaimed. 'It's a bloody nightmare! I want to know! I need to know! I can't bear not knowing!'

Liz stared at Matt, wide-eyed at his outburst.

Matt held up his hand in defence. 'I'm just saying I'd rather know, that's all.'

Liz smiled and reached over to pat Matt's leg reassuringly.

'You don't need to worry,' she said. 'Boy or girl, you'll both be amazing parents. Trust me.'

'Trust you?' Matt replied. 'I need to trust myself first!'

Again, the conversation fell away, but a couple of minutes later, Liz suggested heading back to Eric's house.

'Maybe we've missed something,' she said.

'You mean like there are more dead animals for us to find?' Matt asked.

'No,' Liz said. 'I just mean another look wouldn't do any harm, would it? And you never know, he might even be home by now.'

Half an hour later, Matt rolled them slowly down the track towards Eric's house.

'It really isn't welcoming, is it?' he said, coming to a stop some way off from the place.

The house was dark, with none of the windows giving any sign of life inside.

'Not exactly the kind of place you'd bring someone back to, is it?' he said, thinking it looked dead, a husk. 'If you know what I mean.'

'Maybe he's brought lots of people back here,' said Liz. 'He might be a proper Hugh Heffner.'

'And you know who that is, do you?'

'Actually...'

Matt noticed Liz's voice trail off. He turned to look at her and found her wide eyes staring back.

'What if all those he bought back never actually left!'

She then proceeded to make some rather inappropriate and terrifyingly accurate sounds of someone choking to death.

'Not funny,' Matt said.

'Who's to say his taxidermy is restricted to beast and bird?' Liz said. 'People's private lives can be the scariest of places, can't they?'

'I'm not listening.'

'Maybe he's got a cellar, one filled with all his extra-special works? His prize pieces he keeps for his eyes only!'

Matt was about to tell Liz to shut it, when a Range Rover flew past them to swing around and skid to a halt outside Eric's cottage.

'Who the hell is that?' Matt asked as both he and Liz leaned forward to stare out of the windscreen.

The driver's door flew open and out stepped a large man with an angry face. He was carrying what looked like a fence post and as he walked towards the front door of Eric's house, he swung it from side to side. Then he was at the door and hammering his fist against it.

'If Eric's in there, he's sure to have heard that,' Liz said.

Matt agreed and added, 'Someone needs to call the police.'

'You just did.'

'Come on then.'

UPSTAIRS IN HIS HOUSE, Eric's dreamless sleep was shattered by what sounded like a pack of angry bears trying to crash through his front door. At first, he'd assumed it was just some bad nightmare that he'd woken from, but then, when the sound had come again, followed by the illegible bellowing of a man, he'd known for sure that it absolutely was not. He recognised the voice. And that wasn't a good thing. Though why the owner of that voice was outside his house and trying so desperately to get in, he had no idea, but he was fairly sure he didn't want to find out.

Doing his best to ignore what must surely be the last few minutes of his front door being a front door, Eric slipped from his bed then crept downstairs. In the hallway, he didn't pause to look at his front door, and instead, headed to the back of the house. Where he was going to go once he was outside, he hadn't the faintest idea, but that didn't matter. Wherever it was, it was most certainly better than staying around to find out what it would be like to have whatever was being slammed into his front door hammered into his own considerably less resilient face.

Grabbing a coat, his keys, and, for protection, a walking stick on the way, Eric edged towards the door at the back of the house. He reached for the latch, geared himself up to make a run for it across the back garden and into the woodland beyond, then yanked the door open.

'Hello!' said the smiling face of a woman in a police uniform on the other side of the door.

Eric didn't care who she was or what she wanted. Didn't even ask. Instead, with his head down, he charged. Two, maybe three steps later, he was on the ground and felt cuffs being ratcheted shut on his wrists behind his back.

'Am I under arrest?'

'Not yet.'

'Then why am I in handcuffs?'

'Oh, is that what these are!'

'You can't cuff me if I'm not under arrest! You can't! It's, well, it's not right, is it?'

The policewoman helped Eric to his feet.

'Here's an idea,' she said. 'How about we discuss that back at the office in Hawes?'

ROUND at the front of the house, the large man who had arrived in the Range Rover was still hammering the fence post against Eric's front door. And he was really going at it some, thought Matt, who was now standing just a few feet behind him, between the man himself and the Range Rover, as yet unnoticed.

'Come out, you weaselly little bastard! Come out right now so I can rip your bloody arms off! Come on! Out! Right now! Out!'

Then it was back in with the fence post and Matt was really rather impressed with how Eric's front door was putting up with such a ferocious battering.

'Excuse me!' Matt said, his voice loud and firm.

The man stopped trying to smash the door in and turned around to face the detective sergeant.

'What the fuck do you want?'

'I'm Detective Sergeant Dinsdale,' Matt said.

'Congratulations,' the man said. 'Now piss off.'

Matt ignored him and spoke again.

'Before we go any further, can I suggest that you put that post down, please?'

'And why the hell would I want to do that?'

'Because we don't want anyone getting hurt, do we? By which I mean you, obviously. Not me, in case you were wondering. I'll be fine. You? Not so much. I don't mean that as a threat. I'm just explaining things in simple terms so that you can understand them. I'm nice like that.'

Matt watched as the man's brow creased with a moment of confusion before he then bellowed a laugh filled with disdain.

'A policeman with a sense of humour!' the man said. 'You should do stand-up, mate!'

'For a start, it's police officer,' Matt pointed out. 'Also, and as I've already pointed out, I'm a detective sergeant. Oh, and I'm definitely not your mate.'

'And all of that's supposed to impress me, is it?'

'Not a bit of it,' Matt said, then nodded back at the car he and Liz had driven over in. 'Now, how's about you come with me back to Hawes so that we can have a little chat?'

At this, the man hammered the post into the door once again, roared, 'You weaselly bastard!' then turned around to walk back over towards Matt. He then prodded Matt gently in the chest with the pointy end of the post.

'I'm here to have a word with an old friend of mine,' the man said. 'As it seems that he's not in, I'll be going home now, if you don't mind.'

Matt didn't move.

'You often try and beat down the doors of houses that belong to your friends?'

'You're in my way.'

'I need you to come with me,' Matt said.

'Is that right, then?'

'It is, yes.'

'Can't say that I'm seeing how you've got any chance of making that happen, Detective Sergeant.'

The man poked Matt once again with the post, the wide smile of a bully on his face.

'Just so that you're aware,' Matt said, 'I've run your plates, so I know who you are and where you live.'

The man stopped and his mean smile slipped a little.

'Also, I will obviously be arresting you for what you've just done to that door there. Criminal damage, you see? And we don't really like that, do we? And by we, I don't just mean the police, but people in general.'

The man glanced back at the house, then back at Matt.

'Oh and one more thing, and you're going to love this one I'm sure, you poking me with that fence post is, well, there's no beating around the bush, is there? It's assault. Against a police officer. That's me, in case you were wondering.'

'Assault? But all I did was poke you!'

'With a fence post,' Matt said. 'That you'd just been using to beat down a door. Also, there are all the shouted threats that will need to be taken into consideration as well. So, if I were you, I'd quit while you're ahead. Unless you want to make it worse for yourself, that is. I'd suggest you didn't.'

The man loomed over Matt who saw his knuckles go white as his grip on the fence post tightened.

'I've friends you know,' the man said. 'Friends who can make your life very difficult. Painful even.'

'Are you threatening me?' Matt asked.

'Sounds like it to me,' said Liz, her voice joining in the conversation from over by the house.

The man turned, only as he did so, Matt was into him quicker and smoother than his physique would ever suggest possible. And before he could do anything about it and react, the man was spun around and against the bonnet of his

Range Rover, his hands cuffed behind his back, the post kicked far enough away to be of no more threat to anyone.

Matt, with the man now pinned firmly against the Range Rover, looked over at Liz.

'Eric was in, then?'

'He was,' Liz said, Eric Haygarth at her side. 'Couldn't see why whoever that is you've got there would be over here and that angry about it if he didn't think someone was in.' Then she added, 'Who is that, anyway?'

'This, PCSO Coates, is Mr Peacock,' Matt said. 'The man who sold Arthur Black his dog.'

CHAPTER TWENTY-NINE

WHEN HARRY WALKED INTO THE OFFICE IN HAWES, HE was surprised to find not only the two men Matt had told him about during a call on his way back from his meeting with Sowerby, but a woman as well, though she was waiting outside. Eric Haygarth was currently in the interview room with Jen and Jim, while the other man, a Mr Peacock, who hadn't been on anybody's radar as a possible suspect in any of this, was sitting in the office with Jadyn close by, watching him keenly. Harry also noticed that the boards for this current investigation, and the ongoing one about Neil's murder, had been removed from the walls. Well done, Jadyn, he thought.

'Do I need to ask, or are you just going to tell me?' Harry said, walking over to Matt.

'About what?'

'The individual outside,' Harry said. 'The woman with the enormous hair.'

'Quite something, isn't it?' Matt said. 'Reminds me of

candy floss. I've not had that in ages, have you? Love the stuff.'

'Matt...'

'Oh right, yes, well, she's currently refusing to come inside,' Matt said, his voice low and hushed. 'Says she wants to speak to whoever's in charge. And doesn't want a certain someone to know that she's here either.'

'But who is she?'

Matt mouthed a word.

'What?'

He mouthed it again and this time Harry lip-read the word *wife*.

'Whose?'

Matt gestured with a slight nod to Mr Peacock. Then shrugged.

'Best I go and have a chat with her, then,' Harry said. 'You okay in here?'

'Fine and dandy,' Matt said.

'Where's Liz?'

'She headed out for another look at the barn,' Matt said. 'Always worth having another pair of eyes check something over, just in case.'

'Doubt she'll find anything,' Harry said. Then, remembering that Sowerby had done the same and had found something, he said, 'But yes, you're right. Anything from Gordy?'

'She's in tomorrow. Oh, and apparently Swift is threatening to come over as well.'

'This week just keeps getting better and better doesn't it?'

Harry left Matt and headed outside to find the woman he'd seen upon entering the community centre busy pacing around.

'Mrs Peacock?'

The woman turned and on seeing Harry hurried over. But when she drew close she came up short, her eyes wide and staring.

'I need to speak to whoever's in charge.'

'I'm Detective Chief Inspector Grimm,' Harry said. 'How can I help?'

The woman's eyes continued to stare. Harry ignored it; some people just didn't quite know how to deal with his face. Which was fair enough, he thought, because most times his face didn't know how to deal with people, its expressions generally unnerving pretty much anyone he looked at.

'Is there something you need to tell me?' he asked.

'He can't hear me, can he?' the woman asked, her eyes flicking over to the community centre behind Harry. 'He doesn't know I'm here, does he? He can't. The officer I spoke to, I asked him not to say anything. If he knows I'm here...'

Harry couldn't just see fear in the woman's eyes, it was also in her voice.

'Why don't you tell me what's up and we'll go from there, shall we, Mrs Peacock?' Harry said.

For a moment, Harry thought the woman might just walk off, but then she seemed to calm down enough to speak.

'I followed him,' she said.

'Who?'

'My husband,' Mrs Peacock said. 'I followed him and he doesn't know.'

'Followed him where?'

All Harry knew so far was that Mr Peacock had turned up at Eric's house.

'I breed the dogs, you see,' Mrs Peacock said. 'It's my thing. Always has been. Keeps me busy and I do love animals. How can you not? They're wonderful, aren't they? Which is why I'm here, why I'm so angry, and why I want that man, that monster, arrested!'

Harry kept quiet and allowed Mrs Peacock to find her own way around to getting to the point.

'We moved here five years ago. It was all very quick, very sudden. And I've never asked any questions, you know. None. Because he does look after me, he really does, and that's important, isn't it, to be looked after?'

'It is, yes,' Harry said, if only to encourage Mrs Peacock to keep talking, though about what, he still hadn't a clue.

'But I still had to know, you see? What he was doing, where he was going. Because he's always going, here and there and goodness knows where else. And it gets so lonely, being in that house all the time, on my own. The dogs are company, but still, you get to wondering, don't you? What he's up to? Why he's always off?'

'Mrs Peacock...' Harry began, but she either didn't hear or didn't want to, and kept on.

'I don't think it's just him, because it can't be, can it? I don't know what goes on in there, not exactly, because I didn't get too close, but I can guess, from what I heard. And there were other cars there as well, you know? Expensive ones. And the people in them, I didn't know any of them. Not one. I heard dogs, you see, lots and lots of dogs, and that's why I'm here.'

'What do you mean, you heard dogs?' Harry asked, now taking considerably more interest in what Mrs Peacock was saying.

'I followed him out to some barns. They're hidden in these trees, miles away from anywhere. You need to go and have a look. Immediately. To see what's happening in there. It's not right. It's not. I know it. You have to go and look!'

'What were the dogs doing?' Harry asked.

'I didn't see them, I just heard them,' Mrs Peacock said. 'All howling and barking and whining. It was horrible. Gave me nightmares!'

Harry tried to collect together what he'd heard so far.

'So, you followed your husband, and when he arrived at his destination, you heard some dogs barking.'

'Not some dogs, lots of dogs!' Mrs Peacock said, her voice jumping in pitch. 'I breed dogs. I know what it sounds like when you have lots of them together and when something bothers them. There was howling, so much howling! God, you should've heard it! And I don't want to think about it because if he's involved, then he's broken his promise to me, hasn't he? The promise he made when we moved here. That he was finished with all of that. Every bit of it!'

'Finished with what?'

Mrs Peacock didn't answer. Instead, she just grabbed Harry's arm.

'Please! You have to go and see! You have to! Please!'

'Did it sound like the dogs were fighting?' Harry asked. 'Is that what you heard?'

'They were howling and yapping,' Mrs Peacock said. 'The sound of it, I mean, it just filled the woods, it really did, but it didn't matter, because no one would ever hear. And that's the point, isn't it? To have no one hear? Those barns, there's nothing anywhere near them, is there? No footpaths, nothing! And the land is private.'

Harry didn't want to think it, but right there and then he was starting to wonder if, against all the odds, he was suddenly not only hearing information that would finish this investigation quickly and neatly, but that inside the community centre, they also had the two men at the heart of it all, particularly after what he'd heard from the pathologist. He knew that it had to be too good to be true, but that didn't stop him from hoping. It also had to all be checked out.

'Do you have the address?'

'Here.'

Mrs Peacock removed her phone from a pocket and showed Harry the screen. On it, a pin was dropped onto a map.

'I'll send you the location. But please, you can't tell him I'm here. You can't! He's not a nice man when he's angry. Not a nice man at all.'

As she spoke, Mrs Peacock started to rub her arm.

'How do you mean, not nice?' asked Harry.

Mrs Peacock said nothing, just kept on rubbing her arm, and then the expression she gave him nearly broke his heart.

'Is he violent?' Harry asked.

Mrs Peacock gave the faintest of nods and as she did so her eyes filled up as tears gathered.

'Can you wait here a moment, please?' Harry asked.

Mrs Peacock grabbed Harry's arm.

'He can't know! Please, he can't! He just can't!'

'He doesn't and he won't,' Harry said, gently removing her hand from his arm. 'I promise you. Please, wait here. Just for a minute or two, yes?'

Harry ducked inside the community centre and called for Matt. Outside, he then asked Mrs Peacock to tell the detective sergeant everything she'd just told him and to show him the map.

'You know where that is?' Harry asked Matt.

'Out Cotterdale way,' Matt said. 'There's not much there,

like, as you can see. Some small woodland, moors, that's about it. You need a four-wheel-drive to get there, that's for sure.'

'We can take the Rav,' Harry said.

'We've got our own Land Rover,' Matt said.

'We have,' said Harry. 'But if we go in my vehicle, and if someone's there, it's got less chance of spooking them.'

'I'm not so sure.'

Harry looked back at Mrs Peacock.

'When were you last out there?'

'A couple of days ago,' Mrs Peacock replied. 'I didn't know what to do. Then that polite young PCSO of yours came over and, well, it's just been going around and around in my head, you see, and I've not been able to sleep, and then he was off again today, wasn't he? So I just thought...'

Mrs Peacock's voice broke over her tumbling words and she was unable to finish her sentence.

'Mrs Peacock, I think you should go home and sort out somewhere else to go and stay for a while,' Harry said. 'Your husband will be staying with us. And I will have one of my team go with you, okay? Matt?'

'Boss?'

'Give Liz a bell right now, tell her to come back here and to head home with Mrs Peacock. As for Mr Peacock, we keep him here. We can have Liz take a statement from Mrs Peacock, not just about what she's just told us, either, but about her husband, if you get my meaning. For now, while we sort through all of this, and everything else, I suggest we have Jadyn keep him occupied.'

'He'll be good at that,' Matt agreed. 'Almost too good. What about Eric?'

'I'm assuming Jen has it all under control?'

'She does.'

'Then I'm not worried,' Harry said.

He then instructed Mrs Peacock to remain in her car until PCSO Coates arrived to accompany her home. Harry would then liaise with Liz about what was happening, and to ensure Mrs Peacock was safe and had found somewhere else to stay.

'Liz is still at the barn but should be on her way back now,' Matt said.

'And is there anything to report from the barn?'

'Some fresh tyre tracks,' Matt said. 'Nowt else. She's taken some photos for us.'

Happy that everything was in hand, Harry headed off, Matt at his side. He wasn't one for believing in luck, but as they drove off into the darkening evening, he couldn't help but cross his fingers.

OUT IN SNAIZEHOLME, PCSO Liz Coates was scrolling through the photos she'd taken of the tyre tracks she'd found at the barn. She'd headed out to the place on the off-road police bike they'd been given a good few months ago now, and it had been a lot of fun flying along the lane just a little too fast. The tyre marks were certainly fresh, she thought, and clearly different to the rest of the markings in the dirt around the barn.

Having parked at some trees just a walk away from the barn, she'd then headed in the rest of the way on foot, keeping her eye out for anything unusual. Partway along, she'd been very surprised, and more than a little excited, to see a red squirrel perched up on top of a wall, just staring at her. It hadn't even bounded off when she'd walked past within only a few feet of the tiny creature, instead just staring at her, watching.

At the barn, Liz had hoped to find a barn owl or two, though she'd expected to find none. However, upon entering and having a look around with her torch, the beam had caught something glinting high up in the rafters. And there, staring down at her, had been an owl. The beauty of the creature was breath-taking, and for a minute or two she just stared up at it, wondering what it was thinking, how it managed to just sit there, so calm, so still. Then her phone had buzzed and she'd headed outside for a quick chat with Matt.

With her instructions to head back to Hawes, and to look after Mrs Peacock, Liz had been unable to resist just another quick pop back inside the barn to say goodbye to the owl. Her torch beam traced a line up the wall and there the bird was, still crouching in the rafters, still staring down.

'You take care, now,' Liz said, and turned to step back outside.

Then something hard crashed down on the back of her head, filling her skull with bright lights and pain.

Then nothing.

Nothing at all.

CHAPTER THIRTY

'I'm guessing you've driven with your lights off before,' Matt said, as Harry eased his vehicle along a narrow track cut into the side of the fell.

The evening was dark now, the sun gone, and the green fells and dales around them were now great shadows that crowded above, threatening to swallow them whole.

'A few times, yes,' Harry said. 'If someone's shooting at you, having your lights on is generally seen as a bad idea.'

'You don't talk much about your life before the police,' Matt said. 'The Paras, I mean.'

'You're right, I don't,' said Harry.

'Is that because of what happened? With the IED, I mean,' Matt asked. 'Must've been tough.'

'It was,' Harry said, staring forward, focusing on the way ahead. 'But you deal with it, don't you? You have to. That's life.'

'Hard to see how,' Matt sighed. 'That you came through it at all with any amount of sanity is a miracle.'

'I never said I was sane. I said I dealt with it. Two different things.'

'Don't sell yourself short,' Matt said.

'It's just, I don't see much need or reason to talk about what I've done, that's all,' said Harry.

'The best of times, the worst of times, right?'

'Something like that.'

Harry eased the Rav4 through a narrow gate. Ahead, he saw the darker shadow of a patch of trees set against the grey hulk of the fells behind.

'I've never been shot at, you know,' Matt said.

'I wouldn't recommend it,' Harry replied. 'You've not really got time to think about it when it's happening. Your training just kicks in and you're on autopilot. It's only afterwards, when the firefight is over, when you're out of it and safe, that's when it really hits home. Like a sledgehammer.'

'I bet,' said Matt.

'You can get the shakes from the adrenaline,' Harry explained. 'The shock, the stress, the excitement, all of it hammering through your system at the same time. Sometimes you just throw up. Then the exhaustion really hits you and you get this thousand-yard stare, where you're just dead to the world because what you've just been through, it's something that no amount of training or rehearsal or experience can prepare you for.'

'Do you ever get used to it?'

'Yes and no,' Harry said. 'If you want to survive, you have to deal with it, manage the stress, the panic. You don't want to become completely hardened to it, though. Otherwise...'

Harry's voice trailed off.

'Yeah, I can understand how that would be bad,' Matt said.

'I've lost as many friends after being in combat, because of PTSD as I did from being in actual live firefights.'

'Makes you think, doesn't it?' Matt said.

'Oh, you bet it does,' Harry said.

Harry slowed down, bringing them to a stop.

'So, that's it then, is it?' he asked.

'That's the location Mrs Peacock told us about, yes,' said Matt.

'Nowhere to park out of sight by the looks of things,' Harry observed. 'We'll just have to leave the Rav here and hope for the best. Though I doubt anyone would want to nick it.'

As they climbed out, Matt asked, 'What do you think we're going to find?'

'Haven't the faintest idea,' Harry said, shaking his head. 'But what Mrs Peacock described, well, it sounds like it could be another dog fight location.'

'And you think we're okay going in alone?'

Even in the darkness, Harry could see worry ploughing deep lines on Matt's face.

'This is a recce,' he said. 'We're going to sneak in, have a look, that's it. If we need backup, we'll call it in. No heroics.'

'Thank goodness for that,' Matt said, then added, 'I mean, I left my cape at home.'

With that, Harry walked into the trees, the sound of Matt's soft footfalls following on behind.

The trees were pine, the area a small plantation, though for what purpose, exactly, Harry wasn't sure. He knew though that the small woodland would certainly give good cover to whatever activities Mr Peacock and his colleagues were up to.

A few minutes later, and with the darkness of the trees

around them now so thick that it was almost impossible to see where they were going, Harry spotted a greying of the light just ahead.

'Looks like a clearing,' he said, whispering back to Matt. 'We'll go really steady from here on in. Small steps. Eyes and ears open. Understood?'

'Totally,' Matt answered.

Creeping forward, the trees maintained their thickness, right up to the clearing's edge. Here, the narrow track, mostly hidden from the sky by the trees which lined its sides, widened just enough to allow the placement of four low-roofed timber buildings placed in a row. There were no other vehicles around and considering where they now were, Harry was fairly confident that they were alone. But he was still cautious.

Observing the buildings for a few moments from the cover of the trees, Harry saw that each one had a door to the front, locked by the look of things, and instead of windows, thin mesh-covered slits along their sides. The felt roofs were covered in moss.

'You wait here,' Harry said, turning back to Matt.

'Not a chance of it,' Matt replied.

'That's an order.'

'And I'm ignoring it.'

'No, you're not,' Harry said. 'I'll go and have a look, check that we're clear, then you follow on. If anything happens, you head back to the Rav.'

To emphasise his point, Harry handed Matt his keys.

'You know there's no chance I'll be leaving you, don't you?' Matt said.

Harry wasn't listening; he was already making his way across to the first building. When he reached it, he found that it was locked, so he slipped down the side of the building to see if he could spy anything through one of the slatted windows and get an idea of what the buildings were actually being used for.

Harry stopped, a thin, whining sound bringing him up short.

Blood thumped in his head, all of his senses on fire now, adrenaline dumping into his system, readying him for flight or fight.

The sound came again, from inside the building, another joining it, followed by a faint yap.

Leaning in close to the mesh, Harry brought up a torch and sent a beam of light into the darkness on the other side. For a moment all he could see were shadows dancing, then bright lights reflected back at him, like a cat's eyes.

'Bloody hell...'

The shadows in the darkness of the building took shape, grew fur, and Harry saw then that the reflected lights were eyes after all, and they were all staring up at him.

'Matt! Get here! Right now!'

Matt raced over out of the trees.

'What is it, boss? What's happened? What've you found?'

Harry handed him the torch.

'Have a look for yourself.'

Matt did exactly that and swore under his breath.

'The hell is this?'

'It's a puppy farm is what it is,' Harry said, and the rumble in his voice was of a dark, hot anger.

'But that doesn't make any sense!' Matt replied. 'Mrs Peacock, she breeds dogs, right? So, why the hell would they have this as well?'

'It's not her, it's him, isn't it?' Harry said. 'Her husband. She had no idea this was going on. And it's a perfect cover, isn't it, a legitimate business disguising another more lucrative illegal one?'

Matt had another look, their presence and the torch beam now causing the dogs to stir. Soon, yaps and barks and howls filled the air.

Harry stood and walked round to the front of the building. The lock on the door looked strong, but the latch it was holding, not so much. After a quick look around on the ground, he found a fist-sized rock and smashed it into the lock. The latch gave way after the second try. Then he yanked the door open and stepped inside.

The smell that hit him nearly knocked him off his feet and Harry quickly covered his mouth and nose with his hand. Not that it did any good.

'This is, well, it's horrific,' Matt said, standing at his side.

In the torchlight, Harry saw pen after pen lining the sides of the building, each with a bitch and its pups, all of them bedded down in damp, soiled straw. A bin stood to one side of the door and a quick look inside showed him what happened to any pups that didn't make it.

Harry stepped deeper into the thick, stinking gloom of the building, rage burning through his veins. The pups were all different ages, some just born, others a few weeks old. Their mothers looked exhausted, drawn, so tired that he was amazed some of them were even alive.

'Matt...'

The detective sergeant, who had walked further down into the building, stopped and turned back to face his boss.

'I can't believe this, boss,' he said. 'I just can't. I've seen some awful stuff, in my time on this job, but this? I... I just don't understand it. Any of it. I mean, why?'

'Call Jadyn,' Harry said. 'Right now. I want Mr Peacock arrested. Immediately.'

'What's the charge?'

'Animal cruelty, should do for starters,' Harry growled, and pulled out his own phone. 'But feel free to add in sadistic evil bastard!'

'You calling the others, then?'

'No,' Harry said. 'A vet.'

CHAPTER THIRTY-ONE

'HERE HE IS NOW,' MATT SAID, AS A BRIGHT BEAM OF light bounced through the trees.

Harry, who was cradling the tiny black body of what he assumed was a Labrador puppy, looked up to watch a motorbike speed into the clearing and come to a stop in front of him.

'Didn't take you long,' Harry said, as Andy Bell, the vet, climbed off his motorbike.

'It sounded urgent,' Andy replied. 'Toby's out dealing with something else, so I came straight away.'

'Much appreciated,' Harry said.

'Who's your friend?' Andy asked, walking over. Then he added, 'And what the hell is that smell?'

'In there,' Matt said, pointing at the open door. 'We've opened every building, they're all the same. You may need to call for help. Can't see how you can deal with all of this on your own.'

Andy walked past Harry and Matt and stepped into the first building. He was quiet for a few moments, but Harry watched his expression change from urgency and worry to pure, fiery rage.

'Who the hell did this? Who's responsible? Who is it? Are they local? They have to be!'

Harry moved to stand next to the vet.

'Well, we've got one of them at least,' he said, the puppy in his arms sound asleep. 'Already under arrest and on his way to Harrogate for an unpleasant few hours of terrible food, no sleep, and a lot of difficult questions that I'm pretty sure he won't be able to answer. Not with all this here in front of us. And the fact that we have a statement from someone who saw him here.'

'I'll do a report on everything I find,' Andy said. 'Whatever I can do to help put them away, I will.'

'Good to hear,' said Harry.

Andy pulled off his biking leathers and walked deeper into the building, Harry following. 'You think this is all part of the dogfighting thing?'

Harry shook his head.

'This is something else,' he said. 'Could be connected, but none of these are the kind of dogs you'd throw in a ring, are they? They're all Labradors for a start.'

'Certainly looks like it,' said Andy, scratching the head of the puppy Harry was holding. 'Hard to know where to start, you know? They all look in a bad way. And the conditions! Who keeps animals like this? What the hell is wrong with people?'

'Wish I knew,' Harry said. 'Would make my job a lot easier, that's for sure.'

Andy climbed over into the first pen. Seven small furry bodies rushed over to him, tails wagging. Their mother, however, didn't have the energy, and just laid there. It was to her Andy went first, kneeling beside her.

'You've no idea how angry this makes me,' he said, as he checked the dog over, then gave her a couple of injections.

'Oh, I think I do,' said Harry. 'Trust me on that.'

'I'm going to need help with this,' Andy said. 'I need someone to call the surgery. There's a twenty-four-hour emergency call service. Whoever answers, tell them what we've got and they'll do the rest.'

'I'll do that now,' Matt said.

Andy stood up as Matt headed off to make the call.

'There's just so many of them!' he said, scratching his head. 'I've never seen anything like it. The filth, it's horrendous!'

Harry told Andy about the bin over by the door.

'I'm going to call someone at the RSPCA,' Andy said. 'I've not got the facilities to house this many animals. To be honest, I'm not sure they have either. But they'll be able to help, I'm sure.'

As the vet moved on to the next pen, his phone to his ear, Harry's own phone buzzed in his pocket. With some struggle, and not wanting to wake up the puppy he was carrying, he finally managed to pull it from his pocket and answer.

'Grimm,' he said.

'Harry?'

Harry recognised the voice immediately, but it sounded strained.

'Liz? Is that you? What's up? Are you back in Hawes?'

'Yes, it's me, I mean, it's Liz. I... I'm...'

The PCSO's voice was choked and Harry heard pain in it.

'Liz? What's wrong? What's happened? Are you okay?'

For a moment, all Harry could hear was breathing.

'Liz? Liz, damn it, answer me!'

'I'm... I'm still out at the barn,' Liz replied, her voice quiet, like it was bruised.

'What? Why? What's happened?'

'I... I think someone attacked me. No, I mean I know someone did. Jeez, my head...'

'Attacked you? What do you mean? Who attacked you? How?'

Matt, his own call over, was now next to Harry.

'What's happened? Is that Liz? Is she okay?'

Harry hushed the detective sergeant with a hot stare, trying to focus on what Liz was saying, which so far wasn't that much.'

'I was at the barn,' Liz said. 'I popped back in, just to have one last look at the owl, but when I left, something crashed into the back of my head. Knocked me out cold.'

'And you're still there? At the barn?'

'Yes,' Liz said. 'I came round a couple of minutes ago. I'm okay, I think. Massive headache though. I'll head back to Hawes now.'

'No, you absolutely will not!' Harry snapped back. 'You'll be staying right where you are until I get there, you hear?'

'But what about Mrs Peacock?'

'You don't need to worry about her,' Harry said. 'Her husband is now under arrest and on his way to Harrogate. I'll have Matt let Jen and Jim know what's happened and they can sort her out.'

Matt gave a silent nod, acknowledging the instruction.

'But I'm fine,' Liz said. 'Honestly, I'm okay.'

'You're not fine! At all! And don't even go thinking that

you can get on that bike of yours. You stay put. Have you got something to keep you warm while I make my way over?'

'I've got a jacket,' Liz said.

'Well, get yourself back in that barn,' Harry said. 'Stay out of the wind. I don't want you getting cold and going into shock.'

'I won't.'

'Someone just twatted you on the bonce hard enough to knock you out!' Harry replied. 'So, you'll be doing exactly as you're ordered to from now on, understood?'

'But...'

'No buts,' Harry said, cutting Liz off. 'Whoever did it, they'll be long gone by now. You must've disturbed them. I want to see why, find out what the hell they were doing there at all that was so important they needed you out of the equation while they did it. So, don't you bloody well move until I get there!'

Harry gave Liz no opportunity to respond, killing the call immediately.

'Matt?'

'I heard enough,' Matt said. 'You go. I'll stay.'

'What's happened?' Andy asked, peering out at Harry from another pen.

'One of my officers has just been attacked over in Snaize-holme,' Harry said. 'I'm going to them right now. I'll leave Detective Sergeant Dinsdale here with you, if that's okay.'

'Is that to do with all this?'

Harry shook his head.

'As of this moment, I don't know what's to do with what, and I know that makes no sense at all, but that's where I am.'

'We'll be fine,' Matt said. 'You get over to Liz and make sure she's okay.'

Harry gave a nod and made to walk off, down the track, back to his vehicle.

'Er, boss?'

Harry turned.

'What?'

'You've, er, well, you've got a passenger there with you, haven't you?'

Harry looked down to see the puppy lying in his arms still somehow fast asleep. Then it shuffled itself around a bit and managed to twist its body enough to flip it upside down, baring its stomach.

'So, you're a she then, are you?' Harry said, and gave the dog's stomach a scratch. It was soft and warm and Harry was struck then, not just by the innocence of the creature he was carrying, but its helplessness, too.

'Boss?'

'What?'

'You want to hand it over? Then you can get going.'

Harry stroked the dog's stomach once more.

'She's coming with me,' he said, and turned on his heels and walked off into the dark.

When he arrived at his vehicle, Harry rested the puppy on the driver's seat as he hunched off his jacket and scrunched it up on the passenger seat. He then transferred the animal over to the makeshift bed, climbed in himself and set off through the dark.

As he drove, Harry found himself reaching over to stroke the dog, to give it a scratch, or to just rest his large, rough hand on its side like a protective blanket. The dog responded with faint snuffles and snores, tucking itself deeper into his jacket.

Arriving at Snaizeholme, Harry headed down the track,

past the motorbike Liz had ridden out on, and down towards the barn. As he drew up outside the building, Liz appeared in the door.

Harry was out of his vehicle and over to her in a heartbeat.

'You never said you were bleeding! Why? Why the bloody hell didn't you say? You need an ambulance, Liz! Look at you!'

She had some colour to her face, so that was something, Harry thought, but there was dried blood on her forehead and down the left side of her face, and it didn't half make her look worse for wear.

'It's just a small cut, that's all,' Liz said. 'Look...'

She pointed to a cut on the side of her head, just in her hair.

'Must've hit something when I fell after getting hit.'

'Hit? You were smashed across the skull and knocked unconscious!' Harry said. 'You'll have a concussion. You need checking over!'

'Well, we can do that when we get back to Hawes,' Liz said, brushing herself down as though nothing had happened at all. 'What are we going to do about the bike?'

'The bike? How is that even important?' Harry was doing his utmost to stay calm but it really wasn't working. He was, in pretty much every way possible, baying for the blood of whoever was responsible. 'We'll pick it up in the morning. What matters right now is you.'

'I'm all right, Harry,' Liz said. 'Honest, I am. And I had company, so it's not been all bad.'

'How do you mean?' Harry asked, his eyes darting around, wondering then if Liz's attacker was still around.

'Well, for a start, that owl was here when I arrived.' Liz

said. 'Doesn't seem to mind people at all. It was gone when I woke up. Since then, I've heard it around the place, hooting and being all owl-ish. Sounds a little creepy at first, an owl on the dark moors when you're alone, but after a while? It's kind of nice. And there's been a few squirrels. How can you not feel okay when one of those cute little buggers runs past?'

Harry ducked inside the barn. He flashed his torch up into the rafters and right enough, the owl was gone. He was about to head back outside to deal with Liz, when he spotted something.

'Liz? Was this here when you arrived?'

'Was what where?'

'The ladder,' Harry said.

Liz came into the barn behind Harry.

'What ladder?'

Harry pointed at the floor.

'I noticed it outside the first time I was over here,' he explained. 'And now it's here.'

'Well, no, it wasn't there before,' Liz said. 'I'd remember.'

'You sure about that?'

The expression Liz gave Harry was more than enough to convince him that yes, she was sure, and it was probably best to not question it.

'I know I've been knocked on the head, but my brain didn't plop out of my ears and onto the floor in the process, you know.'

Harry walked over to the ladder for a closer look. As he did so he noticed marks in the dirt on the floor showing where it had been stood up against the wall.

'Where was the owl when you were in here?' Harry asked.

'Up there,' Liz said.

'Interesting,' Harry said, then manoeuvred the ladder to where the marks were on the floor. Leaning it against the wall, it came to rest exactly where Liz had just pointed.

'What are you doing?' Liz asked.

'Answer me this, Liz,' Harry said. 'Why would someone come out here in the first place?'

'How do you mean?'

'Well, let me put it this way, then, why would someone come out to this barn, knock you unconscious, then use this ladder to climb up to where not just you, but I and the pathologist all saw an owl?'

Liz scrunched her face up.

'No idea,' she said. 'Egg stealing? There's money in that, isn't there? Maybe it was that?'

Harry, though, wasn't listening. He was already halfway up the ladder.

'Be careful,' Liz said.

'Careful's my middle name.'

'I very much doubt that,' Liz sighed.

When he reached the top of the ladder, Harry didn't look down. He'd been a rare thing in the Paras; someone who hadn't been best pleased about heights, which was a bit of an issue, seeing as being a Para was linked clearly in their very name to jumping out of planes with a parachute. But that had been the funny thing about getting his wings; jumping from a plane had always seemed just too ridiculous to be scared of. The height out of the back of a plane just didn't look real. But standing at the top of a ladder, though? Well, that was different. Harry was certain it was more dangerous, what with the fact that he wasn't wearing a parachute.

'You okay up there?' Liz called out.

'Fine and dandy,' Harry said, then he turned to look at

where he remembered the owl had been. The wooden beam was old and worn, he noticed, but what struck him as odd was how there was just no evidence of a bird ever having been there at all. No feathers, no mess, nothing. And that was confusing the hell out of him right up to the moment that he spotted some thin wire nailed into the wood.

'Well, now, isn't that interesting,' Harry muttered.

'What is it?'

Harry looked down, ignoring how the floor of the barn seemed to twist and lurch up at him just a little.

'Well, and I know this is going to sound crazy, but that owl? I'm not entirely sure that's what it was exactly.'

'Oh, it was definitely an owl,' Liz said. 'What else could it have been?'

Harry didn't answer, but leaned in for a closer look instead. He saw scuff marks around the wire, which made him wonder if there was a chance of finding some fingerprints.

'I'm coming down,' Harry said, then backed himself down the ladder.

When he got to the bottom he immediately spotted some feathers on the floor, which he picked up and placed in an evidence bag. But as he did so, he spotted something else in the dirt and picked it up.

'I'm not sure I understand,' Liz said.

'I think,' Harry explained, looking at the small object resting in the palm of his hand, 'that there was more to that owl than any of us thought.'

'In what way?'

'In the way that I think it was stuffed and placed up there for a reason, that being to keep an eye on things down here.'

Liz shook her head. 'Wait, you mean like it was a microphone or something?'

Harry showed Liz what he'd found in the dirt on the floor. It was an SD card.

'Or a camera,' he said. 'I think whoever attacked you came back for this. You probably disturbed them and in their rush to get out, they dropped the very thing they'd come back here for.'

Harry then told Liz about the scuff marks and the wire.

'I'll have Sowerby come out and check it over for us. But right now, there's someone I need to speak to.'

'Who?'

'Someone we all know who's rather partial to stuffed animals...'

CHAPTER THIRTY-TWO

HAVING SENT OUT A MESSAGE TO EVERYONE ON THE team to let them know what had happened to Liz and that she was okay, and to also tell them what he'd found out at the barn in Snaizeholme, Harry was now nursing a mug of tea and trying to work out how best to start the interview of Mr Eric Haygarth. So, while he thought on, he finished the large slice of fruit cake that Matt had brought in from Cockett's earlier in the day. That there had been any left was in itself a miracle. He wasn't having cheese with it because, although he'd grown to just about enjoy the combination, he still wasn't sure that cheese and cake went with tea.

He was joined in the interview room by Jen, who was sitting patiently waiting for things to begin. Jadyn was in the process of transporting Mr Peacock to Harrogate where Gordy was then going to take over, once she'd gone through the details and photos of the puppy farm Harry had already sent through.

There would be more to follow as well, from the vet, his

surgery team who had turned up, and the RSPCA, as well as Matt, who was working as a liaison between the police and everyone else.

Jim was on with making sure that Mrs Peacock was okay and staying somewhere else with friends or family and was then going to pop over to Mr and Mrs Hogg to check up on how they were doing after the burglary.

Harry had dropped Liz off at home and called a doctor out to check her over. The worst part of which, hadn't been trying to ignore her increasingly vocal protests, but the fact that he'd left the little sleepy black puppy he'd taken with him in her care. Liz, on the other hand, had been over the moon.

'Right,' Harry said, his tea finished at last, 'shall we get this party started, then?'

'Party? How is this a party?' Eric asked. 'I shouldn't even be here, should I? I've not done nowt!'

Harry reached forward and started the recording device in the centre of the table. He then stated the date and time and who was in the room.

'So, Eric,' he began, 'perhaps you'd like to tell us where you were two nights ago.'

'I'm not answering that!' Eric said. 'You think I did it, don't you? So, anything I say, well, it's only going to make it worse, isn't it?'

Harry glanced across to Jen.

'I don't think I accused him of anything, did I?'

Jen shook her head. 'Not a sausage.'

Harry looked back at Eric.

'Which begs the question, doesn't it, Eric, as to what it is that you think we think you've done.'

Eric folded his arms.

'Now you're just trying to be clever.'

'I promise you, I'm not,' said Harry. 'I've not accused you of a single crime. Not yet anyway. All I've asked is for you to tell me what you were doing two nights ago.'

'No, you asked me where I was two nights ago. That's different.'

'Well, you're listening, so that's good,' Harry said. 'So, why don't you start by answering my first question.'

'I was at home,' Eric said. 'And that's no lie.'

'For the whole night?' Jen asked.

'What?'

'Where you home for the whole night?'

'Yes,' Eric said, and gave a short nod. 'Yes, I was. At home. All night.'

Harry then pulled out a photo from a folder on the table in front of him.

'Can you confirm that this is your vehicle?'

Eric leaned forwards.

'Yes, that's mine,' he said. 'Why are you taking photos of it? What's the point in that?'

'We have a witness who says that they saw this very same vehicle in Redmire on the night in question,' Harry said.

'What witness?' Eric asked.

'I'm not about to tell you that, am I?'

'Well, they're lying, aren't they?' Eric said. 'I was at home.'

'If that's the case,' Harry continued, 'can you tell me why, when I came to find you in the early hours of the following morning, that you weren't at home?'

'I'm a busy man, Detective,' Eric said. 'I'm a gamekeeper you see. It's not a job with sociable hours.'

'This was, I think, around four am. You were out then?'

'I was.'

'Doing what.'

'Work.'

'Where?'

'On the estate I look after.'

'That's rather general, isn't it?' Harry said. 'Estates are large places. You must remember a specific location, I'm sure. And also what it is you were doing while you were there.'

'What does any of this matter?' Eric said. 'I've not done anything wrong, even if I was over at Arthur's, which I wasn't.'

At this, Harry glanced over to Jen.

'Can you just check, Constable Blades, did I mention anyone by the name of Arthur in this interview?'

Jen checked her notes and shook her head.

'Once again, not a sausage.'

'Not even a dickie bird?'

'Not even one of those,' Jen said.

Harry turned his attention back to Eric.

'Can you tell me why you said that name?'

'What name?'

Harry leaned forward, and his calm voice grew gradually less calm as he went on.

'Look, Eric, this is all being recorded by this here fancy device in the middle of the table. If you want me to, I can rewind it and playback your very own voice saying the name Arthur. Do you want me to, or can we just get a wriggle on and stop all this buggering about?'

'It was a slip of the tongue,' Eric said.

'In what way was it?' Harry asked.

'Pardon?'

'Well, a slip of the tongue means you said something you didn't really mean to, doesn't it? So, why did your tongue slip enough to say that name?'

'Arthur lives over in Redmire,' Eric said. 'That's why. Because if someone says Redmire, that's what I think, isn't it?'

'So, it's like word association then, is it?'

'Yes, that,' said Eric.

'Okay, then,' said Harry. 'What would you say if I said, oh, I don't know, how about taxidermy?'

'Taxi what?'

'Taxidermy,' Harry said. 'It's where you get an animal, a dead one preferably, and stuff it. I'm not sure with what, never mind the why.'

'What's that got to do with anything?'

'Constable Blades?'

Jen opened another file and pulled out a collection of photos. Each one showed the various animals from Eric's shed, from the strange partly skeletal dog creation on the table to an owl, a fox, a buzzard, and a red kite.

Eric stared at the photographs and Harry watched the man's face change colour, growing scarlet with anger.

'You... you had no right! They're mine! That's my house! You trespassed!'

'No, you're the one who's trespassed,' Harry said. 'And I mean that in the biblical sense. You know the Lord's Prayer, right? Forgive us our trespasses? Unsurprisingly, it has nothing to do with anyone being on someone else's property. But what it does have a lot to do with is breaking the rules, the law.'

Jen then asked, 'Do you have an Article 10 certificate, Mr Haygarth?'

'A what now?'

'An A10,' Jen said. 'And are you registered with DEFRA, you know, the Department for the Environment, Food and Rural Affairs? What about APHA, the Animal and Plant Health Agency?'

'Are you making this up?' Eric said.

Harry saw Jen's jaw drop just a little.

'Am I making up DEFRA and APHA?' she said, shaking her head in obvious disbelief.

'You see,' said Harry, 'a lot of these animals here are protected. And, to sell them, you need to be registered. And it looks to me like you're not. And that's a little bit of trespassing on your part right there, isn't it, Eric?'

'You've no proof I've sold any of my work,' Eric said.

Harry produced another photograph, this one of a stuffed owl that looked a little worse for wear.

'We've already matched this one to the materials found in your shed,' he said. 'It was found in a house that was broken into last night. As you can see, it's a little damaged, but it's definitely yours.'

'You're losing me,' Eric said, and Harry could see panic in the man's eyes. He was starting to unravel, which was good, because Harry wanted answers.

'I want a list of your customers,' Harry demanded. 'And don't even try to pretend that you don't have any or that you've lost their names or can't remember them. I want them, Eric. And I want them now!'

'What, you expect me to remember them all?'

'I expect you to have some recollection, yes.'

'But all of them? How am I supposed to do that?'

'If we have to, we can send someone over to your house to collect your records.'

'Which I don't have.'

'Then your brain is all that we have,' Harry said. 'Your memory.'

'But all of them, though,' Eric said. 'I mean, I can try—'

'You can indeed,' Harry said.

Eric then looked over at Jen and asked for a pen and some paper.

'I'll write them down,' he said. 'It'll take me a few minutes though.'

Harry smiled.

'See how much easier this is if you cooperate?'

'But I still don't understand what any of this has to do with, well, anything, actually,' Eric said, starting to write on the piece of paper. 'They're just dead birds!'

'They're not though, are they?' Harry said. 'They're birds you purposefully killed to make a bit of extra cash. And as for the dog and fox and whatever else you have in your collection, did you shoot those, too? Did you?'

'No!' Eric shouted. 'I didn't! I didn't shoot that dog! It was roadkill, that was all. It was a waste to just leave it on the road, wasn't it? And while we're at it, I didn't have anything to do with Arthur's dog either, if that's what you're thinking. I didn't steal it. I didn't! And I had nothing to do with whatever happened to it after. Why would I?'

'Constable Blades,' Harry said, and raised an eyebrow.

'No mention of a stolen dog either,' Jen said.

Harry eased himself back in his chair. It creaked and complained ominously.

'So, here's the thing, Eric. We know that Arthur Black called you that night and accused you of taking his dog. Why? Because he told us he did, that's why. We also know that you were seen there by a witness later that evening. So, what I now need to know, is why you attacked Mr Black.'

'I didn't!'

'Eric, you were there! Arthur called you and accused you, didn't he? You were angry, you drove over to have it out with him. Things got out of hand and you got carried away. It'll be easier for everyone if you just admit what you did and come clean.'

'I didn't! I really didn't! It's the truth!'

Harry was starting to believe him, but still, he pushed to see if he would trip up, offer any other information.

'Did you go there to kill him?'

'It wasn't me!'

'Did you honestly think you'd get away with it?'

'It was someone else!' Eric shouted. 'You have to believe me! I walked in and saw him, Arthur, I mean. He was on the floor, and there was this other person, standing over him. And they were wearing something over their face, a balaclava! So, I ran! That's what I did! It's not brave, I know, but it was none of my business, was it? So, I didn't hang around, I got out of there sharpish!'

'You expect me to believe that?' Harry said. 'You disappeared, Eric! You sodded off! Was that guilt? Is that it?'

'I'm not guilty!' Eric replied. 'I'm not! I was scared! And I knew everyone would think it was me. What else was I supposed to do?'

'Call the police?' Jen suggested. 'I mean, that's what someone who wasn't guilty would probably do, don't you think?'

'I'm not guilty!'

Eric shoved the piece of paper and pen back to Jen.

'That's everyone I can remember who's bought one of my pieces,' he said.

Jen glanced down the list.

'This is all of them?'

'Yes.'

'And it took you all that time to remember them?'

'What's your point?'

Jen handed the list over to Harry.

Harry had a read.

'You do know a list is generally something with more than two items in it, don't you?' Harry asked.

'There is more than two,' Eric said.

'You're right, there is,' Harry said. 'There's three.'

Eric gave a disgruntled shrug.

'My work isn't really that good,' Eric said. 'It's the best I can do, like, and it's improving. But most people don't really seem to like it.'

'And of the three names you've given, one of them is Andrew Bell?'

'He's the vet,' Eric said.

'I know who he is!' Harry replied. 'I'm asking why his name's on your list!'

'Because I've donated a few pieces to the surgery, that's why. For their raffles, like. The other two ended up giving me my birds back. Said they'd gone rotten. Which they had, but that's not the point, is it? A deal's a deal, right?'

Harry couldn't believe what he was hearing.

'You thought it was appropriate to give the vets stuffed animals to help them raise money to be nice to animals?'

'Why not?' Eric shrugged.

'And Andrew didn't ask any questions about your license? Nothing at all?'

'They're anonymous donations, aren't they?' Eric said. 'Though I did put a little note on them, you know, saying how they were family heirlooms, that kind of thing. How I didn't really want them in the house, but wanted them to go to a good cause.'

When Eric had provided air quotations with his fingers around the words *family heirlooms* Harry had wanted to reach over and snap them off at the knuckles.

'You lied, then,' Jen said.

'Of course, I lied! I'm not an idiot!'

'Oh, I wouldn't go that far,' Jen muttered just loud enough for Harry to hear.

Harry was staring at the vet's name on the piece of paper. He knew that there was no point tracking down the other two names if they'd given Eric back what he'd made for them. So that left a list of just one: the vet. If Harry thought things hadn't made much sense before, well now he was so confused he didn't know how much more his brain could take.

'Jen?'

'Boss?'

Harry waved Eric's list in the air.

'I need to go check up on this. Can I leave you with Mr Haygarth here?'

'Of course,' Jen said. 'It'll be fun, won't it, Eric?'

Eric said nothing, but the sneer he provided was world-class.

Harry finished the interview, then switched off the recording device.

'Make sure he's comfortable and doesn't cause any trouble.'

'What, and you're just leaving, are you?' Eric said.

'That I am,' Harry said, standing up.

'You have to believe me, though,' Eric said. 'I didn't do anything to Arthur or his dog!'

'Right now, I don't know who did what to whom,' said Harry. 'Which is why you're staying here in case you want to tell us anything else.'

Harry saw Eric's eyes flit between him and Jen.

'There is something else,' Eric said, and Harry heard desperation in the man's voice. 'Well, someone else, I mean.'

'Yes, we know, Eric,' he said. 'Whoever it was, they were wearing a balaclava. Or you were. Which was it?'

'No, not that someone, the other someone, someone outside,' Eric said.

'What someone outside?' Jen asked. 'Who? Why didn't you mention this before?'

'They were in this red car, watching the house.' Eric said. 'Arthur's house!'

Harry stopped dead.

'Repeat that.'

'There was someone else there! I swear there was! I saw them when I was leaving, staring at the house. I couldn't see them properly, like, but they were definitely—'

'No, what you said before, about the car,' Harry said.

'I didn't really see it,' said Eric.

'But you saw its colour.'

Eric gave a nod. 'I did. It was red. Why?'

Jen caught Harry's eye.

'Didn't the farmer over in Snaizeholme say he saw a red car?'

'He did,' Harry said, remembering something else. 'Reedy... doesn't he drive around in something flash and red?'

'Yes, he does,' said Jen. 'A Subaru Imprezza.'

'A red Subaru Imprezza,' Harry said.

Then he was out the door and back in his vehicle, heading once again to Cotterdale and the barns hidden in the woods.

CHAPTER THIRTY-THREE

HARRY ARRIVED AT THE BARNS TO FIND THAT MORE people had turned up to help deal with the hellish mess they'd uncovered. An RSPCA van was there and he saw that Detective Sergeant Matt Dinsdale had been joined by a group of helpers, who were all dealing with the dogs as best they could.

As he climbed out of his vehicle a message pinged through to his phone from Liz.

Sorry, boss, forgot to send you these. Maybe that bump on the head was worse than I thought? Liz xxx PS: Smudge is such a cutie!

Harry was pretty sure the three kisses were unnecessary. And by Smudge he assumed that the PCSO was referring to the puppy. Had she really named it? he thought. Already?

Harry opened the attachments Liz had sent and quickly scrolled through the photos she had taken of the tracks she'd found out at the barn. They were definitely different to any of the others he'd seen, and Liz was right, they were fresh. Though what exactly was different about them he couldn't quite put his finger on. Which wasn't really a surprise, he thought, considering everything that was running around inside his head like a herd of a spooked cattle. The final photo was of the little black puppy, apparently now going by the name of Smudge, snuggled up on Liz's lap.

Putting his phone away, Harry made his way over to Matt, realising as he drew closer that Andrew Bell was nowhere to be seen.

'Vet not here, then?' Harry asked. 'Where is he?'

'Got called away to another job,' Matt said. 'But this lot were here by then, so it wasn't a problem.'

'And how's it all going?'

'Slowly,' Matt said. 'Most of the pups and the mums are okay, but a few have had to be put down, just too far gone, you know? Breaks your heart, doesn't it, that folk can do this? Let animals get into this state. I mean, why would you? What do you have to have wrong inside your head, your soul even, to treat them like this?'

'Maybe some folk just don't have souls,' Harry shrugged.

'We've been sending details over to Gordy,' Matt said. 'Keeping her up to date with everything, for her little chat with that Mr Peacock. The RSPCA are all behind the prosecution and I'm pleased to say that I don't think he stands a chance. They also think they have some idea as to who else he's been working with to do this. Looks like it could be the tip of the iceberg.'

Harry asked, 'Can you remember what car it is that Reedy drives?'

'Impossible to forget something like that,' Matt said. 'Red Subaru Imprezza. Beast of a thing. Why?'

Matt's memory confirmed his and Jen's discussion earlier.

'I think Eric Haygarth saw it outside Arthur Black's house the night he was attacked.'

'You mean Reedy attacked Arthur?'

'Eric says he saw someone in it, that's all we know. Who it was though, I've not the faintest idea.'

'But it has to be Reedy, surely!' Matt said. 'It can't be anyone else, can it? That car, well, it's just a massive dick extension, isn't it? And he doesn't half-love to get it out and show it off.'

'Well, we can't actually do anything about it until we find him. I mean, where the hell is he? And where is that car? People and vehicles don't just disappear, do they?'

Matt said nothing, and Harry was grateful for that.

'I need to speak with Andrew,' he said eventually. 'Do you know where he is?'

'Probably best to just give him a call,' Matt said.

Harry walked away from the barns and made the call. The man answered on the second ring.

'Mr Bell? It's DCI Grimm. Just wondered if it would be possible to have another chat?'

'Not a problem,' Andrew replied.

'Where are you?'

'Home, actually,' Andrew said. 'The call I got wasn't the emergency everyone thought it was. Happens sometimes. You get a panicked call from someone, race out, only to find that whatever animal it is has decided to get up and walk around like Jesus himself has been there and sorted it out. So, I just stopped off to grab some stuff before heading back out to all those dogs.'

'Well, may I ask that you stay where you are?' Harry asked. 'I think they're doing fine. Looks like everything is in hand.'

'Sure, not a problem,' Andrew said. 'You've got my address, yes?'

'I have,' Harry said. 'I'll be there in about twenty minutes.'

WHEN HE PULLED up at the vet's house, rolling past a garage, Harry parked up next to a rather full skip, filled with rubble and dust. Looking at it, Harry thought back to what Sowerby had found in the tyre tracks out at the barn earlier in the week, the tiling adhesive, the granite dust.

To the side of the skip, two large motorbikes were parked. Walking over, he noticed the marks from the tyres in a pile of sand that had spilled from the skip. He pulled out his phone, clicked on the message from Liz, and in one of the attachments saw the same tyre marks staring back at him.

Harry was just about to have a closer look when the front door of the house opened and there stood Andrew Bell.

'Good to see you,' Andrew said, waving Harry into his house. 'Bit of a mess inside, I'm afraid. Still, it'll be worth it when it's done. At least, that's what I keep telling myself. Cost enough.'

Inside, the house was very much in the middle of being renovated, with pots of paint, tools, brushes, lengths of wood, all piled up in the hall, and what furniture Harry could see through open doors all covered in dustsheets.

'Not a fan of DIY myself,' Harry said.

'Neither am I,' Andrew said. 'Which is why I'm paying someone else to do it for me instead.'

Harry followed Andrew down the hall to the kitchen at the back of the house. Alarm bells were ringing, but the sound, to Harry, just didn't sound right, like the notes were off somehow. He just wasn't sure why. Things were starting to click into place, but to each other, rather than in a nice neat line.

'Coffee?' Andrew asked. 'Toby rode over here earlier just as I got back, so I made a pot. And if I drink it all myself I'll be up all night, wired to the moon!'

'No, I'm fine, thanks,' Harry said, on guard now, but making sure he looked and sounded relaxed. 'This is only a short visit.'

Andrew sat down at a small dining table and gestured for Harry to join him in another chair.

Sitting down, Harry noticed that the kitchen cabinets had no work surface installed yet.

'Must be difficult though, living in this mess,' he said, looking around then to see if he could find what was missing.

'Won't be long now, though,' Andrew said.

'Kitchen looks like it'll be nice,' Harry observed. 'Once you get the worktops on.'

'Well, for what it's costing, I bloody well hope so,' Andrew laughed. 'Granite isn't cheap, you know! Don't really know what I was thinking. I could've gone for something a hell of a lot cheaper, but I just got carried away. When you've spent thousands already, a few more just don't seem to matter that much.'

'No, I'm sure,' Harry agreed.

'Now, what was it you wanted to ask?'

Harry edged his chair just a little way out from the table, to give himself space to move, and quickly, should the need arise.

'Can I ask if the name Eric Haygarth means anything to you?'

'Only that he's the worst kind of gamekeeper you could

imagine,' Andrew replied. 'Awful man. How or why anyone employs him, I've not the faintest idea. Why do you ask?'

'I understand that you have raffles throughout the year to raise money,' Harry said.

'At the surgery? Yes, we do. For an animal shelter we support down the dale. It's good business sense, obviously, but it's also, and more importantly, the right thing to do.'

'And some of the prizes have been taxidermy, I believe?'

At this, Andrew laughed.

'We had a few anonymous donations,' Andrew said. 'I was all for throwing them out, mainly because they were bloody awful. Really amateur, you know? But then Toby pointed out that it was pretty disrespectful to the animals themselves and that half the charm of them was that they just weren't that good.'

'Can I ask where you were three nights ago?' said Harry.

'Here,' Andrew said. 'Why?'

'Have you ever been up to Snaizeholme?'

'The red squirrel reserve, you mean? Yes, of course. It's beautiful. But then where isn't around here? Look, Detective, why are you asking these questions?'

'I have my reasons,' Harry said.

'What are you trying to imply? That I'm dealing in illegal goods? Those pieces, terrible though they were, were anonymous and taken in good faith. If you're now telling me they're not legit, then we will do everything we can to get them back and have them destroyed.'

'What about two nights ago?' Harry asked. 'Can you give me your whereabouts then, too?'

'Wait a minute,' Andrew said. 'You asked about Snaizeholme... that's where the dog was found, wasn't it? The one killed in the fight? You're not seriously trying to link that to me, are you? Are you mad? I'm a vet! I carried out the necropsy!'

'Believe it or not,' Harry said, 'we have reason to believe that a stuffed owl was used in the barn to spy on the proceedings, as it were.'

'And now you're here,' Andrew said. 'Why? Because of that thing with the hens when I was a kid? Seriously?'

Harry felt as though he was staring at all the right events, all the correct bits of information and evidence he needed, but that they just weren't in the right order.

'I'm trying to make sense of things,' Harry said. 'We've apprehended the person who I'm fairly confident was behind the stuffing, for want of a better word, of the owl,' Harry said. 'This individual has also admitted to being over at the house belonging to the owner of that dog the following evening. He witnessed a violent attack on the owner, which was enough to put them in hospital, and saw another individual watching the house.'

'And you honestly think I was involved?'

'I'm simply trying to get to the bottom of what's been going on,' Harry said. Then he pulled out his phone, scrolled through to the photos Liz had sent through, and showed Andrew.

'These are fresh tyre tracks, found out at Snaizeholme earlier by one of my team. She was attacked and knocked unconscious. You'll notice that the tracks bear a striking resemblance to those made by your own motorbike.'

'Do I need to point out just how many people in the dales have motorbikes with those exact tyres?' Andrew asked. 'We've got two ourselves at the surgery, remember?'

'There's more, though,' Harry said. 'Some of the tracks we found on the day the dog was discovered, they contained traces of materials used in house renovation. Tile adhesive, for example, and granite dust.'

Andrew said. 'I could give you a list of addresses that Toby and I have visited just this month that are having work done!'

'That would be useful,' Harry said.

'Are we done here?' Andrew asked, and Harry heard anger in the man's voice.

'Yes,' Harry said. 'Thanks for your time.'

The vet stood up and led Harry out of the house.

'You'll forgive me if I don't thank you for popping round,' Andrew said, standing to one side to allow Harry to step out into the evening air.

'Just doing my job,' Harry said, looking back over at the skip, the motorbikes parked close by.

'Toby lives local, then, does he?' Harry asked.

'Why do you ask?' Andrew said.

Harry pointed at the two motorbikes.

'Earlier, you said that he rode over. I'm assuming on one of those.'

'That's correct.'

'So, he either lives close by and has walked home, or someone picked him up.'

Andrew shook his head.

'No, he headed off in his new car. He got it this week and asked if he could keep it in my garage, seeing as it's empty. I generally keep my Land Rover at the surgery, you see, and use the bike as my runabout. The Land Rover wouldn't fit in there anyway. Well, it would, I just wouldn't be able to get out of it once I'd squeezed it in there.'

Harry walked over to the garage, rested his hand on the door.

'A new car?'

'Don't ask me what it is,' Andrew said. 'Cars just aren't my area at all. So long as it can get me from A to B, I don't care what it is, whether it's red or black or—'

'Red?' Harry said. 'Why did you say that?'

'Because that's the colour of Toby's car,' Andrew said.

'How long since Toby was here?' Harry asked.

Andrew checked his watch.

'Twenty minutes I guess. Why?'

But Harry wasn't listening. He was already on his phone and running over to his Rav4.

CHAPTER THIRTY-FOUR

JIM WAS ONCE AGAIN SITTING AT A TABLE IN A KITCHEN he'd known since childhood, with Mr and Mrs Hogg sitting opposite.

'I know you say he had nowt to do with it,' Alan said, 'but I'm sticking to my guns on this. He knew. I'm sure of it. It's the only thing that makes sense.'

Jim caught the look Helen sent to Alan as she then turned to him and rolled her eyes.

'We've talked about this,' Jim said. 'There's no reason or evidence to connect Mr Adams to the break-in.'

'But he knew we weren't here, didn't he?'

'Of course he did!' Helen exclaimed. 'He was the one who invited us over in the first place!'

'Exactly!' Alan said.

'Exactly nothing!' Helen said. 'You need to stop. Right now. No more of this nonsense. We were burgled. It happens. And we're lucky that so little was taken or damaged.'

'Except that,' Alan said, and pointed to what was sitting in the middle of the table.

'You really think you can fix it?' Jim asked. 'I mean, it doesn't really even look like an owl now, does it? Its wings are broken, its head is all scrunched in.'

'I'm going to have a bloody good go,' Alan said. 'How hard can it be?'

'It's not an Airfix kit, is it?' Helen said.

'And there's those wires hanging out of it,' said Jim, reaching out to poke the bird. 'What were they even for?'

'That's how you stuff a bird,' Alan said. 'You skin it, then you make a sort of wireframe for it, and then you put the skin on it, you fill with sand or sawdust or something, and there you go, one stuffed bird!'

'But these wires wouldn't be any use for that at all,' said Jim, showing Alan. 'Look, these are all floppy, aren't they? They're electric wires. Was it fitted up with a battery so that its eyes lit up or something?'

'Not that I know of,' Alan said. 'Though that's given me a great idea! I could have a motion sensor, couldn't I? And then, when someone walked past, I could have the eyes flash! I could even put in a sound thingy, make it do an owl sound!'

'A sound thingy?' Helen said. 'And that's your technical know-how, is it?'

'Well, I think it's a great idea,' Alan said. 'And it's my bird so I'll do what I want with it.'

Jim, though, was still looking at the bird.

'So, it wasn't wired for anything, then?'

'No,' Alan said. 'Why would it be? It was just a stuffed bird we won at the raffle, like I said. I remember, because I didn't know what I'd actually won until I went to collect it, and that new vet, Toby whatever his name is, he gave it to me. We had a good laugh about it, too, mainly because it's not the best, is it? But I liked it. It's a bit of fun, right?'

'A stuffed bird, *fun*.' Helen sighed, shaking her head.

As Alan and Helen continued to talk, Jim was still looking at the owl, or what was left of it. The wires were strange, weren't they? If there was no reason for them to be there, then why were they there at all? And what was it that Harry had said in that message earlier? Something about an owl being used to spy on the dog fight?

Jim stood up.

'Is it okay if I go take another look around Neil's room?'

'Of course,' Helen said. 'Something up?'

'I don't know,' Jim said, then left the kitchen and headed upstairs.

In Neil's room, he sat down on the bed and tried to gather his thoughts, though he was pretty sure he was mad for thinking them. But those wires in the owl, what Harry had said... What if someone had used the owl, now in pieces on the dining table downstairs, to spy on Neil? No, that was insane, Jim thought, it had to be, didn't it? After all, the only people who would've done that, would be the gang Neil had got himself involved with over in Darlington. And if it was them, how would they have even got into the house to essentially bug the place? Is that what all this was about? Had someone broken in to get back whatever it was in the owl? But why leave it till now?

Jim stood up, walked around Neil's room, not really sure what he was looking for, or why. The place had been tidied up since the break-in, but it still had an odd feel to it, almost as though he could sense the intruders from the night before. Through the window he saw the tree, remembering again how he and Neil used to climb it all those years ago, the secret stash of sweets they used to keep up there in an old biscuit tin.

Jim was out of the room and running downstairs to head outside in a flash.

'Hey, what are you doing?' Alan called out. 'What's the rush?'

But Jim wasn't listening. Instead, he was heading over to the tree, because he'd remembered something Alan had said earlier in the week, about how on the day they'd lost Neil, he'd been out here, in his treehouse.

Round the back of the trunk, an old wooden ladder reached up into the branches. It didn't exactly look all that stable. Jim took hold and started to climb. The ladder complained, and some of the rungs felt more than a little spongy, as though they would give way at any moment, but they held out, and soon he was up in the branches.

'Jim? Jim! What the hell are you doing up there!'

Neil's dad had followed him out and was now standing underneath the tree.

'Just give me a minute,' Jim said. 'I'll be down in a sec.'

'It's not safe,' Alan called up. 'I gave Neil a proper bollocking for going up there as well, you know, when he went up there that day. Now, get yourself down!'

Ignoring Alan, Jim climbed through the branches and into the treehouse. It was smaller than he remembered, but then how much bigger was he now than the last time he'd been up here? Inside, it was still surprisingly dry. Jim could see plenty of evidence that the place provided shelter for various furry and feathered creatures, with twigs and feathers and moss all over the floor. And there, in the corner, wrapped in an old plastic bag, was the tin.

Jim reached over and pulled it close. He opened the bag and pulled out the tin.

'Jim, I mean it now,' Alan called up. 'Get yourself down before you fall!'

Jim opened the tin. And inside, in another plastic bag, he found a phone. Keeping it inside the bag, he pressed the power button and watched, amazed, as the screen burst into life. The password it asked for was obvious because Jim knew that Neil hadn't changed it in years: his birthday.

With the phone open, Jim sat there staring at it, wondering why on earth Neil would hide it up here of all places. He opened the emails, flicked through, but nothing stood out. Same with texts, though reading the ones he'd sent to Neil himself brought a lump to his throat. Then he opened the photos and someone he knew was staring right back at him, surrounded by faces he didn't recognise.

A shrill sound burst into the moment and Jim nearly dropped the phone as he went to answer his own.

'Jim, it's Matt.'

'I think I know who broke into Neil's parents' place,' Jim said, but Matt cut him off.

'Where are you?'

'Neil's parents' house,' Jim said. 'Why?'

'I'll be there soon as I can,' Matt said.

'Why? What's up? What's happened?'

'Harry's happened,' Matt said. 'And he's given us an address to check out urgently.'

'Do you know where he is? I need to speak to him.'

'Right now,' Matt said, 'he's probably terrifying everyone on the roads between here and Darlington.'

'What? What's he doing?'

'Catching his prey,' Matt said and killed the call.

CHAPTER THIRTY-FIVE

Having swapped his Rav4 for one of the incident response vehicles the team had parked up in the market-place, Harry had wasted no time in flicking on the blues and twos and booting the accelerator to the floor hard enough to snap it. He'd already put in the relevant calls to have as many police officers as were available looking for a red Subaru Imprezza on every road from Hawes to Darlington. The net would close in quickly, and he wanted to be a part of it.

Given that Toby had left twenty minutes ago, Harry put him at anywhere between Redmire and Richmond. There was no chance that he would catch him up, but he was going to give it a damned good try. And if Toby doubled back for any reason, he'd at least be there to meet him.

The dales rushed past, a blur of greens gradually growing darker as the evening headed into night.

Harry's phone sang to him and he answered, grateful for hands-free, considering the speed he was doing.

'Grimm,' he said.

'It's Jim.'

'Look, I'm a bit busy,' Harry said.

'I know, but I think I've found something. Over at Neil's parents' house.'

'What? What have you found? We had words about this, Jim, remember? Or have you forgotten everything I said?'

'It was that owl you mentioned,' Jim explained. 'What you said about it, remember? The one in Snaizeholme?'

'Of course, I remember!' Harry snapped back. 'It wasn't exactly that long ago, now, was it?'

'The break-in, at Helen and Alan's, there was this stuffed owl. It was all broken and smashed, you see, and Alan wants to mend it.'

'That's very interesting,' Harry said, swinging round a sharp right bend and powering out of it. 'But can this wait?'

'There were wires in it,' Jim said, clearly not listening. 'I think something was in it, a bug or a camera or something, I don't know, but I went out to the treehouse you see, because that's where Neil and me used to play and we'd hide stuff up there.'

'Jim,' Harry said, staying as calm as he could, 'I'm currently chasing down the person I think is responsible for the dog fight and for attacking Mr Black. We'll talk about this when I get back, okay?'

'It was there, up in the treehouse, this old biscuit tin we used to hide sweets in. I think that's what they were after, what they were trying to find, whoever it was that broke into the house.'

'They were after biscuits?'

'No,' Jim said, 'the phone!'

'What phone, Jim? What the hell are you talking about?'

'I found a phone in the tin,' Jim said. 'I think Neil must've hidden it up there to keep it safe. And I think what's on there, that's why the house was broken into, why he was killed. They wanted the phone, what was on it, and Neil had it, you see, as some kind of insurance maybe? A way of getting out of what he was involved in!'

'Jim, you're making massive leaps here,' Harry said, passing the eerie silhouette of Temple Folly on his left.

'There are photos on there,' Jim said. 'Loads of them. All kinds of stuff. And there's someone in them that I recognised. I mean, I probably wouldn't have, if I hadn't met them this week, but then they've not been in the area for long, have they? And we usually deal with Andrew.'

'Get to the bloody point, Jim!' Harry roared, slowing down as he came round the left bend into Redmire, there for the second time that week, only this was going to be a considerably shorter visit.

'Toby!' Jim said. 'Toby Halloway's in the photos! That doesn't make any sense, does it? He's a vet! Here in the dales! But in these photos, he's with all these other people with expensive cars and Neil's there, too. I think some of the photos are in Darlington, but the others I don't know, but it's definitely him. So why would Neil have them, Harry? What's going on?'

Harry was flying through Wensley now, Leyburn just over a mile away.

'Jim?'

'Yes, boss?'

'We need to get that phone to forensics. Give Sowerby a call.'

'She won't like that,' Jim said.

'I've already spoken to her. She'll be fine. She's staying over in Askrigg at her mum's.'

'Right, will do.'

'I want Andrew Bell's garage going over, and there's a skip of stuff outside his house she'll be cross-checking with what she found at the barn. And there's the address you and Matt are off to, as well. Cordon that off.'

'Who's address is it?' Jim asked. 'And who is it you're chasing after?'

'It's Toby's,' Harry said. 'And right now, he's somewhere between me and Darlington.'

Phone call over, Harry sped on and soon found that he recognised a few buildings as Catterick came up to greet him, and with it came memories of his time training for the Paras. It was so long ago now and the place seemed to have hardly changed. But he had. The years, the experiences had carved him into something else. As to what that was exactly, he wasn't really sure, not least, because the dales was having its own go at him as well, changing him further.

Harry hit the A1 and headed north, the road was busy as he threaded his way through traffic, wondering if he'd managed to pull any closer to the one he was after. Then a call came through on the car radio and Harry answered only to hear the voice of Detective Superintendent Swift.

'We've got him, Grimm.'

'Where?'

'Location being sent now.'

'You made the arrest?'

'Not yet. Firearms Unit has been called in.'

'What?'

'He's armed. Refusing to cooperate. Why was this information not passed on?'

'What information?' Harry said. 'I had no idea he was armed! How would I?'

'Well, he is,' Swift said. 'Fired at one of the cars when he realised he couldn't escape! Where are you?'

'About five minutes away,' Harry said, and hung up.

When Harry arrived at the scene, a lonely road somewhere on the outskirts of Darlington, the darkness was being cut through with flashing lights from the half-dozen or so police vehicles blocking the road in both directions. Any traffic heading into the area was already being directed away, but Harry got through and was soon at the scene. As he climbed out of his vehicle, Swift came over to meet him.

'Any progress?' Harry asked.

'Not yet,' Swift said. 'Still waiting on the firearms unit.'

Harry glanced over to where Toby was parked. And there it was, Reedy's red Subaru Imprezza.

'Is there anyone with him?' Harry asked.

'No,' Swift said. 'Why?'

'That car, it's not his,' Harry explained. 'Belongs to a suspect we've been looking for. What's he armed with, then?'

'A pistol,' Swift said. 'Here, look for yourself. He's had it on show from the moment we arrived and he took that pot shot at us. I think he's trying to show off with it, you know? Scare us away.'

Harry took the pair of binoculars handed to him by Swift. Once focused, he was able to see not only Toby sitting in the car, but the weapon he was holding. And Harry recognised it at once.

'It's the Humane Killer!' he said.

'That's what he's calling himself, is it?' Swift said. 'What is it with people and nicknames?'

'No, not him, not Toby, I mean what's he's holding, the pistol!' Harry said. 'It's called a Humane Killer.'

'I don't really care what it's called,' Swift said. 'It's a

weapon and we're not doing anything until the firearms unit is here. There's no telling how many people he could injure or kill with that if he started shooting.'

'Not many, actually,' Harry said.

'What?'

'It's a pistol specifically designed for use by vets to put animals down,' Harry explained. 'Horses, cows, sheep, big animals.'

'Sounds deadly.'

'Oh, it's deadly,' Harry said. 'But it's not exactly practical.'

'How do you mean?'

'It only has one round,' Harry said.

Swift, Harry could see, was confused.

'I don't understand. One round?'

'One shot,' said Harry explained. 'Once fired, you have to reload it.'

'I don't see how that matters,' Swift said.

'You said he fired at you when you arrived, yes?'

Swift nodded.

'And that he's had the pistol on-show ever since?'

'Yes, that's what I said, didn't I? Why are you asking?'

Harry stared down the binoculars, saw Toby sitting in the car, the pistol in his hand, and then he was running.

'Grimm? Grimm! What the hell are you doing? Grimm!'

Harry ducked around to his right, out of sight of Toby, then legged it across the open ground between the police and Reedy's car. He covered the space so quickly that he was almost on Toby before the man realised what was happening.

As Harry rounded the back of the car, Toby tried to bring the pistol round to point it at him.

'I'm armed!' he shouted.

'Like bollocks are you!' Harry snarled and before the pistol was even pointing at him he slapped Toby's hand with the binoculars hard enough to shatter bone.

The pistol spun off through the air to clatter uselessly onto the road.

Toby was screaming.

'My hand! You've broken my hand!'

Harry didn't listen. Instead, he opened the driver's door and hauled Toby out of his seat before spinning him around to pin him to the side of the car. Then he cuffed him and read him his rights. By the time he'd finished, two other officers, along with Swift, had joined him.

'Grimm, you bloody idiot!' Swift yelled as Toby was dragged away, still screaming about his possibly broken hand. 'What were you thinking? Do you have any idea of how much trouble you're in? Do you?'

'The pistol wasn't loaded,' Harry said. 'One shot, remember? And you'd just told me he'd already fired it.'

'But he could've reloaded!'

'You said yourself he'd had the thing on-show ever since.'

'What you did, it was reckless,' Swift said. 'You put lives in danger with your actions! And you hit him? What on earth was going through your brain?'

Harry wasn't listening. He was staring at Reedy's car.

'You smell that, Sir?' he asked.

'Smell what, Grimm?' Swift said. 'What are you talking about now?'

'You smell it though, right?'

Swift stopped raging and sniffed the air.

'Dear God, what is that? Where's it coming from?'

Quiet now, Harry walked around to the back of the car.

'I'd stand back if I were you,' he said.

'I don't take orders from you, Grimm,' Swift said.

'Suit yourself.'

Harry leaned forward and popped the boot.

'Good God!' Swift exclaimed, covering his nose and mouth with his sleeve. 'That's a body! Who is it, Grimm? And what the hell is it doing in there?'

Harry stared down at the corpse. It had been in there for a couple of days, that much was obvious from the smell and the bloating, but it wasn't long enough for it to become unrecognisable, even with the bullet wound it had suffered to the temple.

'That,' Harry said, 'is Reedy.' Then he looked down at Swift and added, 'Looks like we're going to be adding murder to the list of charges, doesn't it?'

CHAPTER THIRTY-SIX

HARRY WALKED OVER TO THE GRAVE AND STOOD NEXT TO Jim. The PCSO had just driven down from the farm in an old David Brown tractor. Fly was with him, sitting at his side. The day was a bright one. April had fallen back to let May push through, which it had done with gusto, thanks to a thunderstorm that had lit up the dales a few nights ago.

'He finally confessed, then,' Jim said.

'Confessed is a strong term,' said Harry. 'It's a word that implies some willingness on the part of the confessor, doesn't it? And I don't think Toby was all that willing. Not really.'

'What swung it for him, then?'

'The evidence,' Harry said. 'It's pretty hard to say you didn't do something when everything says that you did. Namely, a certain pistol kept at the vets.'

'They got a ballistics match, then.'

'That they did,' said Harry. '.32 calibre. And the forensics evidence for the bullet that killed Neil matches that for Reedy. He'd signed the weapon out on both the dates in question, clearly never once thinking he'd be caught.'

'Wrong about that, wasn't he?'

Harry read Neil's name on the gravestone at their feet, his too-short lifespan etched in stone. And beneath it, the simple words, 'Miss you, Son.'

'At least this gives some closure now,' Harry said. 'And that's good for everyone. How are his parents?'

'Helen and Alan?' Jim said. 'Oh, they're doing okay. Alan's finally given up on the idea of trying to persuade the government to give him one minute alone with Toby.'

'He's a bit of a firecracker, isn't he?'

'You could say that,' Jim agreed.

Harry reached down and stroked Fly's head. The dog sniffed Harry's hand, his tail thumping.

Harry laughed.

'I still can't believe it was Toby, though,' Jim said. 'I mean, a vet, of all things, involved with dogfighting? What's that about?'

'Turns out there's more to Toby than anyone thought,' Harry said.

'I feel for Andrew, though,' Jim said. 'He's blaming himself for not seeing Toby for what he was. Says he feels like he's betrayed the dales for hiring him in the first place.'

'I doubt he had much choice in the matter,' said Harry. 'Toby was placed here by the gang or gangs he was involved with. We managed to speak to everyone else who applied for the job. Turns out they were persuaded to back out or just look for something else.'

'Persuaded, how?'

'Jobs came up,' Harry said. 'And a few threats. I mean, nothing you could really trace or whatever, but enough to have them think again.'

Jim reached down and dusted some dirt from off the top of Neil's gravestone.

'Still though, a vet?'

'On the outside, yes,' Harry said. 'It was a good cover story really, that's all.'

'Was it?'

'There's been a few things come to light about Toby's past. Old school reports, that kind of thing, and what his parents had to say. They're heartbroken, obviously, but still.'

'How do you mean?'

'He's got a history of animal cruelty,' Harry said. 'Started when he was a kid, even before he was at school. Pulling the wings off flies, that kind of thing. They thought nothing of it, but then they later found out that he was trapping mice, birds, and doing things to them. Took him to doctors, psychologists, but they all said he'd grow out of it.'

'Wrong then.'

'Just a bit,' said Harry. 'He just got better at hiding it. Passed his veterinary exams with flying colours. Not top of the class, but close. And that just opened the door for him, I suppose, gave him access to all the animals he could ever want. You saw what they found at his house, right?'

'Don't think I'll ever forget it,' said Jim. 'We've gone through and cross-checked everything we found with our own records, returned the animals we could. Some had to be put down, though. Others were already gone.'

Harry and Rebecca Sowerby had been first on the scene over at Toby's house, near Bainbridge. Harry had seen things there that he knew he would never forget, cages containing twisted things borne of a mind too sick to imagine.

'With his work at the dog track, Toby ended up getting in

with people he shouldn't have,' Harry said. 'But then, like attracts like, doesn't it?'

'And that led on to the sheep theft?'

'Not just that, but all kinds of stuff,' Harry said. 'Horse racing, dog racing, dog fighting, dog theft, puppy farms. They needed a vet who could keep the animals alive enough to make money from them. And Toby just needed a few playthings.'

'He killed Neil because Neil knew who he was.'

'Oh, there was more than just Toby in those photos,' Harry said. 'Neil's phone is proving to be very useful indeed. A veritable who's-who of Yorkshire's worst.'

'If only Neil had handed that phone in,' said Jim. 'Gone to the police.'

'That was the worry, I think,' Harry said. 'And that was why Neil's parents won that owl.'

'Toby had it wired.'

'He did indeed,' Harry said. 'To keep an eye on them. He'd have found another way, I'm sure, but when their ticket came up as a winner at the raffle, it was just too easy to put a little microphone inside it and listen in. He was just waiting for his moment.'

'Which was the night they went out with Richard Adams,' Jim said. 'Their first since they lost Neil.' He shook his head and added, 'It's hard to believe all of this happened in Hawes.'

'Crime doesn't really care about location,' Harry said. 'Anyway, Neil must've let on that he had the phone, for insurance, like you said, remember? And they dealt with him in the only way they saw fit, once he'd sorted out that little job for them at your farm.'

'But if Toby killed Neil so easily, what happened with Arthur Black?'

'Organised crime like this casts a wide net,' said Harry. 'Reedy was another contact. Not a major player, but he was a dealer, someone they could sell through. Not just skunk, but other stuff, too.'

'And he got involved with the dog fight then?'

'We've found out that there have been other fights, just not in the dales. Around the area though, always moving locations. This is the first time it's all been able to be tied together, thanks to what was found on Toby's hard drive.'

'The footage from the barn?'

'Who would've thought a stuffed owl could be so useful?' Harry said. 'Anyway, Toby never attended the fights, but watched from afar, and the footage was sold on the Darknet. That night at Snaizeholme, he saw Reedy forget to clean up.'

'He left the dog.'

'Toby knew something had to be done, particularly with the police involved. With Arthur being aware of what had happened to his dog, he ordered Reedy to sort it out.'

'And Reedy thought the best option was to try and kill Arthur.'

'That I don't know,' said Harry. 'He at least went in there with the intention of giving him the kind of beating that would warn him off from asking any more questions or cooperating with the police.'

'But he didn't account for Eric walking in, did he?'

Harry shook his head.

'Toby was with him, waiting in the car. We found his fingerprints on the stub of a betting ticket found at the barn by Sowerby's team, and on the SD card I found after Liz was attacked. I think Toby went back to get the owl and dropped that card in the panic of getting out of there knowing that he'd just clobbered a police officer.'

'Was Toby involved with the puppy farm as well?'

'No, actually,' said Harry. 'That was just a bit of good luck for us and those poor dogs. Not so much for Mr Peacock, though.'

'Who stole Arthur's dog in the first place, then?' Jim asked.

'Toby,' Harry said. 'Phil had told me the vet was out to see his old Shire horse the same day that Jack was taken. Only he forgot to mention which vet.'

'Not Andrew, then.'

'No,' Harry said. 'And as for Reedy, he was just a loose end that needed tying up. When we caught him, Toby was bringing the car and the body over to a group of his pals to dispose of. The car in a chop shop, Reedy I'm guessing in a barrel of acid or something equally effective and no less horrifying.'

When Harry stopped speaking, neither he nor Jim said much for the next few minutes. Instead, they both just stood there, in one of the most beautiful cemeteries in the world, lost to their own thoughts.

A horn sounded.

'That'll be for you, then,' Jim said.

'I reckon,' said Harry. 'How do I look?'

Jim stood back and looked his boss up and down.

'Not quite sure what I'm supposed to say here, if I'm honest, boss.'

'Am I presentable? These are new jeans, you know. So's the shirt.'

Jim gave Harry a grin.

'You look fine,' he said. 'Who's looking after Smudge?'

'Ben and Liz,' Harry said. 'Didn't take much persuading.'

Jim turned away from Neil's grave and walked Fly back to where he'd parked the tractor. Harry followed alongside.

As he climbed up into his tractor, Jim said, 'You'll be fine, boss. You might even enjoy yourself!'

'Sod off,' Harry said, but he couldn't hide the smile.

With Jim and Fly leaving, Harry turned to the car that had beeped its horn. Walking over, he watched as the passenger window slowly slid down into the door.

Harry ducked down to look into the car.

'Hi,' he said.

'Hi yourself,' Grace said back. 'You ready?'

'I'm all yours,' Harry said and climbed in.

'You could be very sorry you said that,' Grace laughed, then she eased the car onto the road and Harry, the smile on his face making his scars ache, joined in.

DCI HARRY GRIMM and the team are back in the heart-pounding crime thriller Cold Sanctuary

---

JOIN THE VIP CLUB!

WANT to find out where it all began, and how Harry decided to join the police? Sign up to my newsletter today to get your exclusive copy of the short origin story, 'Homecoming', and to join the DCI Harry Grimm VIP Club. You'll receive regular updates on the series, plus VIP access to a photo gallery of locations from the books, and the chance to win amazing free stuff in some fantastic competitions.

You can also connect with other fans of DCI Grimm and his team by joining The Official DCI Harry Grimm Reader Group.

Enjoyed this book? Then please tell others!

The best thing about reviews is they help people like you: other readers. So, if you can spare a few seconds and leave a review, that would be fantastic. I love hearing what readers think about my books, so you can also email me the link to your review at dave@davidjgatward.com.

AUTHOR'S NOTE

Snaizeholme, apart from being a wonderfully strange name, is a place I remember from my own childhood in the dales. My dad, like many people up there, did a bit of rough shooting and still does. And one place he would head out to in the early mornings with a couple of friends was Snaizeholme. I went along with him a number of times as well, not just to Snaizeholme either, but down at a farm near West Burton (not the one Harry meets Andy Bell at, though!)

The Red Squirrel trail in Snaizeholme is very much worth a visit, not just because you'll get to see the valley itself, but for the Red Squirrels themselves, and who could say no to that? For more information, just do a quick search on the Internet for 'Snaizeholme Red Squirrel Trail'. There's a good chance that you'll see roe deer, too.

As to the theme of *Blood Sport*, I was very aware from the off that I didn't want the focus to be on the actual dog fights themselves. Instead, and as I hope with the rest of the *DCI Harry Grimm Crime Thrillers*, I wanted this to be about the characters. The idea for it actually came from something I'd read about a serial killer who was also a doctor. It struck me as so strange and more than a little terrifying how someone whose profession was to care and to heal could also be someone who would then kill those they were supposed to look after. So, why not a vet*?

A few other things to note ...

1. Yes, Harry has finally gone on a date! This was actually supposed to happen in book 6, but it just didn't feel right. However, romance has finally walked into Harry's life in the dales, (much to many readers' relief I think, judging by the number of messages and comments I've received about it!) so it'll be fun to see where it all ends up.

2. Harry has his own dog! I resisted this for a good while, because Fly is such a wonderful addition to the team on his own. And I hadn't really planned on Harry getting a dog in this story either. However, when he discovered what had been going on in those sheds, he just ended up with a puppy in his arms. Funny how that sometimes happens when you're writing, the characters just deciding things for you.

3. I've had a few comments/queries about how I write, or don't, a Yorkshire dialect. This was a conscious decision back when I started with *Grimm Up North*. My hope was that the story would be read a little wider than just the UK, so I wanted a broader appeal. Also, and as an example, I felt that dropping every 'H' and 'T' could've become distracting, not just in the

writing, but more so in the reading, as could littering everything with *reet* this and *by 'eck* that! So, what I've tried to do (whether I've succeeded or not is for you to decide!), is ensure that there's a tone to how the characters speak that is reminiscent of the dales. That way, I'm not littering everything with phrases like, 'ow ist 'e?' (How are you?), and, 'ee, that's reet grand, like,' (Wow, that's fantastic!)

*A note here to say that the Wensleydale Vets practice is superb, serving the local community wonderfully. I would also like to especially thank Director and Veterinary Surgeon at the practice, Amy Cockett, for her advice on the .32 humane killer.

ABOUT DAVID J. GATWARD

David had his first book published when he was 18 and has written extensively for children and young adults. *Blood Sport* is his seventh crime novel.

Visit David's website to find out more about him and the DCI Harry Grimm books.

 facebook.com/davidjgatwardauthor

ALSO BY DAVID J. GATWARD

THE DCI HARRY GRIMM SERIES

Welcome to Yorkshire. Where the beer is warm, the scenery
beautiful, and the locals have murder on their minds.

Grimm Up North

Best Served Cold

Corpse Road

Shooting Season

Restless Dead

Death's Requiem

Cold Sanctuary

One Bad Turn

Blood Trail

Fair Game

Unquiet Bones

The Dark Hours

Silent Ruin

Dead Man's Hands

Dark Harvest

Made in the USA
Monee, IL
17 April 2024